THE HAND IN THE GLOVE

By REX STOUT

Novels

HOW LIKE A GOD

GOLDEN REMEDY

SEED ON THE WIND

FOREST FIRE

THE PRESIDENT VANISHES

O CARELESS LOVE!

Nero Wolfe Mysteries

FER-DE-LANCE

THE LEAGUE OF FRIGHTENED MEN

THE RUBBER BAND

THE RED BOX

A Dol Bonner Mystery

THE HAND IN THE GLOVE

THE
Hand in the Glove

A Dol Bonner Mystery

By REX STOUT

FARRAR & RINEHART, *Inc.*

NEW YORK   TORONTO

THE HAND IN THE GLOVE

A Dol Bonner Mystery.

CHAPTER

ONE

*I*T WAS not surprising that Sylvia Raffray, on that Saturday in September, had occasion for discourse with various men, none of them utterly ordinary, and with one remarkable young woman; it was not surprising that all this happened without any special effort on Sylvia's part, for she was rich, personable to an extreme, an orphan, and six months short of twenty-one years. She was intellectually unpretentious but not vapid; physically a fair focus for dreams but not a gasper—though a viscount stale from Oxford had dubbed her so; financially impregnable but not notorious.

As, around ten o'clock Saturday morning, she emerged from an elevator on the 28th floor of the Chemicals Building on 39th Street, her pretty lips were askew in a crooked line of worrisome determination and her lovely brown eyes were dark with trouble. But surely not a trouble that threatened her soul, for obviously she had not been losing any sleep; and, as she turned right and started down the wide corridor, there was no drag at all in the muscles of her happy young legs.

Twenty feet from the elevator door she stopped short. Facing her was a man who, meeting her from the opposite direction, had also stopped.

Sylvia showed surprise. "Well, hullo! I didn't know you ever got as far south as this." She looked down the

3

corridor and back at him. "I suppose you're buying aspirin wholesale?"

The man stammered, "Miss Raffray. Really." He too looked along the corridor and back. "They don't make aspirin, do they?"

She shook her head. "I guess not. I saw you come out of there. Not that it's any of my business—but I didn't know they had begun making chemicals out of brains." She looked doubtful. "I don't suppose that's funny, either. Anyhow, nice to see you." She took a step.

He put out a restraining hand, but without reaching her. He said somewhat loudly, "Miss Raffray!" in a tone of urgency and appeal. She halted, surprised again, and turned the brown eyes back to him. Always pale, he seemed a shade paler, now that she really looked at him. She saw that his stringy hair, objectionably thin for a man not yet forty, was as usual straggling on his forehead, that his large nostrils were faintly quivering from his perpetual mental excitement, which was also definitely objectionable, and that his pale inquisitive eyes appeared, even more than ordinarily, to emerge perceptibly from their sockets in the effort to see more, see deeper, see everything. None of this surprised her, but his tone did, and his hand reaching for her. She raised her brows at him.

He swallowed. "Miss Raffray, I . . . I don't want to be impertinent. . . ."

She laughed. "There's no law against it. But I'm late."

"Yes. You're going to see Mr. Storrs. Aren't you?"

"I was headed that way."

"Yes." The man closed his lips tight. Then opened them again: "I want to ask you . . . don't see him. That is, don't see him now. See him later. He's not—" He stopped, and frowned. "Oh, the devil. That's all. See him later."

Sylvia was staring at him. "What's the matter? Is he lit? That would be good, P.L. lit. Or are you? What's the matter? Are you lit, Professor Zimmerman?"

"No. I'm not a professor. I'm an instructor of psychology."

"But you're an Assistant Professor. Martin told me, kudos from your book. And I haven't congratulated you. May I? But what is this about P.L.? Have you analyzed him and left him limp?" She glanced at her wrist. "Good lord, I'm twenty minutes late! Are you doing an experiment on me, getting a reaction or something?"

"Please." The man raised his hand again, and dropped it. "I merely thought you would realize, if I asked you to postpone . . . but of course you won't. You will, though, later. You will realize, Miss Raffray, that sometimes an injury, an almost mortal injury . . . you will realize what a sacrifice I have made to devotion, that I am profoundly devoted . . ." He stopped, frowned at her, and finally shook his head. He muttered, "No. All right. The devil. Go ahead," and turned and started briskly toward the elevators.

Sylvia attempted no outcry, and allowed only three seconds for astonished gaze at the man's retreating back. Then, murmuring with a tinge of exasperation, "Utterly off his nut," she proceeded to the end of the corridor, where wide double doors proclaimed in gold lettering,

COMMERCIAL CHEMICALS CORPORATION, and entered. So, briefly, ended her first occasion for important discourse that morning, though she had then no hint of its importance.

The second occasion, this one not accidental but by appointment, took place in the private office of Peter Lewis Storrs, president of the Commercial Chemicals Corporation. As Sylvia was ushered in to him by a soft-spoken young woman who obviously, from her lips and eyes and cheeks, did not confine her dealings with chemicals to their business aspect, P. L. Storrs glared at her from behind a telephone transmitter, nodded at a chair, and continued rumbling into the phone. She sat and regarded him with her lower lip caught by a tooth. She saw nothing alarming, nothing to account for Professor Zimmerman's idiotic suggestion in the corridor. Everything seemed quite normal: the brusque impatient bass of his voice, the golf-tanned healthy skin crowned by his thick gray mop of hair, the colored handkerchief showing at his breast pocket, the slight redness in the eyes which she knew was the banner of hay fever.

But when he finished with the phone and pushed it away, something extraordinary, indeed unprecedented, did happen. He said nothing. He sat and looked at her a full ten seconds, pursing his lips. Finally he slowly shook his head, got up from his chair, and walked around his desk to stop where she sat, looking down at her. She sent her eyes up at him, speculating. At length he shook his head again, sighed audibly, returned to his chair, placed his hands on top of his desk with the fingers interlocked, and rubbed the ends of his thumbs together, regarding her. All this was remarkable. He had not reproached her for being late, he had not asked her if she wanted a drink of water, and he was showing no efficiency whatever in the employment of time. She had not dreamed that he had been so disturbed by the little difficulty—little to him—which had arisen, and she bit her lip again. Then she smiled at him:

"I met a man in the hall. Steve Zimmerman. He said I shouldn't see you. He said I should wait and see you later."

P. L. Storrs was scowling. "He did, huh?"

She nodded. "He was stammering. That alone was funny enough, you know how he can talk if you let him get started. I was surprised to see him—I thought you disliked him so much—"

"What else did he say?"

"That was all. Oh, he raved something about mortal injury and sacrifice and devotion—do you think he's cracked? I do. I expected to find you . . . I don't know, he was crazy. I thought you tolerated him only on account of Martin. I thought you disliked him."

"I do." Storrs tightened his lips, then resumed, "Zimmerman is vile. Zimmerman is a mental and emotional scavenger. Call it modern psychology! Pah!" He made an abrupt gesture. "What else did he say?"

"Nothing."

"You said mortal injury."

"He was just blithering. I guess he was anyhow." Sylvia bit her lip again, then released it, and sat up straighter. "But I was late, and I'm keeping you. I had a long talk with Dol last night."

Storrs nodded. "You said you would. And I said—"

"I know. But listen, P.L. Please listen. I know there's no use arguing with you about Dol, because we'd only fight. But I have to tell you what she said. There are three important points. Wait." Sylvia opened her ostrich-skin bag and fumbled in it for a paper, which she unfolded and frowned at. "Now, first, the matter of publicity. Dol says okay. I told you yesterday, that piece in the Sunday Gazette was just an accident. Len Chisholm—"

"It's no use." Storrs was brusque. "Really, Sylvia—"

"You wait, P.L.!" She raised her voice. "You be quiet! And then you can be reasonable. Len Chisholm got those pictures and jollied us about it, and we thought he was only joking, and then the Sunday editor offered him two hundred dollars for it and he needed the money. Dol says"—she squinted at the paper—"she will guarantee in writing that no similar disaster will occur in the future. That's the first point. Next, me being around there too much. I myself think that's silly, because I might as well be there as anywhere else, except maybe in jail, and it's no more vulgar than a dog show and it doesn't smell as bad; but anyway, Dol has written down here, 'Miss Raffray will come to the office no more than three times a week, for conferences.' That settles that. The third and last point—well, this is the big concession *I* make. Dol persuaded me. I don't think to have the firm's name Bonner & Raffray is a disgrace at all, and I'm not ashamed of it, but Dol persuaded me. The new name will be the Bonner Detective Agency, Incorporated, and Dol and I will each own half of the stock, same as before, and she'll be president and I'll be vice-president and treasurer—don't just sit there like that and shake your head at me!"

Storrs' head was moving from side to side too slowly, with too much reluctance, for his typical firm certitude. At her protest it stopped all movement, and he sat gazing at her gloomily. Presently he rumbled, "Sylvia . . . dear child, dear Sylvia. . . ."

"Oh, my God!" She waved an irritated hand at him. "That's the limit, P.L., pulling the softy act on me. This should be man to man. It's not fair."

"It certainly isn't." He shook his head again, and actually heaved a sigh. "I'm not pulling an act. I was thinking of something . . . but not now . . . no, I can't now. You think I was acting soft?" His tone was suddenly grim. "Not exactly. For the first time in my life I really understand murder. I could at this moment kill a man"—his clenched fists were on the desk before him—"with these two hands, without compunction. And feel I had done a good job, and willingly—" He stopped abruptly and with his fist shoved a heavy paperweight so that it slid across the polished desk and collided with a file basket. He glared at the basket, then looked at Sylvia. "I'm a damned fool. I can't now. I suppose you're going to be in the country with us this evening?"

She was staring at him. She said, incredulous, "My goodness. I didn't know you ever got upset like that."

"I don't." He was crisp again. "But this . . . forget it. Until tonight, anyhow. You'll be at Birchhaven?"

She nodded. "Later. We're going to play tennis at Martin's, and dinner, and I'll come over with Janet. Is it money? I mean the murder you're cooking up. Because I suppose I still have a lot. . . ."

"No. It isn't money." He was gazing at her dismally. "God bless you, my dear, and thank you. . . ."

"Stop it! Softy again? Don't do that!"

"I'm not being soft. I'm merely remembering that you insisted on buying two thousand shares of our treasury corporation stock at a time when—"

"But why remember it? Anyway, I didn't lose anything, did I?"

"No, thank God, at the market you show a profit—"

"Then forget it." She smiled at him. "P.L. darling. You'd better forget about that murder too." She arose to her feet and permitted the smile to become more devastating. "That's the first time I ever saw you brought to a boil . . . you'll have to make it a pretty good one. I doubt if Janet and I will get over much before ten, you know what dinner is like at Martin's place—and I'm already sick of pheasant, he'll have to give that up after we're married." She glanced at her wrist. "Good lord, I've spoiled your morning." She moved toward the door, fluttering a hand at him. "I'll tell Dol it's okay with her three points."

"Sylvia!" Storrs snapped from his chair. "Come back here."

She raised innocent brows. "What?"

"You come back here." He glared at her. "You know very well I'm on to your tricks. You will tell Miss Bonner nothing of the sort. I haven't agreed to that, and I won't. You know what was said yesterday. Your connection with that abom—with that enterprise, is to be severed completely and finally."

She stood stiff and frowned at him. "P.L. I don't really like that tone, you know. I suppose it was all right when I was a kid, but now that I've learned the multiplication table . . . after all, in six months . . ."

"I know. You'll be twenty-one in March." Storrs suddenly struck the table with his fist. "Damn it, Sylvia! Must I tell you again? My tone is my tone and you know it. I relinquish absolutely all claim to any authority, though there is still six months before you come of age. Look at you! My God, look at you! I have felt for three years that to assert authority over you would be like . . . like . . . it would be nonsense. History and fiction are full of instances where an elderly guardian has fallen—"

"You're not elderly."

He glared at her. "I'm fifty-three. Middle-aged? What's the difference? Where an elderly guardian has fallen in love with his ward. I haven't fallen in love with you, but it wouldn't take me long if my idiotic wife and daughter would go off to India, where they belong, and give me a chance to get something done besides selling these damned chemicals. I haven't fallen in love with you, but you know damned well that you are the one person anywhere that I love. You were five years old when your parents died. I've been a pretty good guardian. You're healthy and you're beautiful, and you've never been run over and you've never been kidnaped, and you're worth over three million dollars. What is most important, the connections between your brain and your other organs are still intact. Then what happens?"

"All right, P.L., you don't need——"

"What happens is that a Wall Street gambler loses his shirt and kills himself, and because his daughter is an old friend of yours, you want to help her out. Fine so far. But she turns out to be a worse freak than her father, and she talks you into going into partnership with her——"

"She didn't talk me in——"

"Partnership with her to start a detective agency! That was bad enough, it was intolerable. Then she feels she needs some publicity. Naturally. Pah! She arranges to have it splashed all over a newspaper——"

"She did *not* arrange——"

"All over a newspaper! You've seen it. Not only her picture and her history, but your picture and your history, and as if that wasn't enough, by heaven, *my* picture, and *my* history, as the guardian of a lady detective! You will be interested to know that I have threatened the Gazette with a suit for libel, and have at least had the satisfaction of knowing that the man who got it up has been fired."

"You haven't! P.L.! It was Len Chisholm, I told you, he needed——"

"He can go on needing! You, Sylvia, you say you don't like my tone. I claim no authority over you. Not the slightest. I claim no gratitude for my efficiency as a guardian—I've probably enjoyed it more than you have. I claim nothing. I speak only as a friend so old that I once built a wading pool for you with my own hands and then put on a bathing suit and sat down in it with you.

Merely as an old friend who loves you. What I say is that if you continue to have any connection whatever, financial or personal, with this damned detective business, it will be against my will and my wish, and in spite of my absolute disapproval and my strongest indignation. I add, that if you disregard my wishes and do it anyway, I shall continue to enjoy as much of your society as you can spare for me, and I shall love you no less—probably more in fact, as time goes on, if I get a chance."

Sylvia had frowned at him throughout. She demanded: "Is that final?"

"Absolutely final." He scowled. "Over my dead body."

"Damn." She compressed her lips, and after a moment lifted her shoulders and dropped them. "You're too clever for me. I might have known you would be. I hope your hay fever is worse this weekend. See you tonight."

She went out on her happy young legs, not quite so happy.

Down on the sidewalk, in the fine September morning, now approaching noon, she decided to walk. East to Fifth Avenue, and then north, she swung along, still frowning. She was regarding herself as put upon, and the devil of it was that there was no one to blame. She nodded vaguely to two young women who spoke to her as they passed, and, a block further on, to an oldish gentleman who bowed in his stride. She knew how Dol would take it; there would be no blame there, either. The avenue was bright in the sun, and, while the Saturday crowd was of course anything but fashionable, it was certainly not dowdy either in apparel or in spirits. She loved the thousand glances at faces and clothes which the avenue afforded.

Near 44th Street she suddenly brought up short, side-stepped, and stopped square in the path of a man who was plodding along like a tractor. She stood with her nose a foot below his large-scale non-committal face, and smiled up at him as he lifted an enormous hand and clumsily removed an old black derby.

"Delk! How odd to run into you this way! I suppose you're working?"

"Yeah. I'm on a job."

"Tailing?"

"Naw, I'm just looking up some things."

"The smallpox case?"

"Naw, just some junk about a dress a lady never got."

"Oh. It doesn't sound very exciting. Of course, that would depend on the dress. I mustn't keep you. I stopped you—I just saw you and took the opportunity to tell you how pleasant it has been to be associated with you—I mean, it has been a lot of fun—"

The man opened his eyes and demanded from the side of his mouth, "Been?"

"Yes—but of course I shouldn't have said that until— you'll understand later—hey! Bart!" She darted aside. "Bart!" She came back with a young man by the arm, a young man who would obviously feel that he would have to have his coat pressed because the sleeve had been pulled at. Sylvia said, "I want you to meet—Mr. Delk,

Mr. Tavister. Bart you fool. You two should have a lot in common. Talk it over. 'Bye."

She went off without looking back. At 47th Street she turned right, and on Park Avenue entered the lobby of an enormous business hive, took an elevator, and left it at the 32nd floor. A long walk down a corridor, and two turns, took her to a door before which she stopped. She stood and looked at the inscription on it:

BONNER & RAFFRAY, INC.
DETECTIVES

"Damn," she muttered, and opened the door and went in.

CHAPTER

TWO

*T*HE ante-room was small, but neat and handsome. The walls were greenish cream, the lighting indirect, the floor's rubber tiling dark maroon; chairs and a small table and a garment rack were of red and black lacquer with chromium-plated trim, and so was the desk at one end and the telephone switchboard, of toy dimensions, which rested on it; the switchboard alone, specially constructed, had cost a hundred dollars of Raffray money. There were two other doors, near the corners of the partition wall facing the entrance; the glass panel of the one on the left bore the legend, in slim elegant block letters in gold: Miss Bonner. The other said: Miss Raffray.

Sylvia said, "Hullo."

The girl seated behind the desk, obviously a Mediterranean, with a dark, pleasant face and black hair slick on her head, nodded amiably and professionally. "Good morning, Miss Raffray."

"Miss Bonner in?"

The girl nodded. "In her room. Mr. Foltz and Mr. Pratt are with her."

"Oh! Mr. Foltz came? I thought . . ." She crossed to the door on the left, tapped on it with her knuckles, opened it and went in.

"Hello, Sylvia." That greeting was from Theodolinda Bonner, Dol to a few, from her chair at her desk.

The chair might as well have been a stool, for she sat straight without touching the back, as usual. Her curious caramel-colored eyes flashed a glance at her friend and partner from under coal-black lashes—seeming blacker from the cream-tinted transparency of the smooth skin of her rather narrow face.

"Sylvia! Where've you been—" That was from Martin Foltz, as he sprang to his feet to take Sylvia's hands. His own hands were shy and nervous; so were his gray eyes as he leaned to her. His gesture was at once proprietary and unassuming; it was certainly not assertive. Sylvia, her hand released, patted at his hair.

The third greeting, from Silky Pratt, was merely an unheeded mumble. Silky sat in the small chair at the far end of the desk, and stayed in it. He was small and unprepossessing and appeared to be negligible, unless you were observant enough to catch a glimpse of the cleverness in his sharp little eyes.

Martin Foltz, having pulled up a chair for Sylvia and resumed his own, was replying to a question from her: "Yes, I know I said I'd come in Monday, but I changed —I decided to come today." His eyes, nervous and distressed, glanced at Dol Bonner, then back at his fiancée. "They—he came last night. It happened again."

"What!" Sylvia gasped. Her tone was horrified: "Martin! It didn't!"

He nodded. Dol Bonner said, low from her throat but briskly, "Yes. We were discussing it. Pratt just got here. I'm going to put him on it—that is, if you agree—"

Sylvia demanded, "Rabbits or pheasants?"

"Four pheasants. Mongolians. In a shelter roost."

"How awful!" Sylvia was on the edge of her chair.
"I tell you, Martin, the only thing is to wire the whole
place with alarms, runs and all. Either that or get rid of
them."

Foltz shook his head. "You know . . . getting rid
of them . . . and wiring everything would cost too
much. We went into that before. Anyway . . . whoever it is, he's so confounded slick . . ."

"But good lord, you can't let it go on indefinitely!
It's—" Sylvia shivered a little. "It's revolting! Of
course they get killed anyway, but there's something
ghastly about it—"

Dol Bonner put in, "We were discussing it. Do you
want to hear me instruct Pratt, and see what you think?"

"But, Dol, you had Delk—and that other man, the
one with gold teeth—" Sylvia stopped, and sat back.
"All right. Shoot."

Dol Bonner raised her hand and with the tip of her
forefinger touched lightly, twice, a tiny black spot on the
smooth skin covering the jawbone, below her right ear.
It was not an old-fashioned court-plaster decoration, but
her natural property, and was generally considered a
distinction rather than a blemish. She turned to the little
man at the end of the desk:

"Your notebook, Pratt? Put down: Martin Foltz.
That's this man. Two miles northwest of Ogowoc, on the
Castleton road. Wolfram de Roode." She spelled it.
"11 p. m. to 5 a. m., starting tonight. Now."

She swiveled to face him better. "On his estate,
among other things, Foltz keeps hares and pheasants.

He used to do it for amusement, recently he has made money from it, or tried to. There are four outdoor men on his place, not counting a chauffeur, and Wolfram de Roode—you have that down—is in charge of them. One morning last May, in a yard shelter, one of the men found two dead pheasants hanging by the neck on pieces of cord which were tied to a pipe supporting the netting. They had been deliberately strangled. The slip knot had been pulled tight enough to prevent their squawking, but loose enough so their struggles were prolonged; they lost a lot of feathers. Foltz and de Roode investigated, without any success. They were assisted by a man named Zimmerman, a friend of Foltz's who was visiting there. A week later it happened again, this time three pheasants. They put on a night watch—"

Silky Pratt's voice was a thin tenor: "Was Zimmerman there that time?"

"Yes. Not for you, though; you're not going to deduce, you're going to look. Zimmerman is an old and intimate friend of Foltz, from boyhood. After two weeks they discontinued the watch. Ten days later six strangled pheasants were found, by de Roode himself, details exactly the same. They put—"

"What kind of cord was it?"

Dol Bonner shook her head. "Please don't. Didn't I say not for you? All those trails have been followed to a dead end. They put locks on the yards and consulted the police. The police looked around and wandered off. Early in July two hares were found in the same fix. Rabbits. That had required more technique, for rabbits would just as soon squeal at night as in the daytime, and no squeals had been heard.—You don't need to put down the statistics, I'm only telling you so you'll know the situation. They locked the hutches and runs. Three weeks later four pheasants were killed, and the very next night three more hares. Don't ask about keys. They had been kept where even an outsider might have got them if he had done some observing. Of course any of the men could. De Roode could. Even Foltz himself could. What, Martin?"

Her caramel-colored eyes glanced under the black lashes. Foltz didn't smile. He said nervously, "Yes, I could. I could if I walked in my sleep. It's a nightmare." His shoulders jerked a little, and Sylvia reached over and patted one.

Dol Bonner was at Silky Pratt again: "That was six weeks ago, and this firm had opened this office. Miss Raffray persuaded Foltz to call us in. I spent a lot of time on it and got nowhere. Finally I took Delk and hired another man and put them on watch. It's difficult, because some of the yards and runs are portable and cover several acres. It was expensive, and when nothing happened at the end of a month we took the men off. Still nothing happened, until a week ago Thursday night. Friday morning they found two pheasants strangled. They put new locks on; the old ones had been discarded as useless. Last night four more pheasants were killed. The wire had been cut to make an opening in the netting big enough to let a man through. De Roode found them; he'll show them to you tonight if you want to see something."

Silky Pratt's eyes had a glint in them. "I'd like to hear more about that Zimmerman," he said complainingly.

"Forget Zimmerman and all that. I tell you I spent time on it. This is the only failure this firm has had. You will be there at the firm's expense, because Foltz has spent a lot of money and got nothing for it—no, Martin, there's no use arguing, we've got to catch him—or her maybe—and you've paid enough.—There's a train leaves Grand Central at 8:48 and arrives at Ogowoc at 9:40 daylight saving. De Roode will meet you at the Ogowoc station. There's an attic window in the cottage de Roode lives in with a good view of the runs and yards. In case of pitch dark you couldn't see much, but on a clear night, or partly clear, you could detect a man moving. No one but de Roode is to know you are there; you will leave before the men are up. Get plenty of sleep in the daytime, and stick on that job for good. It will be regular eight hour pay, and a hundred dollars extra when you catch him."

Pratt, frowning at her, licked his lips. "But boss. From an attic window. Say I do see him, what's the tactics? How far off will he be?"

Sylvia exploded: "Shoot him!"

He turned up his palms. "In the dark, miss? I'm not that good."

Foltz offered, "Sneak down and rouse de Roode."

Pratt looked doubtful. "Monkeying around in the dark . . ."

Dol Bonner said, "Don't lose sight of him. You will probably see him on his way in, so you will have a little time. Have a rope ready to go out through the window. Have a flashlight and a gun. Get as close as you can quietly. If he runs it will be legal to shoot, but aim low."

"If I aim low I'll hit him in the stomach."

"Don't you dare hit him in the stomach." Dol Bonner's eyes flashed. "Or anywhere else. Just scare him. Then run and catch him. He must be an awful coward to be sneaking around in the night strangling . . ." She shivered. "You can catch him, can't you?"

"I'll try." Silky sighed and was on his feet. "I don't like this on a perch all night. Never have." He moved, and stopped. "This Foltz place, ain't it near that Birchhaven, the Storrs place, where I went for that trunk that time?"

"It adjoins Birchhaven, yes. Now don't start deducing from that." Dol Bonner had left her chair and was beside him. She put a hand on his shoulder. "Get him. Okay, Pratt?"

"Okay, boss. So-long."

"Wait a minute." Dol turned. "How about it, Sylvia? This will cost us money. You're the treasurer."

"Oh, my God." Sylvia looked startled, and helpless. "Oh, Dol—that's what I have to tell you . . . Dol dear. But then—have we got the money in the bank?"

"Of course we have. That thousand you put in Wednesday."

"Good. Go ahead. Unless . . . no, go ahead."

Dol looked at her partner, hesitated, and turned to Silky Pratt and nodded him on his way. When the door had clicked behind him, she walked around the desk again to her chair. Moving, she gave the impression that she was proceeding with the air rather than through it. Unconsciously, seeing her move, or hearing her speak, people settled into their chairs more easily, it was so pleasant to see energy flowing like that, naturally, with no strain and no interruption of grace. She sat down with her back straight, touched the black spot on her cheek with the tip of her finger, lightly, and let her hand fall to the desk.

"Well? The three points didn't work?"

"They did not." Sylvia suddenly grabbed her gloves and hurled them to the floor, then her ostrich-skin bag, harder, to the other side. Foltz reached for the gloves, and got up to retrieve the bag, and sat holding them. Sylvia said bitterly, "I could chew him up."

"But . . ." Dol looked puzzled. "Could he cut you off for six months? Your own money? Is that it?"

"Of course not. I don't know, he wouldn't. That's not it."

"Then . . ." Dol waved a hand. "All right. What does it amount to?"

"Plenty."

"For instance?"

"I am to have no connection whatever, financial or personal, with this damned detective business."

"I see. Just like that." Dol sat a moment, pursed her lips and was so still she seemed to be not breathing. "Well. Then you're not a detective any more. It must be nice to have a man to tell you just what to do. You know I can't return your capital . . . not now."

"Oh, Dol!" Sylvia looked miserable.

Foltz was on his feet. "If I'm in the way——"

Sylvia told him to stay. Dol said, "Not at all, Martin. It will be your turn next to tell her what to do. Stay and admire the virtue of submissiveness."

"Dol Bonner!" Sylvia showed color. "You have no right to say that! I'm not submissive to any man!"

"I don't like men."

"Neither do I! At least—I don't like all of them. But that has nothing to do with it. P.L. didn't tell me what to do. He said specifically that if I stuck here in spite of his disapproval he would do nothing at all, and he would . . . he wouldn't like me any less. That's the devil of it." She sounded bitter. "That's how clever he is. He knows darned well I wouldn't stand for dictation, even from him. He also said I don't owe him any gratitude, because he knows I'm naturally ungrateful and he wouldn't get it even if I did owe it. *But*." She became savage. "He also knows that he has been perfectly swell to me for over fifteen years, and that I have sense enough to know it, and that I'm fair-minded and tenderhearted. After all, that picture of him . . . that piece in the Gazette was appalling."

Dol Bonner asked drily, "Fair-minded? Fair to me?" But at once she added: "No. I take that back. Fair enough. If I had any complaint, which I haven't, it would be against myself, for letting you persuade me . . . as you know, my idea was to go into the detective business alone, in a little room in a cheap building. . . ."

Foltz ventured with diffidence, "If I may—it's none of my affair—but I've often wondered—why did you pick the detective business? A girl of your ability—and

all the people you know—you could have done anything—"

"I know, Martin." Dol sounded patient. "I could
have got a job as a stylist, or an executive secretary, or
started a hat shop or a shopping service. May I just say
I didn't want to? I could add that I wouldn't accept any
man as a boss, and preferably no woman either, and I
made a long list of all the activities I might undertake on
my own. They all seemed monotonous or distasteful except two or three, and I flipped a coin to decide between
detective and landscape design. I had to swallow my
pride to take a favor from one man, to get a license. I
had no family, and my father died owing money, and
instead of taking a thousand dollars from Sylvia to keep
me going a while, I was weak enough to let her come in
for all this." She waved a hand at the handsome room,
with its yellow and blue and chrome, then shrugged her
shoulders and looked at her erstwhile partner. "It's all
washed up, Sylvia dear? Final?"

Sylvia looked miserable again. "Oh, Dol . . ."

"Okay." Dol got brisk. "I'm four years older than
you, I should have known better." She opened a drawer
and took out a sheet of paper with typewriting on it.
"I'm not surprised, and I'm as clever as P. L. Storrs—
I like you no less. I got these figures together this morning. You've advanced nine thousand dollars of the fifteen thousand contemplated as your capital contribution.
It has gone for my salary, office furnishings, payroll,
rent—it's all itemized and I'll give you a copy. We
have—"

"Dol, stop that!" Sylvia's face was flushed. "You don't have to rub it in!"

"I'm not rubbing it in, I'm reporting as president of the corporation. We have taken in $712.83. We have accounts receivable $949.10, all good, they've been slow only because they knew you didn't need the money. Our bank balance is $1164.35. Our net worth is $7219.88, but the furnishings are in at cost, and of course when we sell them—"

"Sell them!" Sylvia gasped. "Dol! Sell these lovely—"

"Certainly sell them. Sylvia dear, you haven't the faintest idea where money comes from. You still think a stork brings it and drops it down the chimney—only in your case it would take quite a flock of storks. Do you suppose I could support this kind of a shebang? The rent alone is eighteen hundred. I don't know what will happen about the lease, but when the corporation is dissolved—and there'll be a lawyer to pay for that—*well!* Get out of here!"

Foltz and Sylvia looked startled, but saw at once that the dismissal was not for them, but for a newcomer. The door had been flung violently open, and an Olympic champion, not of the dark variety, had crossed the threshold. He was tall, built for use, blue-eyed, and as tanned as a nudist on the exposed surfaces. Ignoring the others, he strode across to Dol Bonner's chair, stood there, and said with feeling:

"Nor frighted at the tigress and her claws,
Nor yet the lioness with open jaws!"

He reached down and clutched Dol by her upper arms, lifted her clear of her chair, high above the desk, held her there an instant, and put her back again.

She had offered no struggle. She said calmly but with some intensity: "You darned sadist. I loathe being touched by anyone whatever, and you know it."

The young man looked down at her and shook his head. "Me a sadist? I know where you got the idea, Foltz's strangled pheasants. By gum, I could strangle you, don't think I couldn't. And if you loathe being touched you should conceal it, because it only increases the temptation, which is already irresistible. Anyway, it's the only technique I know, and some day the woman in you will blossom forth and you'll eat it up." He decided to acknowledge the audience. "Hello, Foltz. Hello, Sylvia. Would it interest you to know that when I start strangling in earnest my first customer will be your darling guardian P. L. Storrs? Don't think I don't mean it. The dirty reptile has got me fired." He turned again to Dol: "I want a job. I want to join up here." He spied the chair Silky Pratt had left, went and sat down in it and observed, "I might as well be a detective as a murderer."

"Get out, Len." Dol sounded firm. "We're talking."

"About me?"

"No. Also egotist. Get out."

"And go where? The CCC? The WPA? The Salvation Army? Did you hear me say I got fired?"

"Fired from where?"

"My job on the Gazette. On account of that publicity I gave you, thinking only—"

"Of the money you'd get for it. I know. You mean Mr. Storrs complained?"

"I mean he raised hell. He threatened to sue for libel and they made me the goat." He pounded his chest with his fist. "Leonard Chisholm, goat. I'm nearly broke and I'm a lot madder than you would think to look at me."

"Yes. You mustn't conceal your emotions like that. They erupt." Dol brushed her hair back. "Mr. Storrs is a nice old duffer, isn't he? No more vindictive than Al Smith."

"He isn't!" Sylvia's voice entered. "P.L. is not vindictive, really, Dol. He got mad, I can understand that, and anyway you yourself said that Len ought to have a job on the subway. And he likes Len"—she frowned—"anyhow, he did once." She considered. "Look, Len. We're going to play tennis at Martin's this afternoon, and eat there, and then go to Birchhaven for bridge. You come with us—that is, if Martin—"

Foltz nodded positively. "By all means. Come ahead, Len."

Sylvia went on, "And you come along to Birchhaven, and we'll see. If you can disguise yourself as a member of the human race, it will be all right. P.L. is not vindictive."

Chisholm regarded her doubtfully. At length he shook his head. "Aw, it's going to rain."

"Now, Len! That Gazette piece *was* terrible."

"I'm broke. I've pawned my uniform."

"You have not. You couldn't get anything on it. Anyway, none of us will dress." Sylvia got up and skipped to him, and put her hand on his sleeve. "Do it for me, Len. I feel bad about it."

"You look out. Get away." Chisholm turned indignantly to Dol Bonner: "My God, can *nothing* make you jealous? Don't you see how she's working on me, and her betrothed?" To Sylvia: "All right, go and sit down. I'll come. But little you know what for. Did you hear me say I'll strangle that old bucko? This will be my opportunity. I'll roll him under the bridge table and use him for a hassock."

"You'd much better be nice to him." Sylvia, back in her chair, frowned a little. "And you'd better watch yourself or he may strangle you. I know he would just as soon murder somebody, for he told me so this morning."

"Not me." Chisholm was positive. "He already has me in a state worse than death—I'm broke. On the level, was darling P.L. out for blood? Who, the office boy? Doesn't sound like him. Say, I'll bet he's after Dol. I'll protect her."

"I don't know who it was." Sylvia still frowned. "Unless it was Steve Zimmerman."

Foltz looked astonished. "Steve! Why Steve?"

"Oh, I just said that. But you know P.L. doesn't like Steve; he won't like him even for your sake, Martin. Then this morning I met Steve in the corridor outside P.L.'s office, and he acted—"

"Steve? You met Steve there?" Foltz was incredulous.

"Yes, why shouldn't I? I mean, if he arrived at a certain given spot at the precise moment that I arrived at it, I was bound to meet him, no way out of it. Though I admit I was as surprised as you are. He talked very funny—I know he often does, and what can you expect, a scientist like him with his mind on his genius. But he seemed to me to be raving—for instance, he mentioned mortal injury, and sacrifice and devotion, and all at once he scuttled—left me standing with my mouth open. Then when I got into P.L.'s room I found him in a trance, absolutely, he didn't even invite me to have a drink of water. Later he doubled up his fists and said he would like to kill a man with his two hands."

Len Chisholm nodded. "It must be either the office boy or Steve Zimmerman. It couldn't be Martin, because he thinks Martin is the bubble in the champagne. It couldn't be me, because he knows I'd break his neck. What's eating you, Martin?"

"Nothing." Foltz jerked around to him. "Only— Steve is an old friend of mine, and he does get funny sometimes—I was wondering . . ."

"Nothing to wonder about. Steve went down there to do Storrs a mortal injury, and Storrs wants to bounce it back at him. It's all right. Those things always reach a climax sooner or later. Like the job I had. It took me a year to get on the Gazette. Oh, well." He turned to Dol Bonner. "Let's go get some lunch."

She shook her head. "You're broke."

"No. I just meant that as a euphemism. Anyway, my credit's good at George and Harry's, and I'll win a fortune at bridge tonight if you'll be my partner."

She shook her head again. "I'm busy. You can all get

out of here any time now.—I'll mail you a copy of this statement, Sylvia."

"You'll what?" Sylvia stood up. "Now don't be eccentric, Dol.—How did you come in, Martin, train?—Good. I've got the big car. We'll all have a bite together and drive out to Martin's. Come, comrades."

They got up, but Dol Bonner sat. "Run along and godspeed." She waved a hand.

Sylvia wheeled. "Dol . . . Dol dear . . . won't you come?"

"No. Really."

"Do you hate me?"

"Of course not. I adore you. I like you. I can't go to Birchhaven because I'm taking Dick to a matinee. He leaves Monday for Gresham. At least—" She hesitated. "I guess he does." She shrugged, and smiled. "Piffle. Of course he does."

Sylvia had looked suddenly startled, and now stood with compressed lips. She opened them: "Good Lord. That shows you what I'm like. I hadn't thought of Dick at all. But Dick certainly has nothing to do with the detective business, and there's no reason—"

"No, Sylvia." Dol's eyes flashed. "Really, you know —not even from you."

"And why not?" Sylvia demanded. "Why shouldn't I? Don't be selfish. Just because you've got a kid brother you're proud of, and I haven't got any at all—you were going to pay the darned school out of your salary, weren't you? And now it's all arranged for Gresham, and the fact is I'm as responsible as you are—"

"No." Dol was incisive. "He's my brother and nobody else's, and certainly I'm selfish. I shouldn't have mentioned it. I'll manage."

"Please?" Sylvia extended both her palms. *"Please?"*

Dol shook her head. "Not even you, Sylvia. You know the jolt my pride got two years ago, and I have to baby it. Not even you."

It sounded final. Sylvia stood and stared at her helplessly. After a moment Dol said brusquely, "You folks had better move along. And Sylvia—you'd better tell your room goodbye."

"I won't! I won't look at it! I . . ." Sylvia went to the desk and stood there looking down into her former partner's caramel-colored eyes. After a moment she demanded: "Dol, am I a louse?" After another moment: "Oh, damn!" she exploded, and turned and ran out of the room. Foltz followed her.

Dol surveyed the ex-newspaper man and said, "Go on, Len. Go away."

Chisholm stood looking surly. "I won't if you don't. Come to lunch."

"Len Chisholm." Dol's voice had bite in it. "You need that job. Realpolitik. Run."

Len strode to the door, turned there, extended his long arms as a suppliant, and whined, "Sister, can you spare a dime?" Then he flung the door open and was gone.

As the door banged behind him Dol Bonner winced, just perceptibly. She sat straight listening to the sound of his four steps crossing the ante-room, and the opening and closing of the door to the corridor, then she crossed her arms on the blue-lacquered desk-top and let

her head go down to them. Apparently she was not cry-
ing, for her trim shoulders in a lightweight tan woolen
dress, and her soft light brown hair, all that showed of
her head, were motionless.

She was still like that ten minutes later, when there
was a light tapping at the door and it began to open cau-
tiously.

Dol jerked herself up. "Come in."

It was the Mediterranean girl. Dol asked, "Yes?"
The girl said: "A man wants to know if you will be here
at one o'clock. It's twenty minutes to one."

"What man?"

"He won't give his name. He sounds . . . important."

"Maybe he is. It doesn't matter. I'll be here."

The girl went. When the door had closed again, Dol
got up and walked to a window and stood there looking down at roofs and chasms. After a while her arms
went up and out and she stretched herself thoroughly,
then patted and pulled at the woolen dress, down and
around. She wandered about the room, looking at this
and touching that, finally stopping in front of a picture
on the wall between the windows, a fine engraving of a
stodgy pile of a building with an inscription beneath:
NEW SCOTLAND YARD. She wasn't really looking
at it; she had not liked it, thinking it pretentious or
ridiculous, or both, to have it there; Sylvia had insisted
on it as the display of an ideal. Dol Bonner was thinking of something else; her practical, impatient and
lonely mind had no time to waste on ideals, either as
goals or as decorations. Suddenly she turned and went

to the door, entered the ante-room, and crossed to the desk in the corner.

She said to the girl: "Martha, I ought to tell you. I have to give you a week's notice. Should it be two weeks?"

"Why—" The girl gasped. "You mean—Miss Bonner—" Her face flamed. "I thought—"

"We're shutting the office. Quitting. Dissolving the firm. If it should be two weeks you'll get the pay. You're okay, and you'd earn more than you'd get, anywhere. I know lots of people, and I won't mind doing one of them a favor by telling him to hire you."

"Oh . . . I can get a job any time." So the tears that had appeared in Martha's eyes were not for that. "But it's so wonderful here with you and Miss Raffray . . . you don't really . . . really have to dissolve. . . ."

"Don't you dissolve in tears.—Or maybe you ought to. I've never been able to manage it—it must be convenient for you people, keeping your emotional pipes clean and open with all that flushing—good heavens, you really are—"

Dol turned and fled back to her room and went to her desk. She was definitely uncomfortable and irritated, but not, she thought, depressed. The contretemps had its consolations. She hated to lose Sylvia because she loved and admired her, but it would bring satisfaction to be on her own. A cheaper and dingier office would be less pleasant, since she had all her life been accustomed to desirable things, even elegant ones, but after all a detective agency should not look like a beauty parlor. She might, before getting on her feet, have to borrow money from some other source than Sylvia, but the obligation of a debt ceased when it was discharged with interest. In any event, Dick should go to Gresham and be maintained there—both her brother and her pride deserved that. She sat considering these things, and others connected with them, when she might better have been devoting her talents to the problems of some of the Bonner & Raffray clients: the $400 gown that had unaccountably disappeared between the salon of Elizabeth Hawes and the Park Avenue apartment of Anita Gifford; the whereabouts of the champion Sealyham whose prolonged absence was sending Colonel Fethersee into fits; the strangled pheasants of Martin Foltz; the intentions of a showgirl named Lili Lombard with regard to a youth named Harold Ives Beaton, and his with regard to her. But she was so far away from those problems and the immediate scene that she did not hear the sounds accompanying an arrival in the ante-room.

There was a tap at the door of her room, and it opened, and closed. Martha was there. Her eyes looked red.

"A man to see you, Miss Bonner. It's the man that phoned."

"Oh. Has he remembered his name?"

"I . . . I didn't ask him. Shall I ask him?"

Dol shook her head. "Send him in."

Martha, out again, left the door open, and in a moment a man came through, and Martha, behind him, was at the knob. At sight of the caller there was a flicker of surprise beneath Dol's black lashes. But it was not noticeable in her voice: "How do you do, Mr. Storrs.—You may go, Martha. I won't need you."

"I can stay if you want, Miss Bonner."

"No. I don't want. Behave yourself. See you Monday."

Martha backed out with the knob. P. L. Storrs approached the desk. He removed a handsome topcoat, placed it on a chair and his hat on top, took another chair for himself, and rumbled in his bass:

"You're surprised to see me, I suppose. I didn't give my name on the telephone because I know you're temperamental and you might have run away."

"Run away?" Dol's brows went up. "From you?"

Storrs nodded. "Pique. Resentment. I suppose Sylvia came here from my office this morning. Naturally you're in a tantrum."

Dol laughed a little. "I'm not much on tantrums. I think you have interfered in something that was none of your business, but that seems—"

"That thing in the Gazette was none of my business?" Storrs showed a little color. "That outrageous—" He stopped himself abruptly. "But here now. That's a waste of time. I came here for something else."

Dol observed sweetly, "You started it. Temperament, tantrums, pique . . ."

"Forget it. I didn't come here to quarrel, and I didn't come to apologize. But my attitude toward Sylvia, and toward that infamous newspaper article, has nothing to do with my admiration of your abilities. I've seen enough of you to realize that you are a very competent person.

I can use that competence. I want to hire you to do a job."

"A job?" Dol sounded surprised. "I'm a detective."

"This is a detective job. A confidential and difficult one."

Dol looked at him suspiciously. "I think not." She shook her head. "It's pretty transparent, Mr. Storrs. Congratulations on your kind heart, but if you think you've been tough on a poor young girl trying to get along in the world and want to make up for it—no, thanks. It isn't necessary. I don't despise charity for those who have to have it, but I certainly despise it for myself." She smiled at him and finished briskly, "Thank you very much."

"Don't thank me." Storrs rewarded her smile with a scowl. "And don't jump ahead like that. Your mind needs discipline. I have no notion of making anything up to you. Even if I were inclined that way, at present I am too damned busy trying to make things up to myself. I have never done any talking to anyone about my personal affairs, maybe I should have. I might have saved myself some shocks—and others too. I think it's about time for me to do a little blurting—and at that, I doubt if there's much secret to it. For example, do you happen to know that my wife is an utter fool?"

Dol calmly nodded. "Certainly. It's obvious."

"The devil." Storrs shut his lips tight. He opened them again: "I suppose it is. I like your directness. I have judged that you have discretion. Without regard to any charity, I want you to do a job for me. May I ask a few questions?"

She nodded. He demanded: "What do you know about the League of the Occidental Sakti?"

"A little." Dol summoned her memory. "The worship of Sakti concerns the active producing principle of one of the goddess wives of Siva. They have lovely names: Durga, Kali, Parvati. Siva is a god of the supreme triad, and represents the principle of destruction, and also the reproductive or restoring power, because destruction involves restoration as a consequence. He is also god of the arts, especially dancing. Of course that's all old Oriental stuff; for the League of the Occidental Sakti it has been pepped up a good deal by a man called George Leo Ranth. You know Mr. Ranth."

"Yes." Storrs sounded grim. "I know him. I don't know if you'll do for this, Miss Bonner. It sounds as if you've got it too."

"No, I haven't got it. I've seen Mr. Ranth only at your home, and once I heard him explaining life and the universe and so on."

"Are you completely free of his influence?"

"Good heavens, yes." She shivered delicately.

"When I say I want to hire you for a job, I don't mean bums that work for you, I mean you. Will you work on this yourself?"

"If I accept the job, and if the pay is appropriate."

"It will be. Do you regard the confidences of your clients as inviolable?"

Her brows went up. "Mr. Storrs . . . really!" She shrugged. "Yes."

"Good. I may as well tell you, something exploded in my face today. Something incredible. It made me consider things. It struck me that while I was cleaning up that debris I might as well make a clean sweep. I've been pretty well jolted. I'm going to do some jolting myself. Here's your part of it. In the past year this George Leo Ranth has got around $30,000 out of my wife for his damned league. She has swallowed the hook and there's no way of getting it out of her except to cut her open. I told her a week ago that her bank account is closed and she gets no more cash and I'll pay the bills, but a man can't live like that with the woman he's married to—damn it, there are plenty of women worse than my wife if she would only learn to keep her nose out of the cosmos! I haven't ordered Ranth to keep away from my place, because if I did she would only go and listen to him somewhere else; he has others on the string and he holds meetings. She told me yesterday that unless she can give money to the league she will have to be a pilgrim and dress in a burlap shawl and take long walks to places hundreds of miles off, and it wouldn't surprise me an iota if she had the thing made at Bergdorf Goodman and put on the account. Do you know her well enough to know that?"

Dol nodded. "Yes, I think I know her that well."

"All right. But that's only half of it—" Storrs cut himself off abruptly. He stabbed at Dol with his eyes, with his chin out, and then went on more deliberately, "I'm staking a lot on your discretion, Miss Bonner. Ranth intends to marry my daughter Janet. My wife threatened me with it yesterday. Threatened me!"

"Yes?"

"Yes. I suppose I was a fool, but I hadn't expected

that. As if it wasn't bad enough already . . . and to find that when it comes right down to it I'm absolutely helpless. . . ."

"Have you spoken to Janet about it?"

"She was there during my talk with my wife—most of it. She heard that. My wife insinuated that the wedding might take place next month, next week, tomorrow. Janet is twenty-six years old. She sat and looked at her mother with the devoted expression—you've seen it. It would be useless my saying anything to her. I am a complete failure with my daughter. I have never yet understood one word of anything she has ever said, and only my own vanity has kept me persuaded that she may be sane. And yet she has poetry published in magazines, and she graduated from a college . . . but she can't add, I've noticed that. But she's my daughter, and she was not born and fed and educated to marry a scoundrel like Ranth. And it might be tomorrow! By heaven, it might! You know my wife. I can't lock them in the cellar and feed them through a trapdoor. Can I?"

He spread out his hands. "I'm absolutely helpless, Miss Bonner. I've thought of everything. I've come to you. I want you to remove this Ranth." He sat back.

Dol asked, with no visible smile, "You mean take him for a ride? Bump him off? I myself?"

Storrs didn't smile either. He let down a little. "If he has to be killed, I could do that myself." He was merely somber. "I mean get rid of him, I don't care how. With all her riding around on clouds, my wife is a stickler for conventional morality. Ranth's past must be full of immoralities; prove it and discredit him. He may have been in jail; uncover it. He looks like he may be a Greek; that would probably do it; my wife thinks the Greeks are scum because they licked the Persians and upset their temples. That may sound funny, but it's not, I got over that idea long ago, it may be anything else, but it's not funny. But I want to suggest: you can start someone else on his record who knows how to go at it, and you can start directly on him. You can do that. Tell him you're interested in this damned Sakti; get his mind off of Janet as soon as possible; tell him you've inherited a million dollars, but hold off on him and keep him working—I don't need to tell you—I know you're a clever woman. Maybe you can even ruin him whether we get him on his record or not. You can come out to my house this afternoon and start in; he's always there Saturdays, you'd be sure to catch him around six o'clock, and you could make some kind of an appointment. . . . I'll say I invited you. Or five-thirty . . ."

Storrs stopped, and scowled at her.

She sat regarding him. Storrs let the silence extend far beyond his usual limit, and then broke it:

"Well . . . Oh, would you like some cash? Retainer."

"No, thanks." Dol straightened her back, already straight. "So. Ranth has overplayed. That shows one weakness in him to begin with. Of course, Mr. Storrs, this is rather a nasty job, but if I'm going to be a detective I can't expect to confine my contacts to saints and epicures. I'll do it for you, but I'll send you a stiff bill."

"I'll pay it."

"Yes, I know you're good pay. You know . . . it

seems to me . . ." She hesitated, then went on, "Since you're paying me, I suppose you should have the benefit of what I know as well as what I do. Your wife is a bluffer."

"Bluffer?" Storrs was astonished. He snorted, "You're not making a good start, Miss Bonner. Cleo Audrey Storrs a bluffer? If she once gets steam up on a track you might as well try to derail the Century by jumping in front of it."

"Oh, no." Dol shook her head. "I wish I had a nickel for every time you have given in when you didn't need to. Your domestic life has been one long series of unnecessary surrenders. You no more understand your wife than you do your daughter. Mrs. Storrs has many good points, of course you know that, in spite of her riding around on clouds and using your money to pay the wind for the ride—but she's a colossal bluffer. I knew that long ago, the second time I visited Sylvia at your house."

He gazed at her. "I don't believe it."

"You should. You'd find it a great help. For instance, take her threat of Ranth marrying Janet. She couldn't possibly make that threat good if she wanted to, and she knows it. At least not until after Sylvia is married. Because Janet is deeply and passionately in love with Martin Foltz, and she isn't the kind to resign all hope before the last breath."

This time Storrs was too amazed to speak. He gaped at her. Then he actually stuttered: "M—M—Martin? Janet?"

Dol nodded. "You don't believe that either."

"My God, no!" He was forward in his chair. "But that—and Sylvia—that would be worse than Ranth—"

"Now, Mr. Storrs." Dol was professionally soothing, in her lowest and nicest tone. "You're all confused. It'll work out all right. Your daughter Janet is exactly the type to get the best possible results, including a lot of poetry, out of an unrequited love, once hope is dead. Of course you're thinking of Sylvia's happiness—I know you approve of Martin and I suppose I do too, even if he is a man—but that isn't going to be interfered with. Martin and Sylvia will get married and live happily ever after, and Janet will eat three meals a day and begin to get into anthologies. Not that her passion isn't genuine, but there are lots of different kinds."

Storrs muttered, "Passion. Janet." Scowling with uncommon ferocity, he demanded, "How do you know this? Do you mean Martin has been at her?"

"Oh, goodness, no. Martin has had nothing to do with it. If all the women in the metropolitan district except Sylvia were sick in bed, he wouldn't send a single flower. As for how I know, that wouldn't do you any good. I do know. So the removal of Ranth isn't quite as urgent as you thought. Do you still want me to start on it today?"

"I suppose so. Yes, I do." Storrs abruptly stood up. "I have too much . . . too many . . ." He stared at Dol a moment, apparently without knowing he was doing it, then turned and picked up his hat and coat. And Dol in turn stared at him, for, incredibly, he sounded pathetic: "I was going to play golf this afternoon. I can't do that. There is no reason in God's world why all this . . . this damnable . . ." He stopped, and started again: "I'm sorry, Miss Bonner. I'm usually coherent. I'll see you at Birchhaven later? I'd like to see you when you come."

She nodded. "Around six o'clock."

He went. When she had heard the outer door close behind him she crossed to the picture of New Scotland Yard and told it: "If you watch me on this one you'll get some pointers. This is going to be good."

CHAPTER

THREE

*B*IRCHHAVEN had formerly been a hundred and ninety acres; it was now eighty-five. When the chemical industry had reached the bottom of the trough in 1932 P. L. Storrs had been forced to adopt even more drastic expedients than permitting Sylvia Raffray to buy stock from the treasury of his corporation; among other things, he had sold more than half of the area of his estate to a development syndicate. Luckily they had not yet got around to developing, and he was now negotiating to buy it back. What was still his was the most desirable portion and included all the buildings; it held the wooded hill down to and beyond the brook, the winding drive and park and gardens, the shrub and evergreen plantings of his father's time as well as his own, the pools, one for swimming and one for panfish and lilies, the stables, kennels, lawns and tennis court.

From the peak of the roof of the house, provided you could get there, you would see, for the distant view, ranks and files of far-off hills on two sides, to the east the sound, and to the south the vague horizon flattening for New York and the ocean; for the foreground, mostly the groves and meadows of Birchhaven itself, except over and beyond the stables to the other side of the hill, where the more modest property of Martin Foltz could be reached by a ten-minute path through the trees.

When Dol Bonner, at six o'clock that Saturday afternoon, steered her coupe (one of the assets of Bonner & Raffray, Inc., soon to be dissolved) up the winding drive and onto the graveled space beyond the shrubbery bordering the terrace, she was surprised to hear sounds of activity from the direction of the tennis court. She decided to go there, since not to do so would perhaps occasion conjecture, and, nodding a greeting to Belden, the butler, who had emerged from the door, she banged the door of the car and set off along the path which pointed around the slope. She still wore the tan woolen dress, with a loose red jacket and a little brown hat which might or might not have seemed familiar to a Tyrolese.

She stopped short of the chairs and tables, unperceived. Sylvia and Len Chisholm were at combat on the court, using more energy for shouting epithets and defiance than for the combat itself. Janet Storrs stood near one end of the net, twirling a stem of goldenrod in her fingers. Martin Foltz lounged in a chair, apparently sunk in gloom, holding a glass which contained the remains of a tall drink. Steve Zimmerman, in another chair, was squinting through a sherry decanter at the sun low in the west, either admiring the color or ascertaining the level of the wine.

Dol walked across and brought up beside Foltz. "Hello, Martin. What is that, Irish?"

Foltz looked up at her without surprise and without welcome, being seemingly submerged in some medium which functioned as an insulator. He shook his head.

"Bourbon. There may be Irish. The things are over there by Steve."

Dol said pleasantly, "Grump." A cry came:

"Hey! Theodolinda!"

The conflict on the court stopped abruptly, the ball rolling to the far end. Sylvia trotted across the boundary toward them, with Len Chisholm following. Sylvia was calling, "Dol darling! You got lonesome for us? I'm beating the stuffing out of Len."

Len was there. He had approached staggering, and now declared, "Theodolinda my love, you're late. If you had come two hours ago I wouldn't be drunk. I'm suffering."

"He's not drunk," Sylvia said disdainfully. "It's an alibi."

Dol nodded. "It always is, with him. I'm thirsty— may I find some Irish and water to spread it out?" They moved to the table where the bottles and glasses were. Dol spoke to Zimmerman in his chair: "Hello, Steve, how are brains making out?" She went on, as Sylvia assembled her drink, "I thought you folks would be over at Martin's. Wasn't that the program? I stopped here for courtesy. Around one o'clock P. L. Storrs got magnanimous and telephoned me at the office to invite me out here—"

"Dol! Did he?" Sylvia extended the glass. "Did he say—did he take back what he told me this morning?"

"No, he didn't go that far. He wasn't retreating, he was just being tolerant. Anyway, he asked me to Birch-haven, so I thought I'd better come here before joining

you at Martin's. I stayed with Dick to the end of the
matinee, sent him in a taxi to the Fergusons', and drove
here like a Valkyrie on wheels." She took two healthy
sips, nodded in approval, and sipped again. "And now I
should find Mrs. Storrs for some more courtesy, since
I'm having refreshment out of her glass. Didn't you go
to Martin's after all?"

"Yes, we . . ." Sylvia bit her lip and waved a hand.
"We were there. Men are fools. I know you think that
all the time, but I have lapses. Len didn't behave very
well, and Martin tried to match him. We came away,
and later Martin came. I suppose he and I aren't speaking, but we soon will be."

Len declared, loud enough to reach all around, "He's
plain dumb. Sylvia was trying to console me for your
absence and for losing my job, and I was fighting her
off. Martin started hissing and writhing, and since I only
came—"

"Len, you gorilla!" Sylvia glared. "Martin does not
hiss and writhe, he merely got mad—"

Len turned on volume: "—since I only came to do a
grovel to P. L. Storrs, I took the path over here. He
wasn't in the house and I couldn't find him anywhere
outdoors. I wandered around, and here came Sylvia. She
entreated me to let her beat me at tennis, and sent for
drinks." He smirked extravagantly at Dol. "I tell you
all this because I don't want you to lose any of your illusions about me. If you lose your illusions our whole ro-
mance falls flat. I haven't a thought—how about it,
Miss Storrs? You've been here the past half hour,
haven't you observed that every time I took a drink—"

"Shut up, Len." Dol widened the circle. "How've you been, Janet? Don't mind him. What a nice dress—that scarf thing—did Cora Lane do it?"

Janet Storrs said yes. She was taller than either Dol or Sylvia, and not at all bad-looking, in spite of a nose rather large for her face—whether from adenoids or from patrician blood. Her gray eyes were sleepy—or perhaps smouldering, her chin somewhat pointed, her neck and shoulders magnificent but stiffish, her movements slow legato. She did successfully achieve mystery; it would have been difficult to say on brief acquaintance whether she was Valkyrie, or viper, or merely an unemployed young woman who stayed in bed too late of mornings. Her voice was a thin soprano which was not especially pleasant, but with a quality of modulation which caught attention.

The three girls chattered. Len Chisholm sidled to the table, mixed a highball, and stood holding it, looking down into the face of Steve Zimmerman, who returned the gaze without any indication of his usual interest in physiognomies. Len carefully and deliberately winked at him, shrugged broad shoulders, swallowed half of his drink, then winked at Zimmerman again. Zimmerman, without any change of expression, said distinctly: "Paranoiac."

Len growled at him, "Melancholia. Dementia praecox. Schizo-something. Dual personality. Triple, quadruple, quintuple, and on up. I know words too. Go climb a tree." He turned his back and stood moving his glass in a rapid circle to make the ice go around.

Martin Foltz, in his chair at a distance, submerged

in his medium, had not moved or spoken. But he was now disturbed by compulsion. There was the sound of footsteps on the gravel path, and voices, and a man and woman appeared; and since the woman was the hostess of Birchhaven, Foltz perforce lifted himself to his feet. He moved, spoke, took Mrs. Storrs' hand and bowed over it; but was curt to the man: "Hullo, Ranth." They moved on to the others, and he sat down again.

Mrs. Storrs greeted everyone, and even thought to introduce Chisholm and Ranth. She was sociable and urbane, but her voice never really put anyone at ease, by reason of an intensity which was invariable with it. It was not shortness of breath; rather, it seemed that her diaphragm formed a compression chamber which needed a larger valve than her throat afforded. Her eyes had intensity too; they were never casual; there was obviously something unique and unforgettable about everything and everyone she looked at. But even so, Dol Bonner thought there was more strain, both to the eyes and the voice of Mrs. Storrs, than common, and she hoped that Storrs, on arriving home, had not himself been indiscreet.

Dol let that thought flit by. She was more interested in George Leo Ranth, since she had engaged to ruin him. He was not actually slimy; in fact, seeing him in a theater seat or on the sidewalk, you might have taken him for nothing more sinister than an importer of almonds and olive oil, or a Fifth Avenue shoe salesman. He was a little above medium in size, somewhere between forty and fifty in age, dark-skinned, well-dressed, deferential with women, and dignified and aloof with men. Dol had once seen him maintain that dignity at the Birch-haven dinner table, with P. L. Storrs present and not trying for a record in politeness, and had thought it an extremely smooth performance. Now, observing him unobtrusively as he ignored Len Chisholm (that alone quite a feat), prepared a drink for Mrs. Storrs, and conversed with Sylvia and Janet and Zimmerman, she realized that her boast to the picture of Scotland Yard had been merely a statement of necessity: this operation would have to be good.

A notion struck her. Her enterprise would be rendered doubly difficult, even perhaps impossible, if George Leo Ranth was given any reason to suspect that she was engaged on it; and, while her presence at Birchhaven was by no means unprecedented, the circumstances of her coming today were such that some chance remark might give Ranth a hint. She, and Storrs too, had already been careless. Possibly her explanation to Sylvia of the telephoned invitation from Storrs had already been contradicted by something he had said to his wife or daughter. Also, he had said that he would like to see her when she arrived. He might appear to join the gathering at any moment. She must see him first, for a word or two, alone. Considering the matter, she let her head go back for the last drops of the drink to trickle into her throat. Then she put the glass on the table and turned casually to Sylvia:

"I'll be back in a minute. The simple pleasures of the poor."

Sylvia nodded and Dol trotted off. Past Martin Foltz, back along the sloping path, past her coupe still standing on the graveled space, across the terrace and into the house. In the reception hall a maid carrying a huge vase of gladioli halted to give her gangway. She found the butler in the dining-room, surveying the table with a frown which meant that he was completely in the dark as to how many places would be required, and knew not when light would come.

Dol asked him, "Do you know where I might find Mr. Storrs, Belden?"

"No, Miss Bonner." Belden faced her. "I think not in the house. He went out over two hours ago."

"Away? In the car?"

"Oh, no. I saw him walking—he isn't at the tennis court?"

"No."

The butler shook his head. "I really couldn't say. Perhaps at the kennels . . . or the garden. . . ."

Dol thanked him, and went through another door and along a hall, emerging onto a narrower terrace at the other side of the house. She looked vaguely around at shrubs and trees and the green alley to the swimming pool. This was a nuisance, but she ought to find him. If he had gone for a long walk he would surely be returning soon, since it was going on for seven o'clock. From this side she could get to the kennels and stables without being observed from the tennis court. She started off that way.

At the kennels there was no one at all except the dogs. At the stables milking was going on and a man was telling the horses goodnight, but it was not Storrs, and he was not around. Dol left on a trot. She couldn't comb the estate, and she decided to let it go and wait for him to show up, but on her way back to the house she could try a couple of spots. She knew Storrs took especial pride in the vegetable garden, and she turned aside and went through a gap in a yew hedge to give it a look, but saw only tomatoes and pole beans and tiled celery and late corn and fat pumpkins impatient for the frost. Back through the yew hedge again, she remembered a corner that was peculiarly Storrs' private and personal spot, a nook beyond the fish pool beneath some dogwood trees, near by other trees which concealed a toolhouse and a shed for mulch. She left her course again and took off down the slope. She skirted the pool, dodged a planting of rhododendron, and there, in his personal nook, she found P. L. Storrs. When she saw him she stopped short, stood perfectly rigid, and, wanting to scream, set her teeth down hard on her lip. It looked at first as if he were doing a grotesque dance in the air, three inches above the ground, with his toes pointing downward; it was not easy to see the slender wire which looped around his neck and stretched taut up to a limb of a dogwood tree.

Dol moved, took one step, and stopped again. She was telling herself with desperate ferocity: *You have simply got to control yourself, you have simply got to.* She stood and shut her eyes, tight, thinking she would not open them again until she stopped feeling numb. She had an overpowering desire to sit down, to quit trying to hold herself up, but was determined not merely to collapse, and there was nothing within reach to sit on . . . or maybe there was . . . she opened her eyes.

She ventured a movement and found that her legs would work and did not even appear to be trembling. She took five good steps toward P. L. Storrs, where he danced, and stood looking straight at him.

He was unquestionably dead. If he was not dead the thing to do was to get him down and get help to make him breathe, but surely he was dead. His mouth was partly open and the end of his tongue, dark purple, showed between his teeth. His eyes were pushed halfway out. His face looked swollen and was the color of an eggplant. He was surely dead. She took three more steps, stopped, and stretched out her hand arm's length —a silly and purposeless gesture, since she was still five feet from him. She muttered to herself aloud, "I am too damned fastidious. I always have been. Nurses handle dead people all the time." She was surprised that her voice sounded firm and controlled, and got courage from it. She moved forward and grasped the hand hanging alongside Storrs' body, held it and felt it. He was dead all right. She backed up a little and again spoke aloud: "Here it is. I'm alone with it. I'm not going to run, not for a minute anyhow."

Her blood was calming down, leaving a tingle all over her. She looked around. First at the wire; it went from its loop around Storrs' neck up to a limb of the dogwood tree some eight feet above the ground, passed over the top of the limb, stretched diagonally to a crotch of another limb with the trunk at a lower level, was wound several times around the trunk itself, in a spiral, and had its end twisted in one of those windings. Dol Bonner frowned at the spiral; it was not a way to fasten a wire. She looked at the ground. Beginning at the edge of the concrete walk which led to the toolhouse was grass which carpeted the nook; and to her eye, which was keen enough but not really practised, it was merely grass. There were, though, two noticeable items: some distance back of Storrs' dangling feet, a bench, long and wide and heavy, lay overturned; and near one end of it there was a white object on the grass. Dol circled to get to it—yes, it was a crumpled piece of paper. She stooped to pick it up, but her fingers stopped short of it; she looked at it, but it was too crumpled to make anything of without touching it. She stood up, frowning. Veteran detectives would soon be coming to this place, perhaps famous ones; but she too was a detective; she realized with a shock that that was what she was thinking. She glanced at the paper again but left it untouched. She surveyed the nook again, but not to any purpose, knowing that she had seen all she could see, then turned her back on it and left its gloom, passed again around the curve of the fish pool, and headed up the slope toward the house.

Before she reached the house she had determined on something. She went around instead of entering it, and at the far end, screened by a clump of evergreens, opened her bag and took out her mirror and examined her face. In spite of the swift walk uphill it was not flushed, but she thought it not too pale. She went on, and down the path to the tennis court, trying to collect as she went the loose ends of her agitation, wishing she could know how her face was acting and was going to act.

Apparently her face was all right, and it seemed that

no one had fretted at her absence, not even Len Chisholm. He was standing at the edge of the court with Janet Storrs, demonstrating something. Sylvia was perched on the arm of Martin Foltz's chair; evidently, as she had predicted, they were indeed speaking again, or at least she was. Zimmerman remained as before. Mrs. Storrs turned from her conversation with George Leo Ranth as Dol approached:

"My dear, Mr. Ranth and I were speaking of you! Mr. Ranth has taught me that the essence cannot be invited, it seeks its own residence, it alights upon the crooked twig as well as the straight young shoot! If you should be chosen, as I have been! Mr. Ranth thinks not! They are trying to decide where to eat, and of course Sylvia in particular because she has Martin to manage. Siva destroys husbands with wives, and wives with husbands, even before the rites. Mr. Ranth says you have no insight, you are too lonely for the communion."

Dol protested, "But if I can't invite I can only wait. Perhaps, Mr. Ranth, you don't know how hopefully some people do wait."

"Never in vain, Miss Bonner." Ranth was positive but polite. "Not in vain if they are destined. Drops of water unite always, if they touch, but their strongest reluctance just precedes the union." He raised a deprecating hand. "The enthusiasm of Mrs. Storrs races ahead of me at times. I would hesitate to disturb your bliss in ignorance."

"When better bliss is made, ignorance will make it." Dol was aware that her remark was silly and her voice

pitched too high. She moved. "I think I can use a drink
—no, thanks—please don't—rather do it myself—"

She poured Irish, conscious that Steve Zimmerman,
from his chair nearby, was observing her without turning
his head. She looked directly at him, then turned her
back for another glance at Ranth and Mrs. Storrs and
the others farther off. She perceived the futility of the
little project she had determined upon after she had left
the nook. If P. L. Storrs had been murdered by someone present there in that group, he was not likely,
however unsuspected and on whatever edge of horrible
expectancy, to exhibit any stigmata of guilt which she
could recognize with any assurance. "Someone present
there" meant chiefly, of course, George Leo Ranth. He
was apparently completely himself. So was Len Chisholm, loudly ragging Janet Storrs, who was looking bewildered. So was Steve Zimmerman, who was commonly
either glum and silent or inquisitive and loquacious.
Likewise Martin Foltz, who was suffering Sylvia to be-
rate him and cozen him, in turn, out of a fit of jealousy.
Dol swallowed the Irish straight, shivered, and surveyed them all again, beginning and ending with Ranth.
Detect? Detect nothing.

She put the glass down. Now, then . . . but not any
of them. Certainly not dear Sylvia. Not Len Chisholm.
. . . Dol set her lips. She was apart from them all,
really. She had no strength but her own, and she didn't
want any, neither for trivialities nor for this shocking
emergency. She left them. Abruptly she started back
toward the house. Mrs. Storrs said something, and

Sylvia called after her, but she went on without answering, into a trot along the slope, running by the time she reached the terrace.

The butler was not in the reception hall nor in the dining-room. She found the button and pressed it, and in a moment he entered by the swinging door. She faced him:

"Belden, something terrible has happened. I speak to you because you are the only man this house has got left, and jobs like this are supposed to be for men. Telephone the police—I suppose the state troopers, that will do—and tell them Mr. Storrs has been murdered."

Belden stiffened and stared. "Good God, Miss Bonner—"

"Yes. Be a man—you know how, don't you? When the police come send them to the nook below the fish pool. That's where he was murdered. You know that nook?"

"But good God, when—"

"Don't tremble like that, Belden! Be a man. Phone them at once and send them to that nook. Then you can tell Mrs. Storrs and the others . . . you won't faint. Will you?"

"I—I won't faint. No."

"Good. I'm going to the nook. I'll be there."

She left him, and again sought the exit by way of the side hall. The sun was finishing his day, and, racing down the rolling slope of lawn, her fantastic elongated shadow leaped and staggered before her. As she ran she thought that it had been idiotic of her not to look at that paper on the grass.

CHAPTER

FOUR

*T*HE nook was more somber now. Night was earlier there than on the open slope under the unimpeded sky. Dol, shivering as she entered the shadow, deliberately did not look at P. L. Storrs, and yet saw and felt the presence as she stuck to the concrete walk until nearest to the overturned bench, where she stepped onto the grass. She stood for a moment, considering the technical problem of fingerprints on paper, then moved to where the crumpled sheet lay and bent over to pick it up. Gingerly she straightened it out and frowned at it. It was a promissory note, a printed form filled out in ink. The writing was precise and eminently legible. It was dated Ogowoc, Connecticut, August 11, 1936, and it went on:

On demand I promise to pay to George Leo Ranth or order the sum of Fifty Thousand and 00/100 Dollars without interest. Value received.
Cleo Audrey Storrs.

Dol read it several times, turned it over and looked at the reverse side, which was blank, crumpled it up again as it had been, and returned it to its original position on the grass. She jerked up, startled at a sound, and grimaced at herself as she realized it had been a fish jumping in the pool. She moved to the concrete walk, and after some hesitation went along it to the toolhouse some fifteen yards away. The door was ajar and she pushed at it and entered. The place was neat and orderly, but a hodgepodge: wheelbarrows, lawn mowers, garden tools of all varieties and sizes, bags of fertilizer, raffia and twine, bulb racks, baskets, a shelf with hammers and pliers and heavy shears . . . and Dol crossed to the other side to look closer at something. It was a large reel of wire fastened to the wall, strands of fine wire twisted into a miniature cable, and as she peered up at it Dol nodded. Something stirred inside of her, a tiny glow of excitement and satisfaction; she had not come to the toolhouse for anything at all, and yet she had almost at once uncovered a palpable and important fact; the wire was the same, no doubt of it. The murderer had entered the toolhouse, knowing of the wire, reeled off a desirable length of it, snipped it off with pliers, returned . . . yes . . . returned the pliers to the shelf, proceeded to the nook and—Dol's train of thought jumped the track. How had the wire got around Storrs' neck? Had he put it there himself? With a shock Dol realized that the idea of suicide had not entered her mind . . . why not? Because P. L. Storrs was so pre-eminently not the sort of man who would do that. The notion had not occurred to her. She saw now that it should have; possibly she had made an utter fool of herself, telling Belden . . .

She left the toolhouse and went back to the nook, but stayed on the concrete walk. Her eyes were sharp with irritation at her own stupidity, and surveyed without compunction Storrs' suspended body. She thought it looked stiffer than before—or perhaps the twilight made it seem that way. At all events, it offered no answer to her question. She looked at the grass again, and saw the crushed blades, not yet uplifted, where she had stepped to reach the paper. She looked at the overturned bench and measured with her eye . . . surely it was two yards, or nearly that, from its edge to Storrs' feet. She made calculations and considered possibilities, but saw that her knowledge and her experience were both inadequate. She turned her attention to the wire. From where she stood the knot at the back of Storrs' neck was not visible, but she did not approach; instead, she let her eye follow the wire up to the limb, and diagonally down to the trunk of the tree, through the crotch, into the spiral— and guessed now at the final twisted end, which she had seen plainly before in the better light. She stared at the spiral, frowning, a long steady stare; but turned abruptly at a sound. The footsteps faint on the grass became more distinct, and a man appeared, bending under a dogwood branch. He approached:

"Miss Bonner! What— Ah!" He exclaimed sharply two words that Dol did not know, throwing his head up like a startled animal, standing poised. He stood gazing at the dance of P. L. Storrs, and Dol gazed at him. After some seconds of that George Leo Ranth said slowly without moving:

"Destruction and restoration. The cycle. But the spirit —Miss Bonner! How do you know he is dead?"

"Look at him."

Then, as Ranth moved, she snapped, "Don't walk there! Of course he's dead! Can't you see—"

She was interrupted—a voice calling her name—a rush into the nook through the leaves that curtained it —and Len Chisholm there: "What the devil, Dol, what kind of a—"

Dol said, "There."

Len turned. He leaned forward, peering. "My God." He straightened. "Like that, huh? P.L. darling. And you found him? My God, Dol, what are you trying to do around here? Pretty cool, huh? Me too. Belden told us. I think I had been drunk. He called the police first. I got a laugh out of it. I grabbed Sylvia to keep her from running down here, and Foltz frothed at the mouth and took her away from me. If it weren't for you—" Len stopped abruptly, regarding Dol as if he would like her to tell him what he had been saying. Then he turned from her to look again at the hanging body.

He muttered, "You've got nerve, Dol. I wouldn't be surprised if you've got more nerve than I have. You'd better go up to the house, to Sylvia. I'll wait here for the cops."

Dol shook her head. "Sylvia's all right. I'm all right."

"Good. I'm not. Oh, the devil, I am too." He was frowning at Storrs in the fast gathering twilight. "Look here. I don't see . . . did he do it himself? How did he get up there? His feet are off the ground . . . what—"

He saw, turning, only Dol's back; and she said in her coolest and lowest tone: "Mr. Ranth. Put that back where it was."

Ranth stood on the concrete walk. His voice was likewise cool: "Put what back, Miss Bonner? What do you mean?"

"I mean that piece of paper. I saw you pick it up. You thought my back was turned, but it wasn't. Put it—no. Give it to me."

"Really . . ." Ranth moved a step toward her; she was between him and the exit. "I don't understand . . . possibly the light is deceptive. I picked nothing up." He moved again. "Since Mr. Chisholm is here, I should see if Mrs. Storrs—"

"Mr. Ranth!" Dol squared in his path. "Don't be a fool. Give me that paper."

He shook his head calmly. "You've made a mistake, Miss Bonner." He made to move, but Dol stepped in front, and he hesitated. Without taking her eyes from him, Dol demanded brusquely, "Len, you've got to make this man give up that paper. Can you?"

"Sure." Len was beside her. "What's it all about?"

"There was a piece of paper on the grass by the bench there. I looked at it and put it back. Ranth just picked it up and put it in his pocket. I want it."

"Okay." Len, from six feet two, looked down on Ranth. "Hand it over. She wants it."

Ranth said evenly, "Miss Bonner is mistaken or she is lying when she says I picked up something. That is not true."

"Is it true, Dol?"

"It is. I saw him."

"Then it's true. Hand it over, Ranth, and hurry up. Don't be silly. In four seconds I'll take it away from you."

"I have nothing to hand over." Ranth's voice was quite composed. "If you attempt force——"

"I won't attempt it, I'll use it. First I'll knock you down to save time. Hand it over. I'll count four." Len doubled his fist. "Wait a minute, I can use diplomacy. Which pocket is it in, Dol?"

"His righthand coat pocket."

"Good. You get away a yard or so. Don't move, Ranth." With his right fist doubled, Len reached with his other hand into the coat pocket indicated. Ranth stood motionless. Len fumbled a little, then his hand emerged with a paper between the fingers. He extended the hand off to his side without turning his head and asked, "Is that it?"

Dol took it. She needed only a glance. "Yes. Thanks, Len. I'm glad you—very neat."

Ranth spoke, and for the first time his voice had undertones. "That paper is my property, Miss Bonner. It was taken from my person, and has been constantly in my possession. If you say you saw me pick it up here you will be lying."

"Oh, yeah?" Len growled. "How about it if two of us lie? God knows I can lie if Miss Bonner can. I saw you pick it up too. How does that sound?"

Dol shook her head. "You won't need to do that, Len. Thanks all the same. It will be all right— Oh! They're coming."

She stood listening. Ranth moved a couple of paces and stopped. Len opened his mouth and closed it again. The sound of men talking steadily approached, with strangers' voices and the only familiar one Belden's.

Belden, as they got nearer, sounded out of breath and exasperated. They came brushing through the leaves of the low-hanging branches with no respect for delicate dogwood twigs, three of them in the uniform of the state police, with big hats, cartridge belts and guns. Belden had been in front, and his gasp of horror was probably the first uncultured sound he had uttered in the presence of his superiors for thirty years. One of the police took him by the arm:

"Stand back a little. Don't go closer." He addressed his colleagues: "Hell, it's nearly dark in here."

"There's a lady there."

"Oh. Excuse me, ma'am."

The trio stood with their eyes focused on the hanging corpse. For a while, without comment. Then one of them demanded, "Murder? Who said it was murder?"

Another said, "Don't go closer. If it's murder it won't be our job, except to take orders. There might be footprints, only it's grass. If we'd had any sense we'd have brought the lights. Go get 'em, Jake, make it snappy." One of them went, trotting. The speaker turned to Len: "What's your name?"

Len told him.

"What do you know about this?"

"Nothing at all. I was playing tennis and drinking."

He turned to Ranth. "What's your name?"

"George Leo Ranth. I have a complaint, officer, that I would like you to attend to. This man has just taken my property, a paper that belonged to me, by force. From my pocket, where—"

"What? What man?"

"Leonard Chisholm. He took it——"

"Oh, forget it. We'll get your paper later."

"But I tell you he took it, and this woman lied——"

The trooper demanded of Len, "Have you got his paper?"

"No. He picked it up——"

"Forget it." The trooper looked disgusted. "You folks fighting about a paper with a dead man hanging here on a wire? You will all please go up to the house and stay there. I don't know how long, not very long maybe. Belden, you go with them."

Ranth began, "But——"

"Listen, mister. I like to be polite, but you beat it."

Ranth hesitated, then turned and went without any glance at his adversaries. Belden had already backed off, and now left the nook at Ranth's heels. Len took Dol's elbow, but she moved away and preceded him, and he followed her to the edge of the dogwoods and into the light of the open sky. At the far side of the fish pool she suddenly stopped and turned on him:

"You go ahead, Len. I want to give that man that paper."

He looked sourly down at her. "You come with me. You can give it to him later. Come along."

"No, I'm going back."

"Yeah? Okay. Me too."

"No. I have something to tell him and you haven't. Besides . . . has it occurred to you that you're supposed to be a newspaper man? There are several phones at the house—or you might go by way of the stable and use that one. The Gazette might appreciate it if they heard of this murder first."

"Holy womanhood." Len stared at her. "And me enamored of you! No jelly in your bones, huh, Dol? And refrigerator pipes for your blood to run through. After all, hospitality—"

"Nonsense." Dol gestured impatiently. "Whose hospitality, Mr. Storrs'? He's dead. Mrs. Storrs' or Janet's? No. Storrs asked me to come here . . . but that's his business. It was. As for phoning the Gazette, all the papers will know within an hour or so anyhow—but do as you please. My lord, do you think the murder of P. L. Storrs is going to be hushed up to save Sylvia's feelings? The only thing that could help Sylvia any would be—"

"Who mentioned Sylvia?" Len was frowning. "Did I say anything about Sylvia?"

"No, I did."

"You're a friend of hers. Huh?"

"You bet I am."

"Okay. I am if you are. Also, if you say phone the Gazette I'll do just that, I don't owe any more debts around here than you do. But my head seems to be clearing up, and it don't look to me as if anybody murdered Storrs. I don't see how they could. It looks to me like suicide, and if I sell the Gazette a murder—"

"Don't sell them anything. Tell them where he is, and he's dead. If they want you to do the story for them, tell them you can't because you're one of the suspects, and if they—"

"I'm what? Now what? What kind of a—"

"Certainly you are. We all are. We were all here. At one time this afternoon you were wandering around this place alone looking for P. L. Storrs, to do a grovel, you said. Weren't you? Today in my office you said you would come out here and strangle him. Didn't you? Oh, I know you were being playful, but you do have a temper, and Martin Foltz heard you say it. I know Martin is a decent man, if there are any decent ones, but he is as jealous as the devil, and especially of you at the moment, because Sylvia decided you deserved being sweet to. Martin's imagination is terrific. Sylvia heard you say it too, and she loved P. L. Storrs. You are probably in for it. We all are. Unless . . . one thing. That might prevent it. If you intend to phone the Gazette you'd better go by the stable and do it from there or you may not get a chance. Then go to the house and restrain yourself. I'll be there pretty soon— maybe sooner, if that man is too busy to listen to me." She moved to go.

Len got her arm. "Your mind certainly works, lady. Swell. Some fancy mind. You don't want me, huh?"

"Not now, Len. But—thank you again for taking that paper away from Ranth. That was nice. I couldn't have done that. See you at the house."

She turned and headed for the gloom of the dog-woods. Len watched her until she was under the first branches, then turned and strode off up the slope, swerving right toward the stables. By now twilight had come even on the open lawn; the sun had gone, and a chill was in the air.

Dol did not proceed directly to the nook. She circled a few feet to the left, noiselessly under the branches on the grass, and stopped behind the shelter of a clump of French willows which kept their roots moist in the overflow from the fish pool. She could see the three troopers dimly through the leaves in the semi-darkness. The one called Jake, who had returned with the flashlights, was on the concrete walk, squatted on his haunches, smoking a cigarette. The one with a flat nose, evidently in charge, was standing flashing one of the lights indiscriminately over the scene, while the third one appeared to be merely chewing a blade of grass. The one with a flat nose was saying:

". . . but of course you can't do that until Doc Flanner comes, and the photographer, and I suppose Sherwood, he'll want to see it. If we could move things around we could try it. Maybe the bench could have been a lot closer and he could have kicked it back as he dropped, but it looks heavy and I don't see how he could kick it that far. If he stood it on end and climbed up and jumped from there and kicked it over, it might have rolled that far, but it would have made more dents in the grass, and from as high as that I should think he would break that limb, he must weigh over a hundred and sixty." He moved the light. "Look at it, not much bigger than your wrist. What the hell, jumping from six feet up? Damn it, they ought to be getting here. Sherwood only had twenty miles to do, and if Doc Flanner waited to finish his supper somebody ought to set fire to his pants."

The man chewing grass shook his head. "All I say is,

try to fasten a wire around a man's neck like that. Unless you knock him cold first. There's no bruises on him, and there's no signs of any scrap. Crowder's *Manual of Crime Detection*, which I've read and so have you, says you can't accept any hypothesis if there's a fact that don't agree with it. Like that case up in Buffalo, where there was two bullet holes in the wall in the same side of the room and the guy said he had been shot at before he shot back, and the woman said the same thing and she didn't seem to be lying, but they was able to prove by the science of ballistics that if both shots— Hey, who's that?"

Dol, seeing and hearing that she would be interrupting nothing of much moment, had become impatient and stepped out of her shelter. She stopped at the border of the nook, facing them, and then blinked indignantly as the flashlight swiftly circled and spotted her right in the eyes. She put up her hand and demanded:

"Move that thing."

The light darted away, and the man with the flat nose, who held it, inquired, "Well? Didn't I ask you to go to the house? What do you want?"

Dol had thought that the thing to do would be to start with a smile, but she didn't feel like smiling. Nor any smile in her voice: "I want to tell you some things. I had no idea you would just sit here and wait for doctors and photographers. My name is Bonner. I'm a detective."

There was a snort from the one smoking a cigarette. The one with the flat nose sounded politely amazed:

"You're what? A detective? What kind?"

"I run a private agency in New York. A licensed detective agency."

"You say—you run it? That's a—well—all right. You say your name's Bonner? Then you found this man. They want you up at the house. It was you that told the butler it was murder. How did you know that?"

Dol moved nearer. "That's one of the things I have to tell you. Is it you I should tell? Are you going to do anything?"

"We'll all do what we can. The first thing is to decide whether this man killed himself. Out here in the country it takes a little while to get organized. Go ahead and tell me."

"Very well. First, the wire. Along that walk, about fifty feet back there, is a toolhouse, and on the wall is a reel of wire like that wire, and on a shelf are some pliers and some shears you could cut it with. That's where the wire came from."

"Good." The trooper sounded sarcastic. "We might have found that when we got moving. That don't explain your calling it murder."

"The pliers or shears might have fingerprints."

"Thanks. Go ahead."

Dol made her back straighter. "This is something you couldn't have found out. I don't know whether it has anything to do with the murder or not. When I first came here about a quarter to seven, and found this here, I looked around without touching anything, and there was a crumpled piece of paper on the grass by the end of the bench. I came back here a little after seven, and pretty soon Ranth came, and then Leonard Chisholm. While I was talking with Chisholm I saw Ranth pick up the paper and put it in his pocket. I told him to put it back and he denied he had picked it up. I asked Chisholm to get it, and first he demanded it and then he took it out of Ranth's pocket and gave it to me. Ranth said it had been in his possession all the time and that I couldn't prove it had been on the grass and he had picked it up. Which is silly." Dol opened her bag and took the paper out. "Here it is if you want to look at it."

The trooper took it and straightened it out and put the flashlight on it. Jake moved to look over his shoulder. They took their time over it. The trooper looked up to peer at Dol in the dim light:

"Who is Cleo Audrey Storrs?"

"Mrs. Storrs. Mr. Storrs' wife. Widow."

The trooper grunted, undid a button of his jacket, and folded the paper and stowed it away inside. "What makes you think this had nothing to do with the murder?"

"I didn't say that. I said I didn't know whether it had or not."

"Oh. Was that what you said? Then it wasn't this paper that made you think it was murder. Was it?"

"No. I—" Dol hesitated. She resumed: "You know, I really am telling you things. The way you act, your tone of voice—it sounds as if you were dragging them out of me. You aren't, you know."

"Yeah. That's all right, go ahead. You've been going to tell me why you told the butler it was murder."

"I am prepared to. I told him it was murder because

I was perfectly certain that Storrs was not a man to kill himself under any conceivable circumstances, and absolutely not in any circumstance which I had reason to suppose existed. I knew him fairly well."

"Was that all?"

"That was all."

"Not hardly enough," the trooper said drily. "After all, it's a serious matter to go saying a man's been murdered. And you a detective. There might be circumstances you didn't know about."

Dol nodded. "I realized that. Later, when I came back here after telling Belden to phone the police. I saw that I had jumped to a conclusion when I had no right to, so I looked around more. That was when I found the reel of wire in the toolhouse. Then I came here and looked, and found real proof."

"Proof of murder?"

"Yes."

"Here?" He sounded skeptical.

Dol affirmed, "Yes. Part of it was what I heard you talking about—about jumping off the bench and kicking it back and so on. I thought you couldn't tell for sure about that without trying it. But something else seemed quite certain. May I have the flash?"

He handed it to her, and she aimed it at the trunk of the tree some four yards away, and slowly moved the beam up and down. She said, "You see that spiral—the way the wire winds around. Did you look at that?"

"Yeah, I saw it."

"Well, it seemed to me that was no way to fasten a wire. Not even for a man who never did it before. I thought I was a fair subject for experiment, because I have never fastened a wire to a tree in my life, so I imagined myself doing it. Here I am with a wire I am going to hang myself with. I drop one end over the limb and leave it dangling at the right height, and take the other end to the trunk to fasten it. It is much longer than I need. What do I do? I might bend it around that crotch and maybe pass it around a few times, and then twist it around itself so it couldn't slip; or I might secure it to that limb a little lower—that one—; or I might wind it around the trunk itself and end with a twist, but if I did so I would cerainly wind it straight around, and anybody in the world would."

The trooper muttered, "Somebody didn't."

Dol nodded impatiently. "But not a man who was going to hang himself with it. Not a man who had the wire free and could take his time and fasten it as he pleased. Look at it! Imagine that you are there by the trunk with the wire in your hands, and it passes through the crotch and up over the limb and down again, and there at the end it is looped around the neck of a man you are trying to murder. The man is on his feet now and fighting it, and perhaps trying to rush at you. What do you do? You pull on the wire with all your might. Maybe in desperation the man foolishly tries to jump up and reach the limb. You pull on the wire and catch him that way, in midair, and you've got him. But now there is a terrific pull on the wire because it is holding the man up, and you don't dare to release an ounce of your pull. But you've got to fasten it somehow. What do you do? You pull the wire hard against the trunk of the tree, and you begin to walk around the trunk, holding the wire tight, and when you've encircled the trunk four times the wire is twining around it in a spiral and the pull of the weight of the body is so diminished that it is easy for you to work the end of the wire under the last circle of the spiral and twist it there."

Dol held the flashlight out to the trooper. She said, with a suggestion of a tremble in her voice, "I think that's proof. A man would fasten a wire to a tree like that if there was a heavy weight on the other end that forced him to, and he wouldn't if there wasn't. No man would. Not even a woman."

The man who had smoked the cigarette, and who had snorted at Dol's announcement that she was a detective, had joined them to listen. He now muttered in wondering disgust, "For cripe's sake!" Jake said nothing. The one with the flat nose had taken the flashlight and walked to the tree and was examining the wire spiraling down the trunk. The others stood and watched him. He sidled around the tree, close to it, four times, following the line of the spiral with the spot of light, then for some seconds inspected the final twist at the end, where it looped around the last spiral. He snapped off the light and came back and peered at Dol in the dusk:

"You did that pretty good. You described that as if you had been here and seen it done—now don't get sore again, it's my nature to talk like that. I only meant what I said, you described it the way it would be. And maybe you noticed that the bark is scratched in three places, where he had a hard time poking the end through to twist it and fasten it."

"I didn't go that close."

"Well, it's like that." The trooper was silent; Dol could see his face but dimly. He spoke again: "You say your name's Bonner? Do you happen to know Dan Sherwood, prosecuting attorney of this county?"

"No."

"I thought you might. He'll be here pretty soon, any minute now. I hope. Have you got any more proof of anything?"

"No." Dol had become aware that she was feeling painfully weak in her middle. Over an hour ago, on first finding P. L. Storrs hanging on that wire, she had felt that she must find something to sit down on, and she hadn't sat down yet. She felt her stomach shivering inside of her, and it didn't seem likely that she could control it. She said, "I . . . I think I'll go . . . to the house," and was relieved to find that her legs seemed willing to undertake it as she turned and took a step. She heard the trooper saying something that appeared not to need any reply, and she took more steps successfully. When she was in the open, beyond the fish pool, she stood a moment, then headed up the slope.

Hearing voices, and not caring to encounter anyone, she made a wide circle to the right. It was a group of men coming down the hill, and a smaller group, two or three, behind, vague to her in the dusk; they strode rapidly along, and paid no attention to her. She aimed for the house, where lights now shone in the windows and on the side terrace.

On the ornamental bench at the left end of the terrace sat a trooper in uniform; Dol, passing, tossed him a glance. The living-room was empty, and the reception hall; there seemed to be no noise anywhere; Dol turned back and went to the dining-room. It was lit and Belden was standing there, and the table was properly laid for eight, but only two places were occupied. On the far side sat Len Chisholm, frowning as he dipped meat sauce over a potato, and across from him was Steve Zimmerman, his mouth full, hastily chewing.

Belden advanced, bowing, and the two men stood up. Dol's stomach began to feel queer again. She asked, "Where's Mrs. Storrs?"

"I don't know." Len sounded savage. "I guess upstairs. Come and eat something."

"I don't think . . . not now. Where's Sylvia?"

"I don't know that either."

Zimmerman spoke: "She's up front with Martin. That room with the plants in it."

Len said, "Come and eat while it's hot. Get some nourishment."

Dol shook her head and turned and left them. At the foot of the wide stairs in the hall she stood a moment but could hear no sound from above, then went on through another room to get to the front of the house. In the sun room, on a couch in a recess with palms, sat Sylvia and Martin Foltz.

Sylvia jumped up and ran to her. "Dol! Dol, what is this? Where have you been? Dol, what *is* it?" She seized Dol's arms.

Martin was there. He looked worn out and helpless, and he appealed to Dol: "For God's sake, why didn't you come to her? Why didn't you tell her yourself?

She wanted to go down there. I couldn't let her do that, could I? For God's sake, Dol, what's happened?"

Dol drew Sylvia back toward the couch; there was a seat at last. Her voice, never harsh, was now: "Sylvia dear. You buck up. You too, Martin. It's awful and it's going to be awful. There's nothing to do but take it."

CHAPTER

FIVE

DANIEL O. SHERWOOD was a good politician, of the plump and ruddy type. He was a fairly competent prosecuting attorney but was sometimes handicapped, in his efforts to promote justice, by his incurably benevolent attitude toward persons of standing and repute in the community. He was constitutionally disinclined to severity, except in those cases where it was obviously deserved, and prudence and experience had taught him that people who have servants and three automobiles very seldom deserve it. He was under forty and thought he might be governor some day.

At nine o'clock Sunday morning he sat in the card room of the house at Birchhaven. It was a large room with a piano in one corner and many shelves filled with books, but was called the card room instead of music room or library because, while the piano was never played and the books not often read, it saw a good deal of bridge. Sherwood was on a straight-backed chair at a table; beside him sat a middle-aged man with spectacles and big ears, possibly a good lawyer but not the type that might be governor some day; and across from him was Colonel Brissenden of the state police, tanned and tough-looking but not without military elegance. A trooper was in an easy chair over by the door.

Sherwood was saying, "I understand that, Miss Bonner. I grant that. I believe you and I think Ranth is lying when he says he picked nothing up. As you say, how could you possibly have known there was a paper in his righthand coat pocket unless you had seen him put it there? But you must remember that when we're investigating a crime and we uncover a fact, we must not only uncover it, we must be prepared to prove it. A jury might believe you against Ranth, that you saw him pick something up, but a lawyer would demonstrate our inability to prove that what he picked up was what was later taken from his pocket. There's a connection, of course, but there is also a doubt."

Dol did not look fresh. The whites of her caramel-colored eyes were not too clear, and there was no glow to her. She sat at the end of the table facing the three men, and seemed now to be considering what Sherwood had said. Finally she told him, with no animation:

"Very well. I had not realized that that could be a point. I mean that the paper taken from his pocket was the one he had picked up. I know it was because I had looked at it. I had picked it up and straightened it out and read it, and then crumpled it and put it back again."

Colonel Brissenden growled, "You didn't say that."

"I think I told the trooper that."

"No."

"I think I did. Even if I didn't, what's the difference? That's what happened. That's how I am sure it was the same paper."

Sherwood asked, "You'd swear to that?"

"Of course I would."

"The paper on the grass was the promissory note to George Leo Ranth, signed by Mrs. Storrs?"

"It was."

"All right, it's your word for it. No one saw you."
Sherwood opened a manila folder on the table before
him and shuffled through a pile of papers. Around the
middle of the pile he looked one over, then leaned back
in his chair. "You seem to be quite intelligent, Miss
Bonner. I don't mind saying that last night we felt in-
debted to you. You had that piece of paper taken from
Ranth, and you turned it over to Sergeant Quill. You
called Quill's attention to the way the wire was fastened
to the tree, and that was clever. Very clever. We appreciate that. I had a little talk with you and then I started
in on the others because you hadn't arrived until six
o'clock and so probably were not here when the murder
was committed. Then I had a few more questions for
you, and you took a most indefensible position. That's
why I'm beginning with you this morning. You stated
that you came here yesterday at Mr. Storrs' request, to
see him on business, and refused to tell what the business was. You admitted it might possibly be connected
with the murder. Your idea that it was a privileged
communication is nonsense; you're not a lawyer."

Dol said wearily, "I know it. Quit arguing, I'll tell
you."

Colonel Brissenden grunted. Sherwood said, "Oh.
You've changed your mind."

"Yes. I've thought it over. I'll explain. . . . I
haven't any idea who killed Storrs. I found that paper
there, that promissory note, and then I made Ranth give
it up when he tried to get away with it, but I knew
that didn't prove he had killed Storrs. I have no use

for Ranth, but because I had done all that, I thought it might be doing him an injustice if I told you what Storrs asked me to come out here for."

Brissenden growled, "We'll handle the justice." Sherwood asked, "Well?"

"Well . . . as you know, I am a detective. I run a licensed detective agency. Storrs came to my office yesterday at one o'clock and said that Ranth was getting too much money from his wife and he wanted to stop it. He engaged me to look up Ranth's record and discredit him if possible. Also to go after him myself and see what could be done. He put it that he wanted to get rid of Ranth, get him away from Mrs. Storrs, by any feasible means short of murder. He said that if it came to murder he would do it himself. Of course that was only a man talking." Dol glanced from the attorney to the colonel and back again. "And you understand that his objection to Ranth was only on financial and—well, call it spiritual—grounds. Ranth is the founder and promoter of a thing called the League of the Occidental Sakti, and he gets money—"

Sherwood nodded impatiently and put up a hand. "I know all that. I've heard of Ranth before. We've got some of his record and we're getting the rest." He squinted at her. "So Storrs wanted to hire you to get rid of Ranth?"

"He did hire me."

"And that's what you came out here for yesterday? What were you going to do?"

"I don't know. Nothing definite." Dol lifted her

shoulders and dropped them. "I was going to look at him."

"You had seen him before, hadn't you?"

"Certainly, several times."

"But you wanted to look at him." Sherwood slowly rubbed his plump cheek. "Of course you realize, Miss Bonner, it never hurts any kind of a statement, no matter who makes it, to be backed up by corroboration. You realize that. For instance, since Storrs hired you, I suppose he paid you a retainer? In cash, or a check?"

"No, he didn't. He asked me if I wanted one, and I said no."

Brissenden grunted, and when Dol glanced at him she met an unbelieving stare. Sherwood was saying, "That's too bad. Was anyone else present at your conversation with Storrs?"

"No. We were alone in my office. My secretary had gone home."

"I see. Did you and Storrs discuss anything else? Anything besides his hiring you to get rid of Ranth?"

"No."

"Nothing whatever?"

"No."

"Search your memory, Miss Bonner." Sherwood leaned toward her. "You will reflect that we are investigating a murder, and it was you who furnished the first demonstration of proof that it was murder. You did not attempt to retire behind the shield of feminine delicacy and horror. You have offered us two strong points against Ranth: that paper yesterday, and your story here about Storrs' hostility towards him. If Ranth did it we'll get him. All that can be done is being done. But we can't afford to overlook anything, and we're not going to. As you know, I spent five hours here last night asking questions of everybody concerned, and there are things that need explanation, and I expect you to help explain them if you can. Search your memory. Are you sure that Storrs said nothing to you yesterday about a visit made to his office that morning by Steven Zimmerman?"

"Yes. He said nothing about it."

"Didn't mention it?"

"No."

"And are you sure that he said nothing about threats that had been made against his life by Leonard Chisholm?"

"Threats—" Dol looked astonished. Then she looked contemptuous. "Rubbish."

Sherwood calmly agreed: "Quite possibly. I'm aware that men are constantly declaring their readiness to kill other men; it's a universal safety valve; I do it myself. But the point here is that Storrs did get killed. That's why it may not be rubbish. I am informed that Chisholm stated specifically that he would strangle Storrs, and that you heard him say it. Is that correct?"

"It is. I think it is also irrelevant."

"That may be. Did Storrs mention Chisholm's threats at your office yesterday?"

"No." Dol was getting irritated. "How could he? He couldn't possibly have heard of it—unless Martin Foltz telephoned him as soon as he left my office with Chisholm and Miss Raffray, and that is inconceivable. There are some things that some men don't do. Martin Foltz wouldn't do that."

"But Chisholm might have previously made the same threat direct to Storrs. He could have phoned him or called on him. Couldn't he?"

"No.—Oh, I suppose he could. Did he?"

"He says not. If he did, and anyone heard it, we're likely to find it out. The New York police are co-operating with us. What I am asking you is, did Storrs mention such a threat, or anything about Chisholm, to you?"

"No. Chisholm wasn't mentioned."

"I see. You expect me to believe that."

Dol opened her mouth, then clamped it shut. After a moment she spoke with complete composure: "Yes, Mr. Sherwood. I expect you to believe everything I say."

Brissenden suddenly and explosively barked, "Take her down! You're wasting time, Dan! The others too! You've got to turn on some heat!" The middle-aged man, startled, jerked up his head so violently that his spectacles slid down on his nose. Simultaneously an interruption came from the door. There was a knock, and the trooper opened it to admit a bulky man in a dark blue suit with his hat in his hand who looked like what he was, a county detective. He crossed to the table and nodded separately to the colonel and the attorney. Sherwood asked, "Well?"

The man's voice was husky, flat, and utterly without hope: "I had an idea I thought I ought to tell you about."

"You mean you've found something?"

"Not exactly found something, no, sir. I've been working the places to the north and east, like you said, with Mullins. We haven't really dug up anything. There's a guy owns a cottage over towards Sumac Knolls that's as crazy as a loon, but he was on the sound all day yesterday. What I wanted to tell you: Mullins and I was talking with a couple of wops that work on Foltz's place, down the hill, north. Foltz keeps a lot of pheasants and hares, and there's been something funny going on all summer. It started about the middle of May—"

Sherwood stopped him with a gesture. "I know all about that. The strangled pheasants. What about it?"

"Well, the wops thought it was quite a coincidence. Strangling going on there all summer, off and on, and now all of a sudden a man gets strangled. It looks like it's in the air, and it looks like there might be some connection . . . some kind of a tie-up we could look into. . . ." The detective stopped, looking even more frustrated than he had before. He muttered disconsolately, "If you want me and Mullins to follow it up . . ."

"Was that your idea?"

"Yeah, that was it."

This was a case where severity was obviously deserved, and Sherwood supplied it. Since he was engaged on an important and difficult murder case and time was precious, he made it short, but not ambiguous. The detective received it as if it was no worse than he had expected, without any notable change of expression, acknowledged with a nod the attorney's orders to continue to follow the instructions that had been given him, and departed.

Sherwood said, "You talk about material, Colonel. You talk about *esprit de corps*. But we'll untangle it, you'll see." He turned to Dol: "You mustn't mind Colonel Brissenden. He's an army man, and he's impatient. He hears you say things that are hard for him to believe—and, frankly, I agree with him." He leaned forward again, looking directly into Dol's eyes, in no wise affected or disconcerted by the remarkable combination of caramel irises and jet lashes. "Is it true that you had seriously offended Mr. Storrs?"

Dol returned his gaze. "I see. So Sylvia—but why shouldn't she tell you that? Naturally she would. The poor girl is sunk in remorse."

"Obviously. My question, Miss Bonner."

"Yes. Mr. Storrs had been offended . . . at me, at his ward, Miss Raffray, at both of us . . . no matter."

"But it does matter." Sherwood's voice sharpened. "There was a violent scene yesterday morning between Storrs and Miss Raffray. She has described it to us. He spoke of Zimmerman, who had just visited him. He spoke of getting Chisholm fired from his job. He spoke of you with deep rancor—"

"I don't believe that," Dol snapped. "I don't believe Miss Raffray told you that. She's upstairs. Call her."

Sherwood gestured impatiently. "You don't like 'rancor.' Call it animosity, disapproval, whatever you please. The fact is that Storrs vehemently insisted that Miss Raffray should stop associating with you, and she—"

"I don't believe that either. She didn't tell you that.

He insisted that she should sever her connections with the detective business."

"All right, then he did that. He was violently angry because his name and his ward's name had been disgraced by publicity connecting them with that business. He demanded that she should immediately cease any association with you in that business. He made a vital point of it and expressed himself with positiveness and deep feeling. And in the face of all that"—Sherwood raised a finger and shook it at her for emphasis—"do you expect me to believe that within two hours after his scene with Miss Raffray, Storrs went to your office to ask you to do a confidential job for him, without once mentioning the injury you had done him? You have said that you and Storrs discussed nothing whatever but his hiring you to get rid of Ranth." Sherwood threw up his hands. "Do you wonder that Colonel Brissenden says we should take you down?"

"Oh, my lord." Dol sounded disgusted, and was. "That's what you've been building up to. Mr. Sherwood, you ought to be ashamed of yourself."

Brissenden growled, "Don't let her get cute."

"That's what I've been building up to," Sherwood told her emphatically. "You can't minimize it. Storrs had ruined your business by depriving it of financial support and of a partner who had valuable connections. I'm not being fantastic. I'm not suggesting that to get revenge, and to remove his opposition, you came out here and murdered him. But I do believe that you and he discussed something besides his hiring you to do a job, and I want to know what it was."

"I see." Dol regarded him. She considered. "I still think you should be ashamed of yourself, but I see how your mind works. Because I said we discussed nothing but the job, and because it seems unnatural that we shouldn't mention the rumpus about Miss Raffray, you think I'm deliberately lying. That may be logical, but it's darned silly. We may have discussed the weather, too. We did mention the rumpus, briefly. He accused me of a tantrum and I told him I never had one. He brushed that aside and said that the fact that he disapproved of Miss Raffray being in the detective business had nothing to do with his admiration of my abilities and competence, and he wanted me to do a job. Then we discussed the job." Dol bent toward him earnestly. "Honestly, Mr. Sherwood, I hate to see you wasting time on me like this. You have a lot to do. It begins to look as if the man who murdered Storrs avoided any foolish mistake, and had no bad luck. If you're going to find him, and find proof against him, you have your hands full."

Sherwood stared at her thoughtfully. He turned to Colonel Brissenden and raised his brows inquiringly. Brissenden thrust at him: "Never believe anything a woman says when she's in a hole."

Dol used her coolest tone: "You're being silly, Colonel. I dislike all men anyway, and I particularly dislike men in uniforms with military titles, because I detest war. I am not in a hole. A man got me in a hole once, and no man is going to do it again." She shifted her level gaze to Sherwood without interrupting the flow of her oration: "I presume you're being thorough and looking up the history of all of us who have got caught here by this thing. You will find out, if you haven't already, that mine is pathetic and banal. It followed an old and trite formula. A man loved me and wanted me, and I loved and wanted him. I wore his ring and I was a proud and happy girl, waiting decorously for the day. The day never came, because my father met ruin and killed himself, and I was a poor girl instead of a rich one. He got his ring back. The banality of it didn't make the pain any less, though you might have thought it would have. I tell you this because it is certainly no secret and you'll be hearing of it anyway, and to let you know that I am still crawling out of that hole and no man is going to get me into another one. No kind of a hole. So for goodness' sake, don't waste time trying to push me into one.—You, Mr. Brissenden, I dislike you very much. You are the north wind type, there is nothing to you but velocity; in anything requiring insight or subtlety, you are merely a nuisance.—I could work with you, Mr. Sherwood, if you would let me. I think I'm clever. I'm quite young, and it may turn out that I'm merely conceited and my pride has been hurt, but I *think* I'm clever. I'm going to try to be."

Brissenden might have been expected to blow, but he didn't; apparently, in addition to his velocity, he had a brake on it. He glared ferociously, not at Dol but at Sherwood; the attorney returned the glare with a gaze half defiant and half deprecatory. The fact was that the colonel was saying to the attorney with his glare, "If you repeat that about north wind type in certain circles I'll get your scalp," and the attorney was replying with his gaze, "If I repeat it, it will only be as a good joke, and anyway it *is* clever."

Sherwood abandoned that clash for the business in hand, for Dol. He turned to her with a frown of appraisal and indecision. But the question whether or not to accept her declaration of good faith had to be left open, for the door guarded by the trooper suddenly swung wide, and a shuffling of feet and murmur of voices announced a visitation. The trooper sprang up but hesitated to challenge when he saw that the leader of the group was Mrs. Storrs, the mistress of the house. She walked with assurance and purpose into her card room, and behind her were her daughter Janet, Sylvia Raffray, Leonard Chisholm, Martin Foltz, Steve Zimmerman and George Leo Ranth. As she halted in the middle of the room, her deepset eyes focused on the four at the table as on something unique and unforgettable. The characteristic intensity of her voice seemed heightened, seemed in fact half hysterical, as she demanded:

"Who is in charge here, please? You?—You, sir? I want to discuss this business."

CHAPTER

SIX

*T*HE men at the table were on their feet. Sherwood advanced to greet Mrs. Storrs and to introduce his assistant and Colonel Brissenden. Foltz and Zimmerman pulled chairs around for others and themselves. Ranth, a little pale, stood with his hands thrust into his trouser pockets, obviously under a strong self control. Janet Storrs refused Chisholm's offer of a chair and crossed to one at the other side of the room. Dol had left the table to meet Sylvia, and the erstwhile partners clasped hands without saying anything. Brissenden, scowling, got back to his place and sat down again. Sherwood was saying:

". . . by all means, if you prefer that chair, Mrs. Storrs . . . certainly. I only thought . . . you say you want to discuss . . ."

Mrs. Storrs, seated squarely facing him, nodded. There was no distinction to her costume—a jersey jacket over a pale yellow blouse, and a jersey skirt, with country shoes—but her face, never quite ordinary, aside from the quality of her eyes, had the stiff white dignity of some inner irresistible conviction. Her fingers rigidly interlocked, her hands resting on her lap, a little shiver visibly ran over her, then she sat still and asked, "You say you are in charge here?"

Sherwood said he was. "I am the prosecuting attorney for this county. I am legally in charge of the investigation. Colonel Brissenden here is giving every assistance—"

"Yes, you told me that." Her eyes were boring into him. "I was sorry that I was unable to talk with you last night, and I do not know whether I fainted with weakness at the physical shock, or whether the spirit refused to recognize the child of its devotion, and departed. If that was it"—her voice tightened its intensity—"it is back again. I was told it had been revealed to you that my husband was destroyed."

She stopped, apparently under the impression that she had asked a question. Sherwood hesitated: "Well . . . revealed, Mrs. Storrs? It seems . . . probable, that your husband was murdered. We are, at present, satisfied that that is so. There will be a coroner's inquest on Tuesday, unless Dr. Flanner changes the date. The evidence of violence . . . the evidence that he did not kill himself—"

She shook her head impatiently. "No. I know all about that."

"Ah, you do?"

"I know he didn't kill himself. The impulse to destroy and to restore—but that is beyond your interest and above your understanding. I have come to tell you something, and I have brought these people with me because they were here, and while they too will be unable to understand, they should at least hear what the manifestation has been. You shall know, all of you, that the death of my husband means my own death. He never followed me above the lower planes of comprehension, but he was my only companion in the sphere he reached, he was my only husband, and only in that sphere can I survive him. In confining myself to that, I die, but I owe that to him, for his destruction was never intended by me—"

George Leo Ranth, without moving, called sharply, "Mrs. Storrs! You are giving an entirely wrong impression!—Sir, all of you, I protest—"

"Don't interrupt," Sherwood snapped. "You can correct impressions later.—Yes, madam?"

Mrs. Storrs shook her head. "It doesn't matter. I was offering an apology, but my true apology can never be made now—not even to my daughter—his daughter." She looked at Janet, seated across the room, and shook her head again. "No. I wish to talk to you—quite differently, on your own level. I can do that. My husband knew I could do that, and admired me for it." She was silent, and stayed so for long seconds. There was no change in her expression, no faint visible effort at composure; she merely sat unmoving and silent, and no one stirred. Then she went on, "First I must make sure no mistakes have been made, nor will be. I wish to know why your men are invading all parts of my grounds, disturbing the plantings, ruining the gardens."

"You understand, Mrs. Storrs . . ." Sherwood cleared his throat, and called that off. He told her briefly, "They are looking for something."

"What are they looking for?"

"Things. Specifically, a pair of gloves."

"Whose gloves? I am not protesting, I am inquiring. I wish to have the practical steps, the facts, explained. Have I a right to ask that?"

Sherwood nodded. "You have. If not a right, at least a privilege which we are certainly inclined to grant. If you are sure you can—you want to hear these details—"

"I do. Precisely."

"Well. Last night we decided that someone killed your husband by fastening a loop of wire around his neck and then pulling him up, hanging him, by pulling on the other end of the wire which had been passed over a high limb of a tree. It seemed possible that the loop had been fastened by first assaulting your husband and perhaps knocking him unconscious, but the doctor could find no indication that he had received a blow. We discussed another theory, that your husband had gone to sleep on the bench and the loop had been fastened as he lay there asleep. Questioning the servants and others, we learned that that bench was in fact your husband's favorite spot for a summer nap. Testing the possibility of fastening such a loop without waking a man up, we found that with a man lying in a certain position it was not even difficult; the end of the wire could be passed through under his neck without touching him, pulled through carefully, brought over and a slip knot made with twists just as it was actually done, leaving a large loop. It would take only an instant to run to the tree and grab the other end of the wire and jerk it, taking up the slack in the wire and pulling the noose tight. Being awakened by a wire tightening around his neck, the natural thing for Storrs to do would be to struggle to his feet, and that would offer the chance to pull the wire some more and hold him there. Then he might try to get on the bench, and perhaps kick it over and away. If he tried rushing at the murderer, the wire would hold him. If he tried to jump to reach the limb, that would finish it—"

An agonized cry sounded: "My God, why must he— why must we—" Dol Bonner squeezed Sylvia Raffray's shoulder hard: "Now. Now hold it." Martin Foltz was there: "Sylvia dear, please dear—"

Mrs. Storrs' gaze did not waver from Sherwood's face. She said, in the tone of a priestess declaiming a dogma, "My husband would have tried to reach the man pulling the wire. He *would* have reached him."

Sherwood shook his head. "No, madam. We have tried this thing out.—But you asked about the gloves. It was obvious that to pull that wire as hard as that would bruise a man's hands badly—it would certainly mark them. That was why last night we examined the hands of everybody here, except yourself. We have examined hands all over this countryside. But I may say here, and I mean only what I say"—Sherwood glanced around at all the occupants of the room—"that we have been able to find no evidence of the presence here yesterday of any outsider. It is pretty well established that no one approached that spot from the east. Other considerations —the unlikelihood of anyone going there at all unless he already knew of the place, the difficulty of a stranger's getting in here without observation, the fact that Storrs had over three hundred dollars in his wallet and it hadn't been touched, the method of committing the crime—no. We have about given up the idea of an outsider."

There was a stir and a murmur. Mrs. Storrs said,

"Only Siva destroys. You mean the agent is here. I believe you. And the gloves?"

"There must have been gloves. No one's hands are marked, as they must have been without gloves. We have also been examining gloves, all we could find. Last night one of my men, wearing a pair of heavy buckskin, pulled up a 170 pound weight with a piece of that wire passed over the limb of a tree, and those gloves are marked and bruised ineradicably." Sherwood looked around the room again. "Somewhere there is a pair of gloves marked like that. There must be. That's what the men are looking for. I realize that on a place of this size such a search is next to hopeless, but we may find them . . . and by the way, Mrs. Storrs, I have a request to make. I intended to make it of you this morning, but your bringing everyone in here simplifies it a little. While we are here, I would like to instruct the men to search this house. May I do that?"

Mrs. Storrs, without any hesitation, said, "I think it may not be necessary."

Sherwood frowned. "You'll have to explain that. You don't mean you know where the gloves are?"

"Oh, no. I mean . . . but then, you need proof. In your sphere . . . you will require proof?"

"Proof? Certainly."

"Very well. You may search the house."

Sherwood looked at Brissenden. The colonel nodded and called, "Peterson!" The trooper approached and saluted. Brissenden told him, "Tell Quill to take five men and search the house from top to bottom, and don't mess things up. I understand you've already searched this room and in front? All right, tell Quill to cover the rest and do it thoroughly. Any gloves that are found are to be brought to me, with a tag telling where they are found. Step on it, now."

The trooper went. Mrs. Storrs spoke to the room:

"I know that the proof of fools is an impertinence to Siva and to the principles. This is a concession I am making, and if I have to pay for it I am willing to do that. Even Siva may be held to a bargain once it has been made, and the destruction of my husband was not intended. I suffer for it." Her voice went suddenly high, half hysterical, the words forced through her constricted throat: "I tell you, I suffer for it!"

Janet Storrs, sitting with her hands clasped tight, cried softly, "Mother! Mother!"

"Yes, Janet. You too, child." Mrs. Storrs nodded at her daughter. She looked back at Sherwood and controlled her voice to its normal intensity: "You say the agent is here? You know that? Do you know him? I would like to hear what you know."

The attorney was regarding her steadily. "It might be better, madam," he suggested, "if you would tell me what *you* know. I have not asked you any questions—"

"You may. But you granted me a privilege. Do you know who killed my husband?"

"No. I am counting on you to help me find out."

"I will do that. But first I must know—I do not intend to attempt to destroy your facts. Only Siva can create facts, or destroy them, and it is Siva I am betraying, for my husband's sake. I must know your facts.

You know the agent is here, among these people. What have you found out about them?"

Sherwood glanced at Brissenden and saw by the colonel's fierce scowl that he was hopelessly sunk; and, remembering the $50,000 promissory note among his papers, signed by Cleo Audrey Storrs, Sherwood himself would not have risked a nickel on the question, whether he was confronted by cunning guilt, or determined remorse, or complicated idiocy. He considered, and at length turned to her with an air of frank sympathy:

"I'll tell you, Mrs. Storrs. I can only say that it seems to us likely that the man who murdered your husband is at present in this room." He disregarded a gasp from Sylvia Raffray and a muttering from the group, and went on, "We have narrowed it down to about fifteen people, any one of whom might conceivably have got to that spot yesterday without being observed. We can find no support for suspicion against any of the servants here, including the outdoor men, and no trace of a motive. One of the workmen from Foltz's place could have come by the path through the woods, but there is no reason to suspect them and they give mutual alibis—except for the man in charge, Wolfram de Roode. He seems—but we're looking into that. Of the eight left, four are women, including yourself. They are not absolutely excluded, but it seems improbable that a woman could have pulled that wire. None of the four men can prove lack of opportunity."

The attorney shuffled among his papers and drew out one. "Your daughter has told us that at about a

quarter past three yesterday afternoon Mr. Storrs left
the house by way of the side terrace. Bissell, your assistant gardener, says that at about that time he saw him
going down the path near the base of the slope, toward
the fish pool. We have found no one who will admit
seeing him between that hour and the time Miss Bonner
found him dead, a little before seven o'clock. But as I
said, neither do we find anyone who could not have had
an opportunity. Ranth did leave this house around four
o'clock, and returned some twenty minutes later—and,
according to his story, went to see you in your room.
Your daughter Janet was out of the house for over two
hours previous to the arrival of guests. Leonard Chisholm came here alone from Foltz's place, by the path
through the woods, about four-thirty, perhaps a little
earlier. He says he looked for Storrs but didn't find him.
Sylvia Raffray also walked here alone, some fifteen or
twenty minutes later, and about an hour afterwards was
followed by Foltz. Zimmerman had left the group at
Foltz's place before four o'clock, for a walk in the woods,
and was seen by no one until half-past five, when he suddenly appeared at the stables, talked a little with one
of the men, and then went to the tennis court. Those
are the stories we get. I've made up a complete time-
table of yesterday afternoon from 3:15 to 6:45, and it
proves nothing and eliminates nobody."

Sherwood shoved the paper aside, looked slowly
around the room, at each face, and back at Mrs. Storrs.
"We are of course being deliberately obstructed. We
expect that. Those obstructions must be removed. We
are told things we do not believe, and we are refused

information we have a right to ask for. We are not satisfied with Miss Bonner's explanation of her peculiar conduct, in going to the tennis court after finding the body, and spending ten minutes with you there, before returning to the house and telling Belden to notify the police. We are not satisfied with Chisholm's statement of his failure to find Mr. Storrs when he looked for him, nor with his statement of his purpose in looking for him. We are not satisfied with Wolfram de Roode's contradictory assertions regarding the sequence of events at Foltz's place yesterday afternoon. We are not satisfied with Foltz's explanation of how his woolen jacket came to be on the back of a chair in the reception hall, when the butler found it there and then found Foltz in the dining-room pouring himself a drink—Foltz having previously told us that he had entered the house by way of the sun room. We are not satisfied with Zimmerman's flat refusal to tell us the subject of his talk, which he denies was a quarrel, with Storrs in his office yesterday morning. We are not satisfied with Ranth's denial that he picked up a piece of paper from the grass by that overturned bench, and tried to get away with it, since we have Miss Bonner's unequivocal testimony that he did so—"

Mrs. Storrs demanded sharply, "What piece of paper?"

Sherwood gazed at her a moment, hesitating, then turned to the pile on the table and found the promissory note. He leaned forward, extending it in his hand: "This, madam."

She took it, glanced at it, nodded at it, and handed it

back to the attorney. She leveled her eyes at him: "You say Mr. Ranth picked that up from the grass?"

"Yes. Miss Bonner saw him. He put it in his pocket, and Chisholm took it away from him."

Mrs. Storrs looked at Ranth, who had stood throughout as if waiting for something, and knowing what. Composed, he met her eyes, and said nothing. She asked in a breath, "Twice, Mr. Ranth?" Still he said nothing. She returned to Sherwood:

"Twice, yesterday, Mr. Ranth had that paper taken from him—as if that could matter, since it is a debt to Siva and I shall pay it. There was a discussion—my husband, Mr. Ranth and me—which ended badly. My husband left the house—you say my daughter saw him go. Mr. Ranth received a demonstration from Siva, which you would not understand. He too left the house, to find my husband, to assert the debt; I agreed to it. Soon he returned, and his rage passed into me, I received the spirit of it, when he told me that my husband had refused all offering to Siva, had kept the paper, had again insulted the principles of the cause. But he did not tell me that Siva had closed the cycle of destruction, that my husband was dead."

Ranth said in a tone of ice, "I did not tell you that, Mrs. Storrs, because it was not true. Your husband was alive and unhurt."

Sherwood wheeled on him: "But you did tell her that Storrs had kept the paper?"

"I did."

"You had seen Storrs at that spot where he was found, and had quarreled with him?"

"I had."

"You lied when you told us you had not been there, you had not seen him, you had had that paper constantly in your possession, you had not picked it up from the grass, you had not attempted to conceal it? You lied when you told us all that?"

"Yes, I lied."

Colonel Brissenden licked his lips. There were movements among the others; Sylvia so gripped Dol's arm with her strong tennis hand that Dol had to pry at her fingers. Len Chisholm stood up and sat down again. Sherwood, with his head sunk into his shoulders, purred at Ranth, "If you want to, you may tell us exactly what happened."

Ranth looked at Mrs. Storrs and spoke to her: "What I told you yesterday was the truth. I found your husband there in the nook and told him our decision. He would concede nothing. I showed him the note you had signed. He seized it and would not return it. I demanded it. He became . . . he would not listen. I left him there. You know that my spirit has forsworn violence."

Mrs. Storrs retorted to his eyes: "Siva, for his violence, must have instruments. You are the instrument of Siva."

Ranth raised both his hands and slowly and firmly pressed the palms against his chest. "No. I am a part of Siva, and Siva has many parts. I know you are betrayed by weakness, and I forgive you." He turned to Sherwood: "Yes, I lied to you to protect the universal principle which I serve. I know that before all unbelievers

I am in danger. I knew that you could show that I got money from Mrs. Storrs, and that Storrs was attempting to make that impossible. I knew that you could show that with Storrs dead and Mrs. Storrs in possession of his property, I would benefit. I knew all that yesterday, when Belden told us Storrs had been killed, and when I went to that place and saw him hanging there. I thought I wasn't a fool, but I was a fool twice, first when I tried to remove that paper without being seen, and second when I failed to foresee that Mrs. Storrs, by the shock to her blood and her nerves, could abandon all the hope I have furnished her and the truth I have taught her. So in that foolishness, I lied to you. I am not an instrument of violence. I could not be."

Sherwood looked at Brissenden, and at his assistant beside him. The colonel growled, "Charge him!" The man with spectacles pursed up his lips and raised his brows, moving his head slowly in indecision. But Mrs. Storrs was talking:

". . . and I could share the guilt if it were mine or if there were guilt to share. But there can be guilt only where it is felt, and while I could feel it I know that Siva could not. I know that the Sakti ritual of Kamakshya, which includes the *pancamakara,* includes also human sacrifice. Siva, the destroyer-god, must fulfill his godship; but I am not Durga or Parvati, I am not ripe. They were pregnant of the world and of life; I am only a woman. Siva should have known that. Mr. Ranth should have known it. The cycle of destruction and restoration is in my spirit, and I would have sacrificed much to its demands, but I could not leave entirely behind me the sphere . . ."

Sherwood was only half hearing her; he was calculating shrewdly to himself, "She would be a knockout for a witness, with that cycle of destruction stuff—I could get it in by relating it to Ranth's tie-up with her and therefore his motive—a jury would eat it up, they'd love it—charge him now, I think—yes, I think so. . . ."

But Colonel Brissenden was on his feet. He did have velocity. He moved swiftly around the table, around Mrs. Storrs still justifying her personal petty remorse to the cosmos, squared off in front of George Leo Ranth and, red-faced, stuck his chin out:

"Come on, you, cough it up. Get it over. We've got you cold. Where's the gloves you used?"

Ranth moved back a step. Brissenden followed him, chest to chest, towering: "Come on, let's have it. Where's the gloves? We've got you! You realize that? Get it over—"

"Wait a minute!"

Everybody turned. Brissenden halted, glaring. Len Chisholm, with no haste but with purpose evident in his face, arose from his chair and repeated gruffly: "Wait a minute with that stuff." He abandoned Brissenden and addressed Sherwood:

"You said Ranth left the house around four o'clock and returned twenty minutes later. Is that right?"

But the colonel had steamed up. He exploded, "You sit down and we'll tell you what's right when we get to you! There's been enough of this damned—"

"Okay." Chisholm waved him off. "Go ahead and put your foot in it, and if you break a leg I can stand it. I'm only telling you something."

Sherwood put in, "Please, Colonel. Just a minute." To Chisholm: "Go ahead."

Len growled at him, "This makes me a princess. I know that. But if I get the idea right, that Ranth got back to the house at 4:20, and he is supposed to have killed Storrs before that, there's nothing doing. Storrs was in that place alive at 4:40. I saw him there, on that bench."

Brissenden glared. There were murmurs. Sherwood snapped: "You told us you looked for Storrs and couldn't find him."

"Yeah, I know." Len grimaced. "I lied too. That may give you a lot of exercise, but the real point is that I saw Storrs asleep on that bench at twenty minutes to five."

CHAPTER

SEVEN

*A*s George Leo Ranth had previously exhibited no despair in his peril, he now displayed no exultation in his relief. All he did was sit down, for the first time since entering the room. He gazed a moment at Chisholm's determined and truculent face, then retreated in good order to a chair behind Foltz and Zimmerman. An exclamation of surprise had come from Dol Bonner, from the others only an astonished silence. Brissenden frowned at Ranth's retreating back as a hawk at a rabbit that had reached the brush. Then he wheeled on the attorney and demanded:

"Get 'em all out of here but this bird Chisholm. We can handle him better alone."

Sherwood shook his head. "Not yet." To Chisholm his tone was not friendly: "You got the jump on us, didn't you?"

Len walked to him. "I don't get you. I'm just telling you—"

"Yes, I heard you. Sit down.—Will you please sit down?"

Len shrugged, moved to the chair Dol Bonner had previously vacated, and sat. Sherwood was speaking to the room:

"I'd like to tell you folks something. All of you. I believe in frankness. That's the way I like to work. I don't set traps. You are all welcome to know anything

I have found out about this. If one of you is guilty it
won't help him any in the end, and it would be no advantage to me to try to be slick with the rest of you.
Nor will it help you any to try to be slick with me. It
won't get you anywhere." He turned sharply to Chisholm: "Where has it got you? Last night you told me
you looked for Storrs and couldn't find him. Since then
you've remembered that the assistant gardener saw you
coming from the direction of the fish pool between
4:30 and 5 o'clock, and you know I've questioned him,
so you decided to get the jump on me by telling me
calmly that you lied. So I'm going to believe you now.
Am I?"

"I don't suppose so." Len sounded morose. "I don't
know anything about any assistant gardener. I spoke up
because I had reason to know you were pulling a foul
on Ranth. Little as I love Ranth."

"You didn't know the gardener saw you yesterday?"

"No."

"You didn't see him?"

"I wasn't looking for gardeners. I was too mad to
look for gardeners."

"Mad at who? Storrs?"

"No. Oh, I suppose him too. Everybody. At 4:40
yesterday afternoon my anger was universal."

"But you were mad enough at Storrs to threaten
yesterday morning, in the presence of three people, to
come out here and strangle him."

"Was I?" Len's brows lifted. "Maybe I did that.
But the ratio of murders threatened to murders accomplished is probably a million to one, so look at the odds

against your getting anything out of that. Anyway, I'm admitting that you've got a legitimate complaint against me; I told you a lie last night, and I shouldn't have done it. Now I've got to explain, I realize that, and my explanation is no good. I mean, there's nothing creditable about it, and nothing discreditable either. I was just too lazy to tell the truth."

Brissenden emitted a sound that was half snort and half snarl. Sherwood asked, "You're being slick, Chisholm? Don't do it."

"I'm not being slick. Yesterday, when I met Miss Raffray here at the tennis court and she asked me if I had talked with Storrs, I didn't happen to feel like explaining that I had found him sound asleep and hadn't disturbed him, so I just said I hadn't found him. Later, when Miss Bonner asked me the same question, naturally I told her the same thing, and others heard me. And when you asked me last night, it didn't seem worth while contradicting myself and doing a lot of explaining. I wouldn't call that slick—the fact is, it was pretty dumb—look at me now, yelling for you to let me up."

"And that is the only reason you give, that flimsy excuse, for telling a deliberate lie, on a vital point, to the authorities investigating the murder of a man whose life you had threatened on the very day he was killed?"

Len nodded. "Yeah, that's the only one. You framed that question swell. I told you it wasn't much good."

"You have nothing to add to it?"

"Not a thing. I'll play it like that."

"And your story now is, that you saw Storrs there, in

that spot where he was found dead, and he was on the bench asleep?"

"That's it. What I told you yesterday was correct, except for seeing Storrs. I left Foltz's place a little before 4:30 and came here by the path through the woods. I intended to find Storrs and smooth him down and maybe get the job back which he had got me fired from. The butler told me he had left the house. I looked around the front gardens and then remembered Miss Raffray had told me that he often took a nap in that place down by the fish pool, and I went there. He was there on the bench, dead to the world—I mean he was asleep. I went up within a few feet of him, and decided not to wake him up because he would probably be in a bad humor if I did. I looked at my watch because I was thinking vaguely of getting someone to drive me to Ogowoc, to catch a train to New York, and it was twenty minutes to five. I came back up the hill and around the front of the house and met Miss Raffray—she had just come over from Foltz's—and she suggested some tennis."

Sherwood was studying him. "Storrs lying there asleep—was he in such a position that you could have passed a wire under his neck without disturbing him?"

"I don't know. I didn't try."

"Did you have any gloves with you?"

"No."

"Did you go to the garden house?"

"No."

"Did you know there was a reel of trellis wire in the garden house?"

"I didn't know anything about the garden house, or if I did, I wasn't thinking about it. I don't know this place very well; I've only been here a few times."

"Which way was Storrs' head pointing?"

"To the right—my right as I faced the bench."

"Did you see the piece of paper on the grass?"

"Huh?—Oh. No, you wouldn't set a trap, would you? Anyway, I didn't see it."

"I wasn't setting a trap. Was the paper in his hand?"

"I didn't see it."

"Did you see anything else—notice anything? Is this your whole story this time?"

"That's it. You've got it all. This time and any other time."

"Not last night."

"Okay. I asked for that one."

Sherwood sat a moment, pulling at the lobe of his ear, without taking his eyes from Chisholm. At length he resumed, "About that threat of yours yesterday morning against Storrs. You're pretty hot-tempered?"

Len said drily, "Yeah, I'm emotional. I get worked up. You mean I might get mad enough at a man to kill him? Not if he was asleep. He'd have to wake up first."

"I suppose he would. But about that threat. I'm aware that men talk like that all the time, but this time there was a curious coincidence. You didn't say you would kill Storrs, or shoot him, or poison him; you said you'd strangle him. Would you care to account for that?"

"I would if I could." Len frowned. "Maybe it was

because I did strangle a man once—in a play I was in at college. Only I didn't use wire, I did it with my fingers.—Look here—your name's Sherwood? There's no sense in going on with this till you get me sore. This junk about me threatening Storrs. If you get me sore and I blow up, what good does that do you? I walk out on you, and then what?"

The attorney purred at him, "You won't walk far, Chisholm. No one here will leave these grounds, for the present. That's understood. As for your getting sore, I'm investigating a murder, you did utter that threat, you did lie to me last night, and you were, by your own statement, the last person to see Storrs alive. I'm not prepared to accuse you of murder; if I were, I would be advising you to get an attorney. But I don't believe you want to refuse to answer questions. Do you?"

Len muttered, "I'll answer questions. But quit reminding me that I said I'd strangle Storrs. I know damn well I said it, but I didn't do it. What do you want to know?"

"I want to know everything." Sherwood looked around again, surveying each face. "I wish all of you would realize one thing. If the murderer is among you, I'm not expecting anything from him—or her. But for the rest of you, you ought to understand that if I knew for certain what each one of you was thinking and doing yesterday afternoon between 3:30 and 6:15, that would tell me who the guilty one was. I say 6:15, because from that time on you were all together at the tennis court, until Miss Bonner left. I say 3:30, because at that hour Storrs was seen by the butler, walking from this house, and a few minutes later he was seen by the assistant gardener. If we accept Chisholm's story as he tells it, we know that Storrs was alive at 4:40, and we substitute that for the 3:30. That would mean that Storrs was killed during the 95 minutes between 4:40 and 6:15. All right; what led up to it? What were the actions and thoughts of all of you who were innocent during that period?"

Sherwood suddenly shot out a hand and pointed at the face of Steven Zimmerman. "Take you! You appeared at the tennis court at 5:45. What had you been doing during the preceding hour? You say, walking in the woods, and I can't disprove it. But what were you doing yesterday morning in Storrs' private office? You weren't walking in the woods then, were you? You have refused to tell me. If you're a murderer I wouldn't expect you to tell me, though I might suppose you would furnish some explanation instead of a flat refusal. If you are innocent, can you really justify your silence— to me, to yourself, to society—to God? I am the prosecuting attorney of this county; I represent the law; but I also represent P. L. Storrs and his dependence on the law to defend his life and to avenge his death. Can any of you say"—Sherwood circled with his outstretched hand, his pointing finger—"can any one of you, except the one who killed him, say that Storrs deserved to have his murderer shielded from the law?" The attorney paused.

He leaned back in his chair. "Well. Any one of you who lies or evades or withholds information regarding what happened here yesterday, or elsewhere as a preliminary to yesterday, you are shielding the guilt of a murderer, whether that is your intention or not. I hope I make that clear?" He surveyed the circle again, meeting each pair of eyes, none refusing him, then abruptly returned to Chisholm: "You say you'll answer questions. You told me that yesterday afternoon you were mad at Storrs and also at everyone else. What about?"

Len grimaced. "Different reasons. You want me to go down the list? It's an empty haul, but you can have it. I was sore at Storrs because he had got me bounced. I was sore at my boss because he hadn't given me two weeks' pay. I was sore at Miss Raffray because she had let Storrs bully her into ditching Miss Bonner, and also because she was using me to badger Foltz and she thought I was too dumb to know it. I was sore at Foltz because he was jackass enough to let her work it, and anyway, he and I aren't compatible, he thinks life is beautiful and I'm a pessimist. I was sore at Miss Bonner because she had stayed in New York. I was sore at myself because I had come out here without Miss Bonner, since the only reason I have anything to do with these people is because they are her friends." Len looked around belligerently. "If it helps you any to know it, I would have been sore at the rest of this bunch too if I had happened to think of them."

Sherwood nodded. "You said your anger was universal. It sounds like it. Why were you thinking of taking a train to New York, since Miss Bonner was coming at six o'clock?"

"I didn't know she was coming. She had said she wasn't."

"When she arrived, did she say why she had changed her mind?"

Len's eyes flickered. "She's right there, ask her."

Dol's voice came: "Don't be silly, Len, tell him."

"Okay. She said P. L. Storrs had phoned her an invitation."

"Did she say Storrs had come to her office?"

"Not that I remember, no. I didn't have my notebook. I wasn't a newspaper man any more."

"No. You had been fired. You said you were sore at yourself because you had come out here without Miss Bonner. Are you an old friend of hers?"

"Fairly old." Len looked across to where Dol sat close to Sylvia, Sylvia's hand in hers, and blinked at the sun which was in the window behind them. He squinted at the attorney: "I am in love with Miss Bonner. I am trying to persuade her that she is in love with me." He paused, and finished with a growl, "She is the only woman I have ever cared for. Ask me that question again next year, and I'll answer it the same way."

"I doubt if I'll be asking you questions next year. I hope not. Since you were sore at everybody, why did you come out here without Miss Bonner?"

"I've told you that. Miss Raffray suggested that I come and wheedle Storrs. I wanted my job back."

"It was not your declared intention to wheedle. Was it? Your declared intention—"

"Hold it." Len had a palm up at him. "I told you to quit reminding me that I threatened to strangle Storrs. And I'm also telling you, the longer you spend fooling with me, the colder you get. I've let you go on only because I lied to you last night and I thought I ought to make it up to you."

Sherwood's reply was forestalled by Brissenden. The colonel leaned across the table toward the attorney and demanded, "Let me have him a while. I'd like to try something."

The reply to that was also interrupted. There was a knock at the door and a trooper entered—the one with a flat nose to whom, the evening before, Dol had demonstrated the significance of the wire spiraled around the tree. At a nod from Sherwood he advanced, and placed on the table, diplomatically between the attorney and his own superior officer, an astonishing array of loot. It was a flat market basket filled with gloves, all colors, all materials, men's and women's. Brissenden glared at it and muttered, "What the devil!" The trooper told him:

"There they are, sir. Those at this end are from the servants' rooms. The others all belong to members of the family, except two pairs—they're all tagged—we found in the closet of the front hall, which the butler and the maid can't identify. None of them was used to pull that wire; there's some riding gloves with marks, but not the kind the wire made. The boys are finishing upstairs—there's a few things, bags and chests, the butler couldn't unlock. What'll I do, let 'em go?"

Brissenden grunted bitterly, "Mr. Sherwood is in charge." The attorney said, "No, I think . . ." He fingered gingerly at the display. "If you've examined all these—perhaps the colonel would like to go over them—they might as well be returned." He raised his head to Mrs. Storrs. "Would you be willing, madam, to unlock the bags and chests and remain to lock them again? Or your daughter perhaps? I think it is our duty to make this search as thorough as possible."

Mrs. Storrs sat unmoving. She declared, "It is useless. I warned you—the proof of fools—I will do it, but it is useless. I have heard all this foolishness. Do you think to entrap Siva with a pair of gloves? What are paltry facts to his wisdom, when he creates facts? What are the hands of a watch or the eyes of a foolish youth? I know the cycle has been closed!"

Sherwood nodded impatiently. "All right, Mrs. Storrs. You leave it to us. We are aware that the cycle could have been closed after 4:40 as well as before, even fools like us. If you will just go with the sergeant and unlock those things . . . and Quill! Has de Roode come, that fellow from Foltz's place?—Good. Send him in, and then I want to see that assistant gardener. —Yes." He looked at Len. "Colonel Brissenden would like to speak with you—will you go to that next room with him?"

Len lifted his shoulders and dropped them. "He'll only bark at me, and I'll bark back."

"Will you go?"

"Sure. I'll control myself."

Sherwood turned again. "I'd like to see you, Mr. Zimmerman, in about half an hour. Please stay within call, and I'll send for you." Another turn: "You may go to your home, Mr. Foltz, if you wish, but no further, please, for the present. I would like to talk with you later.—The rest of you will please remain on these grounds, I don't know how long—oh, and Quill! Tell those reporters I've changed my mind and get them off the place and keep them off. They can wait at my office. —If you don't mind, Mrs. Storrs?"

CHAPTER

EIGHT

*D*OL BONNER hadn't slept much, and she had a headache. In the friendly sunny September morning she walked along the path skirting the top of the east slope, thinking that outdoors she might breathe the headache away. The evening before, she had eaten nothing; this morning she had been starved and had breakfasted on two enormous peaches from the Birchhaven orchard, cereal, finnan haddie, rolls and coffee. While at the coffee she had been summoned to the card room by Sherwood, without a chance to step to the terrace to look at the sun. Now she walked in it, but it only glared at her and made her head ache worse.

She was proceeding on the assumption that she was a detective. She had in fact come to Birchhaven in that role, hired by P. L. Storrs, and even if she had been more strongly inclined to abandon it than she was, her obstinacy would probably have prevented her. She was aware of the picturesque incongruity of an attractive young woman—for her self-assurance had not been so mortally injured that she denied an obvious mirrored fact—undertaking such a career, but since the first week in the office of Bonner & Raffray it had not been prominent in her thoughts. She was a pretty good realist, and it was obvious that she must either seriously endeavor to establish herself in the profession she had chosen, or be prepared to admit to herself that she was a phony.

The latter, for Dol Bonner, was not likely. So she had attacked earnestly and energetically the problems that had been presented to her for solution, even the messy affair of Lili Lombard and Harold Ives Beaton.

Now here she was, up to her neck in a murder case. Not her case, but she was in it.

Strolling along the path, passing a large and luxuriant clump of cotoneaster, her eye was arrested by an impression of something dead brown in color, a color not appropriate to live twigs and green leaves—the color, for instance, of brown leather. She stepped off the path and pushed the cotoneaster branches aside to get a look, and saw that the object was an abandoned bird's nest. She became aware that so simple an incident had made her pulse jump up, and she sneered delicately at herself. So! Without really being conscious of it, she was looking for a pair of gloves, was she? *That* was a likely enterprise, among all these acres, even for the throng of troopers and detectives on the job, let alone for one woman. Not that she disapproved the effort from a professional standpoint; it was clearly worth trying, no matter how hopeless it seemed.

She decided to see what the nook and the tree looked like in broad daylight, and headed down the slope. But, arriving there, she did not actually enter the nook; first, because a trooper was standing at the entrance, by the low-hanging dogwood branches, chewing gum and obviously a Cerberus; and second, because her attention was caught elsewhere. Voices came from the direction of the fish pool and men were moving around there. She approached, ventured further and stood where the

THE HAND IN THE GLOVE

water-line had been, and no one gave her any notice, because they were engrossed in their task and the curious sight it afforded. The pool had been completely drained, to the bottom, and thousands of fish, mostly blue-gill and perch, were flopping frantically about, while men with rakes worked their way through the muck and mire, sweating, grunting, calling sarcastic encouragement back and forth. On the opposite bank stood a gray-haired man in faded blue overalls, looking distressed and indignant as he puffed spasmodically at his pipe—Watrous, the Birchhaven head gardener.

Dol went away, back up the slope, reflecting that it had occurred to someone besides her that it would have been simple for the murderer to stick a stone into each glove and toss them into the pool. But my lord, what a job! Also, the outdoor housekeeping at Birchhaven was impeccable, and there really were no small stones lying around loose, and if you have just hanged a man and want to get somewhere else quickly you haven't time to hunt around much—unless you have provided yourself with stones or weights beforehand, which didn't seem likely.

Passing the elaborate and extensive rose garden, she saw that two men with dark suits and black derbies were in there, armed with spades, crouching and darting around, presumably looking for evidence of recently overturned soil. She went on to the stable, told a man there good morning, and received his permission to pat the horses, one of which she had several times bestrode. From the loft above came gruff voices and grunts and the sound of men forking hay and—she listened—apparently pawing at it. She muttered, "Needle in a haystack," and sought the sunshine again. Retracing her steps, she turned aside through the gap in the yew hedge to the vegetable garden, and walked along the central path of turf. She thought she saw evidence of a search here too—celery tiles crooked, watermelon vines trampled, pepper plants and eggplants rudely bent—but there was no one around. She continued to the far border, where there were low brick-walled compartments for compost heaps, and stood looking at the conglomerate mass ready for decay on the heap most recently begun: corn husks, spoiled tomatoes, cabbage leaves and roots, celery tops, carrot tops, a little pile of watermelon meat, faint pink and unripe. . . .

She thought, "So recently living and growing, and now no good for anything until it rots. . . ." She put her hands to her temples and pressed; apparently the sun wasn't going to help her head any. She went back to the house.

In the reception hall, Sergeant Quill appeared from somewhere and put himself in her path: "Oh, Miss Bonner, I've been looking for you. The back of your car's locked. If you don't mind . . ."

"What?" Dol's brain slowed up when her head ached. "Oh, of course. The key's in the dashboard compartment."

"I know it is. I saw it there, but it would be better if you'd come along."

Dol shrugged, and followed him out of the house, across the main terrace, and onto the graveled space. He opened the door of her coupe and stood back, and she opened the dashboard compartment and fished out the key and gave it to him. Around at the back, she stood and watched him as he unlocked the panel and raised it and began pulling things out. There was a sweater, a kodak, two tennis balls, a leather jacket of Sylvia's, a copy of a book by Ogden Nash and one of the third volume of Gibbon's *Decline and Fall of the Roman Empire* . . . then the trooper brought forth a leather case, not large but handsome and sturdy, of light pigskin with chromium hinges and clasps, with "T. B." stamped in gold beneath the handle. Not wanting to scratch it on the gravel, he rested it on the sweater to open it, and as he did so Dol felt herself blushing and could do nothing about it. Immediately disclosed, strapped to the under side of the lid, was a little blue-metal Holcomb automatic pistol and a box of cartridges.

The trooper said solemnly, "Of course you're a detective."

Dol snapped, "I have a license. I mean for that gun."

He nodded and examined further. As his eye took in the significance of the case's contents, he muttered admiringly, "By golly, quite an outfit." Dol felt sure that in another minute she would kick him. That case was not Bonner & Raffray property, it was her own, a gift from Sylvia, who had taken the trouble to meet and consult with two New York inspectors of police in order to determine what it should hold. Possibly Sylvia had overdone it a little, but that was her way. . . .

The trooper was observing, "Tannic—muriatic—three magnifying glasses in there—fingerprint powders, squirters, pads—yep, litmus paper—envelopes, that's for clues—empty bottles, you never can tell when you might need one—gauze and tape—say, that flashlight's a pippin—" He looked up at her: "But that gat—of course it's all right to keep it here ordinarily, but I should think you ought to have it right on you when you're on a murder case like this—"

Dol said, "Put the key back when you're through," and left him. She thought to herself, as she sought the winding walk to the tennis court, that the annoying little incident was without significance, since she already disliked men to the limit of her capacity. She tossed it off.

In two bright yellow chairs near a corner of the tennis court sat Martin Foltz and Sylvia Raffray. As Dol approached Sylvia sat leaning back, with her hands up covering her eyes, and Martin was talking with a man who stood before his chair looking down at him. The man presented a rather singular appearance. If you looked at him only from the neck down, it would scarcely have been far-fetched to say that you saw an enormous ape in a suit of clothes and shoes; it was an inescapable impression from broad shoulders slumping to dominate the chest, the hips stuck onto the trunk like a mammoth jointed doll, the hang of all the muscles giving you the feeling that uprightness was a strain. Then, looking up, you were startled to see the uneasy, enigmatic, intelligent face and eyes of a sensitive and sapient man, around sixty years old. The way his shoulders slumped, he was not much taller than Martin Foltz.

Martin interrupted his talk with the man: "Here's

Dol, Sylvia.—I'm glad you came, Dol. De Roode wants to ask you about that man you sent down—"

"Dol darling, you're a bum." Sylvia had uncovered her eyes and sat up. Her eyes looked deep, her gay aggressiveness was gone, and there was gray in the accustomed loveliness of her skin. "You are always going off. What the dickens are you doing?"

Dol put her hand on Sylvia's shoulder and looked into her face. "I'm having a headache, that's all. I suppose we all are." She straightened up, and around to Martin. "You mean Silky Pratt watching the pheasants. I thought of him last night. It seemed—I don't know—ridiculous. Did he come, de Roode? Did you get him at Ogowoc?"

The man nodded. "Yes, miss." His voice was husky and guttural. "I couldn't sneak him into my attic like I was supposed to, because when I got back with him there was police there—from here—and they had the men, talking to them. They questioned your man too, and of course they questioned me. He spent the night watching anyhow. I told him you'd let him know today. It seems sort of useless, since everybody knows about it."

"I suppose so." Dol's forehead was wrinkled. "What do you think, Martin?"

Foltz hesitated. "Well . . . I don't know . . . since you said you wouldn't let me pay for it . . ."

"You mean it's my money we're wasting. Or rather, Sylvia's. All right, I say go ahead. I know we all feel right now that we're in an earthquake, but if we've started a job we ought to go on with it." She looked at de Roode. "I'll phone him to come tonight. Meet him at Ogowoc on the same train."

Sylvia burst out, "Dol, it's so silly! After what's happened . . . a man sitting there all night watching those pheasants. . . ." She stopped, then abruptly went on, "Anyway, there's no sense in it. Martin and I mentioned it this morning, and we're going to get rid of them right away."

De Roode muttered, "That remains to be seen, Miss Raffray."

"No, it doesn't." Sylvia looked straight at him. "There's been enough of this foolishness, de Roode. You're too darned stubborn. Martin's a nervous wreck. Oh, I know you've been in the family fifty years, or maybe a hundred, and you rode Martin piggy-back, and you'd give both arms to save him from a bad cold, and you hate me, but if you like those pheasants you'd better go off with them somewhere."

"I don't hate you, Miss Raffray." The man's face twitched. "But you're very young, and it's not my duty to let you interfere——"

"De Roode!"

"Yes, Mr. Martin."

"Don't argue with Miss Raffray."

"Yes, sir." A tremor, just perceptible, ran over the man's frame, then he was still. "I didn't start it, sir."

Sylvia insisted, "You did start it. You said it remains to be seen. It does not remain to be seen. It's decided."

"Yes, Miss Raffray.—Is it decided, sir?"

"Suffering saints!" Martin threw up both hands.

"You get. Beat it. Go on home. I'll have a talk with you later."

De Roode moved only his eyes, to Dol. "And about the man, Miss Bonner. Am I to get him tonight?"

Dol said, "Yes, until further notice. I can let you know."

De Roode turned and went, without celerity, but with no retardation of age in the power of his great muscles. Dol looked at his back as it receded—his sinewy rounded shoulders, the smooth vigorous swing of his legs.

She said to anyone, "He's a strange beast, that man." And to Foltz, "If I were you, Martin, I'd send him away at the same time as the pheasants. He is obviously so insanely jealous of Sylvia they couldn't possibly live in the same establishment. He gets worse all the time." She shrugged. "He has idolized you long enough anyhow, he should have a vacation." She sat down on the footrest of Sylvia's chair. "Well, Raffray, what about it? How goes it?" She patted Sylvia's ankle.

"Rotten, thank you, Bonner."

"I suppose so. You're young, and you were just a kid when your mother and father went, and this is the first real sock life has handed you."

"It isn't only that." Sylvia drew a long deep breath, with a trembling catch at the end of it. "P.L. was a swell guy and . . . you know what he was to me . . . and it's awful that he's dead." She bit at her lip, looked down at her twisting fingers, looked at Dol. "But this is worse than awful." She bit at her lip again, then suddenly burst out, "Don't they know that man killed him?

Why don't they take him away from here? Why don't they let us go? I hate this place!"

Martin leaned to her: "Now Sylvia. Don't do that."

Dol said, rubbing Sylvia's ankle, "You're a spoiled child. So was I, once. Even you, you have to learn you can't just snap your fingers. There are some doses you have to swallow even if you are fortune's darling. I swallowed one and darned near choked on it."

"But dragging it out like this—making us sit there and listen to him—and to that crazy woman—"

Dol shook her head. "You're taking too much for granted. They do not know that Ranth did it. Even if they knew it—"

"Of course they do! Who else could? Of course they know!"

"No, Sylvia dear." Dol was gentle. "They don't know at all. They are up a stump. They prefer Ranth on account of motive, but as it stands now, after what Len said, they haven't a particle of evidence. And there's a strong point in Ranth's favor: if he went back there after 4:40, and did it, surely he wouldn't have left that paper there on the grass. It's possible, he might have gone off in a panic, but it isn't likely."

Sylvia was staring at her. "But . . . I supposed of course it was him. If it wasn't him . . ."

"That's just it," Dol agreed. "If it wasn't him. It might have been somebody we never heard of, but Sherwood is convinced it wasn't. It might have been you or me or Janet or Mrs. Storrs, but he thinks it wasn't a woman. It might have been Len, losing his head, or Martin, mistaking him for a rival, or Steve, to observe a reaction—now hold your horses, Raffray, I'm not talking just to hear myself or to pile anything on. I didn't come here as your guest, either, it was P. L. Storrs who invited me." Dol abruptly switched to Foltz. "What do you think, Martin? Have you got any more opinions than you had last night?"

"No. I haven't." Martin slowly shook his head. "I guess there's nothing very rugged about my nerves, but I can't help it. Last night I was so shocked I wasn't capable of doing any thinking. When those troopers wanted me to go down there and look . . . look at P.L. . . . and I didn't want to go, they actually got suspicious, but I couldn't help that either. I've got too much imagination . . . I didn't need to go there to see it." He put up his hands and pressed his fingers against his eyelids, then looked at Dol again. "I would be better off if I could be hard. Maybe more manly."

Sylvia fluttered a hand at him. "Please, Martin. You are you. Such as you are, you are mine."

He gazed at her and muttered, "God knows I am."

Dol, not caring for love manifestations with a certain poignant memory still too acute, put in brusquely, "And such as you are, I'd like to ask you a couple of questions. May I?"

"You mean me?" Martin's gaze left Sylvia reluctantly.

"Both of you. You first. What happened over at your place yesterday?"

"What happened?" Martin's brow folded. "Why, nothing. We played a little tennis. . . ."

"Something must have happened, to make you come

over here through the woods in groups of one, at lengthy intervals. Sylvia told me that Len misbehaved. Len said that Sylvia was badgering you and you were a jackass.— But wait, I suppose I ought to tell you, this isn't just friendly curiosity. I am investigating the murder of P. L. Storrs."

Sylvia stared at her in astonishment. Martin stammered, "Why . . . of course. If you want to know—"

Sylvia interrupted him: "Don't humor her, Martin. She's wonderful and I love her, but she is a prima donna. —Dol Bonner, this isn't—it is *not* in good taste."

"On the contrary," Dol declared calmly, "it is. I merely didn't want Martin to misunderstand and think he was speaking under the protection of private confidence, which naturally I couldn't betray. But I would like to know what happened over there yesterday."

"It is still bad taste. What happened there has nothing to do with P.L.'s death."

"All right, forget it." Dol abruptly rose to her feet. "Don't think I'm grandstanding, Sylvia. The firm of Bonner & Raffray, which is not yet dissolved, is investigating the murder of P. L. Storrs. If you don't like it, I'm sorry. About yesterday, I can ask Len Chisholm." She moved to go.

"Wait a minute, Dol." Martin groaned. "My god, you girls! What's the difference whether it's friendly curiosity or what it is? Nothing happened yesterday except that I suppose we all made fools of ourselves. We got to my place around three o'clock. I had forgotten about Steve, and he was already there when we arrived, and he was grouchy and I spent half an hour smoothing

him down. When I finally went outdoors I suppose
Sylvia had decided I was neglecting her, and she under-
took to teach me a lesson by pretending there was no one
there but Len Chisholm. I suppose I showed that I didn't
enjoy being taught, and Len made some remarks, and I
also made some. Len blew up a little, and left, headed
for the path over here. Then Sylvia and I went at it—
and I may say I *was* a jackass—and pretty soon she left
too. I sulked a little while, and looked around for Steve
and couldn't find him, and then I came over here too. I
heard Sylvia and Len on the tennis court and didn't care
to join them, so I went around by the evergreens and
got to the house from the south, the sun room, and went
to the dining-room and had a drink. Belden came in
and told me there were supplies at the tennis court, and
I couldn't stay away anyhow, so I came out and sat in
that blue chair—that one—and had another drink, and
I was still there when you showed up."

Dol nodded. "And Steve was there too."

"Not when I got there. He came a few minutes later.
That must have been about a quarter of an hour before
you came."

"What was Steve grouchy about when you got to
your place yesterday and he was already there? If you
want to tell me."

"Nothing in particular. You know Steve. He's touchy.
He thought I had forgotten he was coming, and I had."

"Did he say anything about his visit yesterday morning to Storrs' office?"

"No, he didn't mention it. I had intended to ask him
about it, because I couldn't imagine what he had gone

there for, but in the—the confusion—I forgot about it."

"What time yesterday did you get here to the tennis court?"

"I don't know. It must have been, I would say, about twenty minutes before you did."

"That was six o'clock. So you got here about 5:40."

"I suppose around that."

"Did you stop anywhere on the way? In the evergreens for instance, to listen to the gayety from the tennis court?"

Martin colored a little. "I may have stood there a minute or two."

"And you went to the house and got a drink. Then—let's see—you must have left your place about 5:15 or 5:20. Where was de Roode when you left there? Did you see him?"

"De Roode?" Martin looked surprised. "Why de Roode?"

"I'm just asking."

"Well, I suppose he was around. They feed at 5:30. I didn't see him."

Dol kept her eyes obliquely down at Martin's face, and stood, silent. Finally she spoke: "Thanks, Martin, for indulging me. I hope it turns out to be Ranth. It was hardly you. Len—I can't see Len. If it was Steve Zimmerman or de Roode, that would hit you, and if I can find generosity to wish any man on earth peace and happiness it will be you, for Sylvia to share it." She compressed her lips and took a slow breath, and looked down at the junior partner of Bonner & Raffray. "It wouldn't hurt you, Sylvia dear, to indulge me too, even if you do think I'm a prima donna. I want to know about yesterday morning: did Steve Zimmerman or Storrs, either one, tell you what their talk had been about?"

Sylvia gazed up into the caramel-colored eyes, biting her lip. She extended a hand and let it fall again. "Dol . . . tell me. Are you just doing this? What are you doing? You can't make a game . . . asking these questions about all of us. . . ."

"I'm not making a game. I'm working." Dol suddenly stepped forward, leaned down to put her hands on Sylvia's knees, and looked into Sylvia's face. "You poor kid. Damn it, I know. Everything hurts you worse because you've never been hurt before. And me—I'm me, that's all. If I'm adding to your hurt by making a job of it, I'll go and sit on the terrace and read about the Roman Empire. I'll let it alone—if you want me to." She straightened up, made her back straight.

"No." Sylvia shook her head. "It isn't what I want— I want you to do whatever you think you ought to do."

"Okay. That's the girl. I think I ought to ask you to answer that question—whether Steve or Storrs told you—"

"They didn't."

"But you said Steve spoke about a mortal injury."

"He did, but I thought he was just maundering. He didn't say anything specific."

"And Storrs didn't either?"

"No." Sylvia frowned. "It all seems cloudy now. It seems a year ago. . . ."

Dol nodded. "All right. I hope it's Ranth." She pressed her palms to her temples. "I'm going to the house and find some aspirin. I'm going to find a hat too, or stay out of the sun." She turned to Martin: "I'll phone Pratt and tell him not to come tonight. Maybe we can try again later, if you still have the pheasants."

Martin agreed that that would probably be best, and Sylvia expressed concern about the headache, then, as Dol moved off, leaned her head against the back of the chair again and shut her eyes. Martin sat and looked at her. . . .

CHAPTER

NINE

CROSSING the main terrace to enter the house again, Dol saw that the door was being opened for her by a trooper in uniform. So they were even usurping the domestic functions. Inside, in the reception hall, stood another trooper, apparently for adornment. She supposed that the movements of everybody were being kept more or less under observation, and that exasperated her until she realized, with a little shock, that she would like to do the same thing herself.

She moved around the obstruction of the broad staircase and stood looking at the closed door to the card room, from behind which came an indistinct murmur of voices. She frowned at hearing no words, and she was frowning, too, from irritation at something that was eluding her memory. It was like a face which she could remember without being able to fit a name to it; a fact that she wanted, and knew was in her mind, but could not get hold of. She felt that it was trivial and yet might be important; something she had that morning seen or heard or felt which had struck her, below the surface of consciousness, as a contradiction or incongruity which needed to be explained; and she had at the moment failed to call it up for examination, and now could not find where it was hid, in some secluded recess of her mind. It was something someone had said . . . or a

gesture not apropos . . . or some object she had
seen. . . .

She gave it up, knowing it would return to plague
her; and heard, behind her, her name pronounced.

It was Belden, bowing, with slips of paper in his hand.
There had been telephone messages for her. Mr. Tavister, having learned of the predicament at Birchhaven
through the newspapers, wished to know if he could be
of any service to her. She could get him at his apartment
until noon, after that at the Biscuit Club. Miss Eldora
Oliver . . . a similar message. Mr. Malcolm Brown
wanted Miss Bonner to know that he was at his place
near Westport for the weekend, and that he could drive
to Birchhaven in twenty minutes. Dol thanked Belden
and asked him if there was a phone available—since the
only one she knew of was in the card room—and was
conducted by him to the pantry. She consulted a memo
book from her handbag for Silky Pratt's number, got
him, and told him to forget about the pheasants for the
present and to join Gil Delk in the search for Anita
Gifford's dress.

She returned to the reception hall frowning again.
What the dickens was it she was trying to remember?
What measly little fact was eluding her? She tossed her
head in exasperation—recollecting too late that her head
was in no condition to be tossed—and mounted the
stairs.

The wide upstairs corridor was intersected at its middle by a narrower one. Around the corner, at the first
door on the right, Dol stopped and tapped softly on the
panel. After a little wait she tapped again; then it

opened and Janet Storrs was confronting her. Janet, as Dol had observed previously, either felt no grief at her father's death, or grief was not with her a matter for tears and lamentations; rather, she had withdrawn from it, or with it, there was no telling which; her surface had frozen into a pale mask, and the blood flowed beneath with its secrets. Her gray eyes slept or smouldered as they had before.

Dol said, "I wanted to see Mrs. Storrs. Just for a minute."

Before the other could reply a voice sounded from within: "Who is it?"

"It's Dol Bonner, Mother."

"Let her in."

Janet stepped aside and Dol entered. But in three paces, she stopped in amazement. The sight that met her eyes was not really extraordinary . . . or was it? Mrs. Storrs, bare-armed and bare-legged, dressed only in an athletic jersey and shorts, stood on the platform of a complicated exercising machine, grasping the rubber handles. She was not young nor slender, but neither was she unwieldy or misshapen. Disregarding, or not seeing, Dol's open-mouthed surprise, she spoke in her normal voice, which always in its first sentence startled by its intensity:

"I have not missed doing this in three years, but this morning I didn't feel like it. After that . . . downstairs . . . I came up and lay down, but I couldn't lie still. Do you want something, my dear?"

Dol was impelled to leave the room without a word. The woman was manifestly crazy; at the very least, simple-minded. She abandoned as useless the questions she had intended to ask, but there was nevertheless something to say. She approached the machine.

"There's nothing I want, thank you, Mrs. Storrs, but there are two things I thought I should tell you. First, I am not here as Sylvia's guest. Mr. Storrs asked me to come. He engaged me, hired me, to discredit Mr. Ranth. To get rid of him. I have told the men downstairs about it, so I thought I should tell you."

Janet stood there motionless, looking on, no change on her frozen surface. Mrs. Storrs said, as calmly as the compression of her vocal chamber would permit: "Thank you, my dear. My husband would do that. I understood my husband. It is of no consequence. He acted in his sphere, and by his death I am confined to it."

Dol hastily agreed. "Yes. It's too bad you couldn't—" She checked herself. "The other thing I wanted to say: I am staying in your house, of course, because I have to, but I still am not a guest. Nor a friend. I am investigating the murder of your husband."

Janet faintly stirred, then was motionless again. Mrs. Storrs released the rubber handles and declared, "That sounds foolish. What is there to investigate about it?"

"Several things. For one—who killed him?"

"Nonsense." Mrs. Storrs stepped from the platform. "Who are you? What can you know? I have told that man . . . he says he looks for proof. Do you mean you help him? Do so, my dear, but do you know what Siva says? *The camel leaves a track, the sun does not.* I could show him the truth, but I could not imprison it for him."

Dol only half heard her. She was thinking that anyone who could stand there in linen shorts with a Saks label showing, and talk like that, was either a mahatma or plain dotty; and that, at the moment, was not the dilemma that engaged her. And there was, after all, one question which might be favored with an intelligible answer.

She asked it: "If you don't mind, Mrs. Storrs, there's one thing I would like to know. Ranth came back to the house at 4:20 and told you Mr. Storrs had kept that paper. Was he with you from then on? All the rest of the afternoon?"

"No."

"How long did he stay with you?"

"Ten minutes. Perhaps fifteen."

"Do you know where he went?"

"Yes. If Leonard Chisholm, as he says, saw my husband alive. He went back to my husband."

"Did he say he was going there?"

"No."

"Did you see him go?"

"No. He said he was going to the card room, to write a letter."

"Was Janet here with you?"

"No. She left long before that, when my husband did."

Janet put in, with her soprano that was at times toned and musical, at others almost a squeak: "I gathered some flowers and put them in vases. Then I went to the rose garden and read there in the pergola. Because my mother is strong, do you have to torment her like this?

Or me? When you have forfeited your right to courtesy . . ."

"I know I have. Courtesy is no good anyway, just at present." Dol sounded firm, but not unpleasant. "Would you mind telling me—while you were outdoors, and in the rose garden, did you see anyone going toward the fish pool or away from it? Len Chisholm, for instance?"

"I saw no one anywhere."

"Okay.—And Mrs. Storrs. Please. You came with Mr. Ranth to the tennis court a little after six o'clock. Had he rejoined you?"

"No. When I went downstairs at six he was on the terrace, the side terrace. We went together to the tennis court."

"Were you upstairs all afternoon?"

"No. I was with my husband."

Dol gasped. "You were what? When?"

"I was with my husband when he left the house. I was with him as he slept, and after he was destroyed. I am with him now."

"Yes. Of course." Dol felt uncomfortably that crazy or not, the wretched woman was pitiable. Standing there in her linen shorts, her bare arms and legs . . . what had Storrs said . . . sticking her nose in the cosmos. Dol said abruptly, "Thank you both, very much. I hope I will be able to show that I am not merely a nuisance." She turned and left the room.

Descending the stairs, she reproached herself for not having made one small demand of courtesy and asked Janet for some kind of a hat. Her own turban was useless in the bright sun, and she did want one. She asked the trooper in the reception hall where the butler was, found him, put the problem, and was directed to a closet in the side hall beyond the dining-room. There she found a shelf of floppy straws and cotton helmets, picked a decent fit, and proceeded to the side terrace. She had learned from the trooper that Ranth was in the card room, and that Zimmerman had emerged from it a few minutes ago and had left the house. She had decided to tackle Zimmerman.

It proved to be her most dismal failure of the morning. The assistant professor of psychology was indeed to be found, but he might as well not have been. After wandering in the grounds on two sides of the house and thinking it as well not to make inquiry of a trooper on the main driveway and another who looked down on her from the roof of the summer kitchen, heaven knew why, she finally ran across Zimmerman out at the kennels. He was seated on an upturned box, staring through the wire netting at a Doberman lying with his head on his paws and blinking in the sun. He offered no greeting, made no movement, though Dol went up and stopped within a yard of him. She stood, also silent, and gazed through the netting at the dog.

Finally she said, "His name is on that plate there. Gulken Prince Birch."

No response. Continued silence. Dol swallowed exasperation and turned on him: "Steve Zimmerman. You're a darned fool. Either what you and Storrs talked about yesterday morning is connected with his murder, or it isn't. If it isn't, you ought to tell it. If it is, and you won't tell it, you should have made up something to tell that man Sherwood. You don't seem to realize that Sherwood can do really unpleasant things. He can lock you up as a material witness, and keep you locked up. He can make you notorious. He knows that just after you left Storrs you said something to Sylvia Raffray about a mortal injury. Now I want to tell you, I'm in on this. I am investigating Storrs' murder. If what you and Storrs said to each other is something that you can't disclose, but had nothing to do with his death, and if you won't tell Sherwood because you think you can't trust him to keep it confidential, you can trust me. That would do until the inquest Tuesday. At the inquest is when you'll really get it. You'll testify or you'll get it.—But maybe I'm talking too fast. You've just been in there with Sherwood. Maybe you told him about it. Did you?"

Slowly Zimmerman's head turned, tilted, and he looked up to meet her gaze. His thin stringy hair was lifeless in the sun, his wide nostrils looked permanently distended, and his pale eyes, no longer inquisitive, gave the impression that they saw nothing whatever and did not expect to. They remained fixed on Dol a moment, then abandoned her and went back to the dog.

He said, in a tone devoid of any concern in the matter, "I don't see that it's any of your business. However . . . I told Sherwood nothing about my talk with Mr. Storrs. Nor will I tell you. Or anyone else."

"Sooner or later you will. You'll have to."

Zimmerman shook his head. "No, I won't." He spoke without animation, with dead finality. "The human mind has given countless proofs of its capacity for resolution. I shall betray nothing that I choose to conceal, unless I change my resolution. It is my own affair whether I act for my own defense, or as a shield either for innocence or for guilt, or merely from caprice. It is psychologically fascinating, but I am not enjoying it. I told Sherwood that."

"Good lord." Dol stared at his profile. "You *are* a fool."

"No, I'm not a fool." Zimmerman picked up a crumb of biscuit which lay on the gravel and tossed it through the netting. The dog eyed it, and decided it wasn't worth the trouble. "You suggest that I invent something to appease Sherwood. Something fanciful? You forget my scientific devotion to the truth. But I suppose I might manage it with the play instinct—the simplest and most effective incitement to the imagination. Should I perhaps tell him that I called on Storrs in my capacity as an alienist, to inquire into his sanity? And as a result of my inquiry, condemned him to annihilation? Should I describe to him how yesterday I got to that place unobserved, and fastened the wire around Storrs' neck, and pulled on it, held him up when he jumped—is that what you would like? Only I don't know where the gloves are; I couldn't tell them that; and I understand the law won't take a man's word for it when he confesses murder, it suspects him of bragging; he has to furnish corroboration. I'm sorry, I must have mislaid the gloves. . . ."

Dol said, "You're as goofy as Mrs. Storrs. You babble. Or are you—" She stopped, and regarded him through narrowed eyes, under the brim of the floppy straw. "I'm not apt to imagine I can guess anything from your silly camouflage, so don't bother about it. But you deserve to hear my opinion. I don't believe you killed Storrs and are acting for your own defense. I doubt if your talk with him yesterday had anything to do with his murder, and I doubt if you have any reason to think it had. I suspect you hit it when you said caprice. You would call it that. You are constantly digging around in other people's brains, even common decency doesn't restrain you, and I actually believe you are mean enough to regard this as an opportunity . . . to practise . . ."

"When you finish with my mote," Zimmerman put in, "I'll help you with your beam. It seems that you also seize opportunities for practising your profession."

He picked up another crumb and tossed it to the dog. Dol, speechless, watched him do that; then, disdaining a reply, she turned and left him. Dismal failure indeed.

Striking off across the lawn, she was hotly denying the justice of Zimmerman's thrust. She thought of arguments: hadn't she herself discovered the body? Hadn't she come here to work for the man who had been killed? Hadn't she deduced the significance of the wire spiraled around the tree? Hadn't she prevented Ranth from getting away with the piece of paper? Hadn't she been told by Sylvia to go ahead? Hadn't she . . .

But, veering away from a perennial border where two men were scratching in the peat moss, she admitted to herself that all those arguments, if not exactly dishonest, were at best specious. She didn't need them anyway. For whose approbation were they required? No one in the world, except possibly Sylvia. For herself . . . She stood looking down at a flaming patch of phlox and muttered aloud, "I'm a detective or I'm not." She dismissed it at that, and a recurring trivial annoyance assailed her, like a persistent buzzing gnat: what the dickens was it that had happened this morning, that she wanted to remember and couldn't? She concentrated on it futilely, then tried to dismiss that too. . . .

She wanted to see Len Chisholm.

After going to the house and learning that he had been dismissed from the sun room by Colonel Brissenden some time ago, and looking for him in vain on the western and southern slopes, she finally found him in the rose garden, in the pergola with his legs stretched out on a bench, reading a Sunday newspaper. As she approached he greeted her and moved to make room, but she sat on another bench across the path from him. Her head felt better, but her muscles were weary.

"Where did you get the Gazette?"

"One of the troopers went to Ogowoc."

"Anything in it?"

"Yeah, half the front page." Len held it up. "Picture of him. Picture of the house too, I wonder where they dug that up. Want it?"

Dol shook her head. "I'll read it later maybe. What did the uniformed colonel do to you? Was he tough?"

Len grimaced. "Honest to God, Dol, I don't know how it happens those babies don't get smacked in the puss oftener."

"Good heavens, did you smack him?"

"No, I only wanted to. I reprimanded him. I let him have it straight. I even told him I was an American citizen. Don't you worry, I acted like a gentleman."

"I'm not worrying." Dol frowned at him. The whites

of his blue eyes looked bloodshot, he had obviously not shaved, his shirt collar was wrinkled and his tie askew, and his hair was more than ordinarily chaotic. "Yes, I am too. Of course I'm worrying. I am taking advantage of this opportunity to practise my profession. I am investigating this murder."

"Fine." Len leaned back and clasped his hands behind his head. "You'll do better at it than that tin soldier. That damn fool pretended he thought *I* did it."

"Maybe he does think so."

Len grunted. "Don't frighten me out of my wits."

"I won't. I want you to use your wits. For instance, tell me what happened yesterday at Martin's place. I understand you got there around three o'clock. Then what?"

"Aha!" Len sat up. "So that's it. You pretend you're investigating a crime, and what you are really doing is prying into my conduct with other women. Thank heaven you have betrayed yourself at last! Jealousy like yours reaches a point where it is uncontrollable, and then it explodes. I refuse to defend—"

"Please, Len, postpone it. I want to know what happened."

He spread out both hands. "You insist? All right, we got there at three o'clock, Martin driving like a demon. We found Steve Zimmerman there on the porch, looking as if somebody had fed him ipecac. Martin excused himself and went in with Steve, and Sylvia found shoes and things, and rackets and balls, and that what's-his-name put up the net for us—"

"You mean de Roode."

"Right. Sylvia and I volleyed a little, and then she wanted to sit and talk, she said about my job. What she really wanted was to put her sign on me. She was waving the wand when Martin came out, and kept it up on account of momentum. I was like stone, I wouldn't give an inch, I was thinking of you all the time. Martin got nervous and butted in, I made one or two appropriate comments, Sylvia got frustrated and bitter, and finally I saw it might end in bloodshed, so I merely bowed to them and came over here. No man was ever more faithful—do I go on?"

"No, not that way. Talk sense. Then—as you told Sherwood—you came here and looked for Storrs, and found him there on the bench asleep, and came away without waking him up, and walked around the front of the house and met Sylvia near the tennis court. Is that right?"

"You heard me say it." Len put up his brows. "Sylvia again, huh? But we didn't sit and talk then. We played—"

"Don't do that! Please. As you came up the slope and around the front of the house, did you see anyone? Janet or Ranth or anybody at all?"

"Dol my love." Len twisted his body around and put his feet on the ground. "What do you think you're doing?"

"I told you, I'm investigating Storrs' murder."

"But not . . . my dear lady . . . not like this. I mean you're not serious. Asking me about the little events at Martin's place? What the devil has that got to do with it?"

"I don't know." Dol kept her eyes level at him. "I'm asking about everything I can think of. I would especially like to know what Steve went to see Storrs about yesterday morning . . . yes, I still would. And I'm still wondering why you told all of us yesterday that you looked for Storrs and couldn't find him."

Len waved a hand. "You're cuckoo. The sun's got you. You actually sound as if you meant it."

"I do mean it. Oh, I know your explanation of that lie was perfectly simple and natural, but I wonder anyhow. I am a detective, Mr. Chisholm. And I happen to be aware that you know how to conceal your feelings quite effectively and that you are a practised and accomplished liar. After explaining to Sherwood why you had said that you hadn't found Storrs yesterday, you went ahead and told him another lie this morning. In front of all of us."

"Me? You're crazy. I was the soul of candor."

Dol shook her head. "You told him a lie."

"Name it."

"You said that you are in love with me and that I am the only woman you have ever cared for."

"Well by God!" Len jumped up. "That's gratitude for you! Just because I don't turn on Hearts and Flowers and whine around like a sick calf? Do you think you can crush my passion like that? Do you think you can blow it away with a puff? Do you think—"

"Cut it out." Dol looked unimpressed. "Stop it, Len. The horse play was all right as long as it merely helped you to hide what you didn't want to show—I didn't mind—some times I really enjoyed it—but not now.

It may have nothing at all to do with this business, but I thought I ought to tell you I know all about it. You are no more in love with me than you are with the Empress of China."

"There is no Empress of China. You play with my heart as a cat plays with a mouse. China became a republic—"

"Len, will you stop? Do you think I'm an imbecile? Do you imagine I don't know that you are completely bewitched by Sylvia?"

It hit him, quite unprepared as he was for it, and, with her eyes on his face, she saw that it did. But he made a good and almost instantaneous recovery. He stared, and got incredulity into his voice: "Say that again? I wouldn't have believed it. You *are* jealous! I've got demons, you've got demons . . ."

Dol shook her head. "No good, Len. I saw it months ago. I suppose you fell for Sylvia the first time you met her, that day last spring at the Giffords'. I don't know why you didn't try to trip Martin up and make a play for her—or maybe you did and it didn't work. You have a fine equipment of words and postures to cover up with, but I've been educated and I'm hard to fool. She put her sign on you all right, so much so that you couldn't resist the desire to see her, just to look at her and listen to her, but you weren't going to make an exhibition of yourself, so you got the idea of pretending I was the attraction. I suppose you figured you couldn't hurt me any, in spite of your charm, because you knew I had been inoculated and was immune. I credit you with that consideration—"

"Dol, you darned fool——"

"You're another. If I hadn't been immune I wouldn't have seen through you so easily. Why do you think I've tolerated all your clowning? Why else would I, except from compassion? I do feel sorry for you. Maybe I wouldn't bother to, if it were anyone but Sylvia, but she is so lovely and desirable and honest and sweet, that if I were a man and as madly in love with her as you are,—— if I wanted her as much as you do and couldn't get her, ——but that's the point I'm coming to. Why all the abnegation? You don't owe Martin anything. You don't regard the ties of betrothal as sacred, do you? Since you've used me for four months as a peg to hang your hat on, and I haven't kicked, I think I have a right to ask that. Why haven't you had the spunk to make a try for it?"

Len growled, "It's not a question of spunk."

"What is it then?"

He shook his head. Abruptly he got to his feet, shoved his hands deep in his pockets, and scowled down at her. He shook his head again, turned and strode six paces down the path, picked a rose from the vine on the trellis——a yellow everblooming climber——crushed it in his hand, and tossed it to the gravel. He came back to her:

"Look here. Have you noticed that I'm going off my nut? What am I going to do about it?"

"Well, Len, what have you tried?"

"Nothing. I thought for a while it might go away. Along in the early stages I kidded with her——I thought I was kidding——and she beat me at it because she is full of devils. Once I asked her why she wasted herself on a guy like Foltz when material like me was available, I

said surely she didn't love him, and she looked at me—
you know how she can look—and she said oh no, she
didn't love Mr. Foltz, she was going to marry him only
because her guardian wanted her to and she always
obeyed her guardian, and she began making suggestions
how I might displace Foltz in her guardian's affections,
she said first I should learn to play the piano because
Storrs was fond of music. That was how far I got kidding with her."

"You might have tried just telling her how you felt.
That might have interested her."

"Yeah, sure." Len sounded bitter. "I did try that
once, and she was clever enough to pretend she thought
I was kidding again, and began making plans how I
could write to her after I got into a monastery. And anyway you're wrong. I'm not in love with her, it's only
some kind of delirium. Infatuation maybe. I wouldn't
marry her if she mounted an altar on wheels and followed me around with it for ten years. She's worth
what? Three or four million? What would be my title,
Equerry of the Steering Wheel? I wish to God she
would go ahead and put the loop on Foltz and lead him
away; with her guardian gone she might forget why
she picked him."

He gazed down at her. He demanded abruptly,
"Why did you stampede me with this now?"

"To show you that I know what an accomplished liar
you are."

"Does anyone else know about it?"

"You mean about your delirium?"

"Yes."

"I imagine not."

"Does Sylvia?"

"I don't think so. Sylvia's conceit is quite superficial; she is really very modest about herself."

"Does Foltz?"

"I doubt it."

"You haven't discussed it—with her?"

"Certainly not."

"You'd better not. Forget it. Don't bother about the compassion; I wouldn't know what to do with it. You haven't time anyway; you're investigating a murder." He turned and strode away, down the path; at ten yards he wheeled to call to her: "And I won't annoy you with any more clowning!" Then he went.

Dol sat and watched him go. The back of his coat was badly wrinkled. He swung to the right, into a cross-path; then, above the intervening bushes, she could see only his head and broad shoulders as he passed through the arch at the far end.

She had thought for weeks that it would some day be amusing to inform Len Chisholm how transparent his antics had been—and now it had happened this way. Nothing very amusing about it, and nothing revelatory either, as far as she could see. Detective? Piffle. She was nothing but a darned female quidnunc.

A breeze stirred gently, and the air around her was fragrant from the roses. She looked at the Gazette with its sections scattered on the opposite bench, and was momentarily minded to reach for it, but didn't. She looked at the ravished rose Len had plucked and crushed and tossed away; and by some obscure communication in her brain it was the sight of those discarded petals, abandoned there on the path, which brought into consciousness the trivial little fact which had been eluding her for two hours. There on the compost heap . . .

Relieved but not elated, she smiled commiseratingly at herself. So that was it! Certainly not worth all her cerebral searching. Probably worth nothing whatever; all the same, she would go and take another look. She got up and shook down her skirt; and discovered how jumpy her nerves were by the sudden start she gave when the loud sound of a gong came from the east terrace; Belden announcing lunch.

CHAPTER

TEN

LUNCHEON, naturally, was a complete failure socially, and not a marked success biologically; plates went back with rejected contents far in excess of the politeness percentage. Meals are the times above all others for household solidarity, not only as a preservative of civilization, but also for digestion's sake; and they can be horrible and dismal affairs when hostility or apprehension or any acute disruptive emotion has invaded the breasts of the partakers. They were all present, even Mrs. Storrs, and including Martin Foltz, who had apparently not taken advantage of the permission given him to go home. The hostess informed them that Mr. Sherwood and Colonel Brissenden had declined her invitation and gone to Ogowoc, but would return shortly.

They were eating in the shadow of death, but not with the reliquiae under the roof with them; the body of P. L. Storrs had been taken to Bridgeport for an autopsy.

The ordeal over, Dol got away and outdoors again, alone. Forlornly, without any expectation of the event, she intended nevertheless to satisfy herself regarding the phenomenon which she had finally dragged into memory. Once more she took the path to the kennels, turned aside at the gap in the hedge, entered the vegetable garden and followed the central path to the other end where the compost heaps were. Glances both ways had assured her that for the moment no one else was exercising any curiosity regarding this part of the grounds; nobody was in sight.

She stood and looked at the compost heap in recent use. It did not appear to have been disturbed since she had seen it three hours previously; there were the corn husks, the spoiled tomatoes, cabbage leaves and roots, celery and carrot tops, the little pile of pink and unripe watermelon meat. . . .

She didn't want to walk onto the mess, nor did she wish to disturb it. Lifting her skirt, she stepped on top of the low brick wall enclosing the heap, and edged around it, bending over, peering. She went clear around, inspecting every inch, arriving at the other side and jumping back to the ground. She stood frowning, thinking, "Of course I'm a fool. Probably they forked this thing over before I was here this morning and covered up the rind. But the fact remains that that's not more than a fourth of a watermelon, and it's not ripe, and there's not a speck of rind or the white part in sight. If somebody tried one and threw it away . . . anyhow, what the dickens, what else have I got to do?"

She returned along the central path, near its middle turned left, and stood surveying the patch of watermelon vines. It was a mat of luxuriant foliage perhaps sixty feet square, with here and there, for a sharp eye, a glimpse of the rounded, rich green top of a melon. She saw that she could expect no hint from displaced vines or trampled leaves or stems, because those signs of recent disturbance were all over the patch; men that morning, she presumed, stepping, stooping, brushing the foliage aside . . . and possibly also conceiving the same idea that had occurred to her, and testing it . . . only with her it was not merely a wild conjecture, she had arrived at it logically. . . . She looked around again, in all directions, saw no one, stepped off the path into the foliage, pushed leaves aside to disclose a melon, and getting her fingers under it, turned it over to look at its bottom.

She shook her head and went on to find another, and another. It became apparent that she would have to look sharp at every step, bending to thrust the foliage aside in a wide circumference, not to miss any. After ten minutes of it she began to feel silly, but she also felt stubborn, and she kept doggedly at it. She straightened up to take a kink out of her back, then muttered to herself, "Leave no melon unturned," and squatted again as she found another one. . . .

She was at the right edge of the patch, near the strawberry bed, when, rolling a large fine melon partly over and squinting at its bleached bottom, she gasped in astounded disbelief. It was as though, opening oysters with an idle pretense of looking for pearls, she had, incredibly, actually found one. She sat back flat, crushing foliage and stems regardless, trembling all over. She saw that she was trembling, and couldn't stop it; then suddenly she was stiffened by a dreadful thought: "What if they've been here and found it? But no . . . surely . . . they would have taken the melon. . . ." She scrambled to her feet and looked around. No one to be seen. She needed some kind of a tool, a nail file

perhaps, and had left her handbag lying on the path.
She reached to her hair and pulled out a bobbie pin,
stepped close to the melon, squatted, carefully turned
it over on its side, and looked again at the irregular
rectangle, as big as the palm of her hand, which a knife
had made cutting through the rind. She pushed tenta-
tively at the rectangle of rind; it was loose; she stuck
the bobbie pin into it diagonally and pulled, and the
piece of rind plopped out. Her hand was trembling
again as she inserted it into the cavity; was it empty?
Was it just a melon plugged to see if it was ripe? The
answer was in her hand as she pulled it out: a pair of
heavy tan leather gloves.

She thought: "I must stop this damned trembling;
I'm a swell detective, I am." She replaced the rectangle
of rind in the hole, pushed it in too far and let it go, and
rolled the melon back to its rightful position. She sat
down on the foliage where she had already ruined it,
extended her legs straight out, pulled up her skirt, and
stuck one of the gloves under the top of her left stocking, and the other under the right. On her feet again,
with her skirt smoothed down, a glance around still disclosed no eye observing her, and she made her steps un-
hurried as she went to the path and got her handbag,
sought the central alley, and followed it to the gap in
the hedge. There she stopped, indecisive. Which way
to turn? To the house, of course, to see Sherwood, or to
await him if he had not returned. But no—she compressed her lips—not of course. Those gloves were, at
least for the moment, her own private loot, her private

and personal discovery, and she would at least examine
them. Not outdoors; she wanted walls, opaque to curious eyes. Not in the house, with troopers and detectives
all over the place. The stable? That would do. She
emerged from the gap in the hedge and turned right.

There was no one there. She stood on the concrete
floor and called, and there was no answer. But one of the
men might come through the door unexpectedly, so she
moved to the other end, beyond the stalls, beside a dusty
window, and got the gloves from their intimate con-
cealment, damp with watermelon moisture. They were
brown, looked new, heavy for driving or country, and
stamped on the inside of the cuff, "Genuine Horsehide."
She did not recognize them as any she had ever seen. She
looked at the palms and, if proof was needed, found
it. Deep marks cut into the new leather, diagonally
across from the little finger to the crotch of the thumb,
on both of them. Circumstantial but conclusive evidence
that P. L. Storrs had not killed himself, for she held
there in her hands the gloves that had been worn by the
man who had murdered him.

Who?

A thought struck her. She rejected it as capricious; it
came back. She admitted it to consideration, and it possessed her. She could do it, or at least she could try,
and there was no reason why she shouldn't. Hadn't she
found the gloves? It would mean at most an hour's delay, if it came to nothing.

But where to leave the gloves meanwhile? They were
certainly too precious to take any chances with. Hide

them . . . where? There was no place good enough. She lifted her skirt again and carefully and thoroughly tucked the plunder back beneath her stockings, and felt no delicate discomfort at the touch of the moist leather against her skin. Then she went back past the stalls, left the stable, and headed for the house.

Instead of entering, she veered to the right and approached, from the rear, the graveled space where her coupe was parked. Other cars were there too, three or four of them; a trooper and a man in a brown suit sat on a running-board talking; and as Dol arrived another car, a large sedan, drove up and rolled to a stop, and its door opened and Sherwood and Colonel Brissenden got out. Dol was right there; Sherwood lifted his hat; Brissenden ostentatiously did not see her. For a split second Dol weakened; she could feel against her legs the two objects which those men would give a night's sleep for; then her resolution returned and she let them briskly cross the terrace. Paying no attention to the two on the running-board, she went to the coupe and got the key from the dashboard compartment, opened the panel at the rear, took out the pigskin case, relocked the panel and returned the key. With the case in her hand, she entered the house.

She knew she was taking the long way around; she should have started at the other end, the melon, but that was not practical. She knew too that this was an undertaking for an expert, and she was not an expert, but that was beside the point—*her* point. So she asked Belden where Ranth was, thinking he would be a good one to begin with, and found him downstairs in the billiard room, alone, with no cue, rolling the balls around with his hands.

He bowed as she approached: "Miss Bonner! Am I to be spoken to?"

She felt pressed for time. She rested the pigskin case on the edge of the billiard table and took his eye: "Why not, Mr. Ranth? Especially since I want to ask you a favor. No reason and no recompense; just a plain unadulterated favor. I am doing an experiment and I want samples of the fingerprints of everyone here, and I'm starting with you. Will you let me take them?"

He looked surprised. "Well!" He rubbed his cheek. "My fingerprints? It . . . it seems one of those requests where one can say, why should I? or why shouldn't I? with equal propriety." He looked at her keenly a moment, then lifted his shoulders and dropped them. "*Sans peur et sans reproche.* So why shouldn't I? You have paraphernalia there? Go ahead."

Dol opened the case, again disclosing to a rude gaze the Holcomb pistol and box of cartridges strapped to the lid, and fished for what she wanted: the ink-pad, the tablet of paper with tissues between, the bottle of ink-remover, the gold pencil with indelible leads. While not an expert, she was not utterly a greenhorn, for she had read a good treatise and had spent quite a little time practising. She uncovered the pad and said, "Right hand first, please." She showed him how: the thumb, then the fingers consecutively; and without comment he followed her instructions. She marked on the slip of paper, "Ranth RH." When the left hand too was finished she took the stopper from the bottle of ink-remover, with its swab on a wire, and dabbed the tips of his fingers. As he got out his handkerchief he murmured, "Thank you so much. Your equipment is quite complete, really professional."

Dol, repacking the case, lifted her black lashes to permit her caramel-colored eyes a curious glance at his dark-skinned face. She protested, "I should thank you. You were very nice about it, to humor me. Gallantry does have its advantages." She snapped the case shut. "I have told everyone else that I am investigating Storrs' murder. They think I am fiddling at a funeral, but I'm not. I have not told you because you could not reasonably suppose that I was asserting a privilege of friendship, since we are not friends."

He bowed. "I was unforgivably stupid about that piece of paper. It was better for me that it should be found there. You did me no harm, and I am sure you are not trying to make opportunities." He gestured at the case in her hand. "You are welcome to that small civility." He bowed again as she turned to leave him.

Upstairs, she sought Belden, and learned that Mr. Foltz was in the study with the members of the family—presumably a consultation. She sent the butler off with a request to Mrs. Storrs, and shortly he returned with the response that she was to go right in.

The study at Birchhaven, as is the case in so many well-to-do American homes, was the room permitted to the master of the house for such petty privacies as his repertory might afford, and was called that, by unintended paradox, because he would never have dreamed of doing any studying in it. Dol had never been in it, but knew where it was. Entering it under the present circumstances, she had no time to inspect its treasures: the mounted rainbow trout, the hunting prints, the radio cabinet, the framed college diploma, the Rocky Mountain sheep head. . . .

Mrs. Storrs was seated across by a window; near her on a stool, erect and still frozen, was Janet. Martin and Sylvia were on a built-in leather divan alongside the radio, and in the big chair at the desk, with a legal-looking paper in his hands, sat a man with a clipped gray moustache, darting gray eyes, and an air of sad but unavoidable importance.

Mrs. Storrs said, "Yes, my dear? This is Mr. Cabot. He is . . . he was my husband's lawyer. Miss Bonner, Nicholas. You want to see me?"

Dol was gripping the handle of the pigskin case. She nodded. "All of you. I'm sorry to interrupt, but it won't take long. I'm doing an experiment." She moved to the desk and lifted the case to it. "Please don't ask me to explain, and don't think I'm a Pulcinella." The case was open. "I've just taken Mr. Ranth's fingerprints, and I'd like to take yours—all of yours. You first, Martin?"

There were sounds—a little exclamation from Sylvia. Mr. Cabot demanded in irritation, "Who, may I ask, who is this young woman?"

Dol had an exaggerated dislike of lawyers, on account of her dealings with them as an aftermath of her father's ruin and suicide. She put out her chin at him: "I am a detective whom Mr. Storrs hired to come out here yesterday afternoon. I am attending to my business and would suggest that you stick to yours." She turned her back on him: "I'm not playing tricks or making mud pies, I really do want your fingerprints. There's no reason you shouldn't give them to me, is there?"

Martin stood up. "You can have mine if you want them. You say you took Ranth's?" He moved to the desk.

"Yes, he was very obliging. Here, this way." She showed him how, took all ten fingers, removed the ink for him. His hands were nervous but strong, long-fingered, sensitive. He looked at the prints with interest. Dol asked, "You next, Sylvia?"

Sylvia came over. The lawyer interposed, "Just a minute, Miss Raffray. This seems to me—"

"It's all right." Sylvia had done it often before and was going about it almost professionally. "This is Dol Bonner, my partner. I don't know what the dickens she's up to, but I can see she means it, and that's enough for me. . . . That all right, Dol? You'll explain when you get around to it . . . to me. Won't you?"

Dol patted her shoulder. "You're okay. I'll explain when the time comes. If it comes.—May I, please, Mrs. Storrs?"

Cabot merely sat back and frowned as his new client, the widow of his client, got up and approached. She acquiesced with her normal intensity: "I have no reason to refuse. You know, Nicholas, Peter always said I had no respect for facts.—This way, my dear?—He was wrong. He was wrong about many things.—Oh, I see, I pressed too hard.—I merely would not let them interfere with acroamata which went far below the depth of

facts, and soared far above their horizon." She lifted
the print of her left hand. "See that? That poor meager
fact? Do you suppose I could admit it as a witness to
contradict my soul?" She put it down.

Dol said, "Janet? If you don't mind?"

Janet offered no discussion of facts and souls; she
said nothing. She walked to the desk in stately indiffer-
ence and followed instructions, and did it more neatly
than any of the others, even Sylvia. When Dol cleaned
her finger-tips she extended the right hand again for an
infinitesimal smudge on the thumb.

Dol put the things back in the case and closed it,
thanked them collectively and apologized for intruding,
let the lawyer have a curt nod as a minimum of courtesy,
and left them. Before she returned to the reception hall
she lifted her skirt for a brief glance to make sure that
the gloves were secure.

She still had to get Len Chisholm and Steve Zimmerman. They proved to be equally amenable and almost
equally unpleasant. She found Len in the rose garden
pergola again, where he appeared to have assumed squat-
ter's rights, and he was, in a word, grouty. She ignored
his rudeness and sarcasm; what she was after was fingerprints, and she got them. Zimmerman was finally discovered in the peach orchard back of the garage, sitting
on the bottom rung of a stepladder, moodily splitting a
fruit. When Dol explained what she wanted he sat and
stared at her for a full half a minute without any effort
to conceal his contempt; then, without a word, he put
down the peach, wiped the juice from his fingers on the

grass, extended a hand to her and held it there. She was, in fact, surprised; she had rather expected a refusal from him. He was last on the list.

She stood again in the vegetable garden, debating on her procedure, and decided not to complicate matters by trying to lug the melon off somewhere. If someone came up she would have to call on her wits. She went to the compost heap and put the pigskin case down there, then went to the patch and found the melon. The stem was tough and hard to break, and she had trouble lifting it, because she had to be careful to touch as little of its surface as possible. It was big and heavy, and carrying it with her hands at the ends, and held away from her dress, was not easy. At the compost heap she put it gently down on the brick wall, opened the case, and got out the white powder, the spray gun, and a magnifying glass. She was not trembling at all now, quite cool and efficient.

She tried a couple of shots with the spray on a cabbage leaf, then turned it on the melon. Delicately and evenly she spread the film; nothing showed; then there was a large blur extending along the side; then she got two good impressions. She looked at them through the magnifying glass, and saw that they were her own; she knew her whorls; but later she could make sure. She became precipitate and got the film too thick and swore under her breath. Then, after turning the melon a little, she got several good prints, and then some more. She covered all the exposed surface before she took the glass again; and, after an examination, she got from the case the envelope holding the samples she had collected, and began comparisons. Some of the prints on the melon were definitely not her own.

Nor any of her samples either? That was quite possible, she thought, indeed, more than possible, but she went on comparing. One paper of specimens after another she laid aside with a shake of her head; then, after one look through the glass at the next one, she smothered a cry of incredulity and peered at it again: the left hand, index, middle, ring. She placed the paper close to the prints on the melon and bent over, close, for a detailed comparison—back and forth with the glass, this one, that one, this one, that one. . . .

There was no room for doubt. She stood up and muttered in an incredulous whisper, "I will be damned."

The total surprise of it bewildered her and made her knees weak. She sat down on the edge of the brick wall. Well, she thought, there she was. The gloves that had been used to murder Storrs were there under her skirt under her stocking-tops, and that was all right, she could go to the house and turn them over to Sherwood. But the devil of it was that she knew who had hid them in that melon, and she devoutly wished she didn't. Whether she really hated men or only thought she did, assuredly she did not hate women; and especially, under the circumstances, to know that that particular woman . . .

It was bad, it was very bad. To turn her over to Sherwood, to the inquisition, to that military creature Brissenden . . .

It was not Dol's custom to dally long over decisions.

She knew that this was a serious one, even possibly peril-
ous, but when she had made it she didn't hesitate. She
arose energetically, her knees no longer weak, took a
piece of gauze from the pigskin case, and began method-
ically to wipe the melon clean. She knew that no matter how thoroughly she wiped, a microscopic examination would betray traces of the powder she had used,
but she hoped it wouldn't come to that, and anyway she
couldn't help it. When she was sure that no spot of the
melon's surface had been missed, she picked it up and
carried it back to the patch and replaced it in the spot
which nature had selected for it, and rolled it back and
forth, handling it so that it would show as many of her
own prints as might reasonably be expected. She left it
there and, returning to the compost heap, collected her
accessories—the powder gun, magnifying glass, speci-
men prints, gauze—and packed them in the case and
closed it. There was a detectable film of powder all
around—on the bricks, the edge of the compost heap,
the ground at the other side—but she decided that nothing satisfactory could be done about it.

Gripping the handle of the case, she left the scene of
her questionable triumph, passed again through the gap
in the hedge of yew, and pointed her steps for the house.
Trying not to look too determined, she entered by the
east terrace, passed down the side corridor to the study
door, and rapped sharply on the panel.

CHAPTER

ELEVEN

SHE opened the door and went in. The same five were there. Three pairs of eyes were on her inquiringly; one pair, Janet's, indifferently; another, the lawyer's, with irritation. He snapped, "Really, this is a private family—"

"I'm sorry." Dol spoke not to him. "I know I'm a nuisance, but I must ask Janet about something important. Will you come with me, Janet?"

Janet's mask relaxed enough to express mild surprise. "Come with you where? Can't you ask me here?"

"No, I can't. It may take too long. And I want to show you something. I wish you would come. I think you ought—"

"This is preposterous!" Judging by his voice, Mr. Cabot's irritation was preparing to blaze. "Miss Storrs is engaged with us—"

No one paid any attention to him. Martin was frowning at Dol, and Sylvia, who knew Dol's ways and tones, was gazing at her with eyes narrowed in puzzled solicitude. Mrs. Storrs, apparently by now resigned to any fact and unimpressed by any, told her daughter, "Go with her, child. See what she wants."

Janet, without comment, got up and crossed to the door. Dol had got there and opened it, with a nod declining Martin's polite approach; they passed through into the hall and Dol pulled the door to.

"What is it?" Janet demanded. "What do you want to show me?" Then she looked startled as she felt her arm being pinched, and puzzled as she heard Dol saying: "I never do have enough powder along. If you wouldn't mind . . . you use Valery's Trente-trois, don't you? That will be close enough. . . ."

The trooper, whose approach down the hall had caused this warning and camouflage, stopped near them and nodded at the study door.

"Is Miss Raffray in there?"

Dol told him yes; and as he thanked her and knocked she took Janet's arm and started her down the hall. "We'll go to your room and I'll take my pick. You're sure you don't mind? I hate to bother you. . . ."

The reception hall was empty, and the door to the card room stood open. They mounted the stairs together and went down the upper corridor to its end, the last door on the right. Dol, whose trips to Birchhaven had been as Sylvia's guest, formerly when she had lived there, and latterly when she had come out from her town apartment for week-ends, had never seen Janet's room before. It was old-fashioned, feminine but not frilly, comfortable but not cluttered.

Janet said, "You don't really want powder, do you?"

Dol shook her head. "Let's sit down."

Janet shrugged, moved, and lowered herself to the end of a blue silk chaise longue. Dol put the pigskin case on the floor and pulled a chair around. She sat and looked straight at Janet and said, "I've found the gloves."

Janet indubitably had control, but it was not perfect.

Her jaw moved perceptibly as her teeth clamped, and her fingers tightened on the silk of the chaise longue. Her eyes betrayed nothing, and her voice didn't because she didn't use it. She sat and met directly the gaze of the senior partner of Bonner & Raffray.

Dol repeated, in the same low imperturbable tone, "I say, I've found the gloves."

Janet said, her soprano more musical than Dol had ever heard it, "I heard you. What gloves?"

"You don't know what gloves?"

"I don't know what you're talking about."

Dol sighed, carefully, for strength. She was not liking this. "Listen, Janet. I suppose you figured that no one would think of the watermelon. Anyway, you left your fingerprints all over it. At least two dozen, and every one of them yours. There's no use in our talking unless we take, as a basis of discussion, the fact that you took the gloves which had been used for murdering your father, and hid them in that watermelon. I'm not going to ask you about that; I already know it."

Janet's eyes smouldered, inscrutably. Her fingers had pressed deep into the cushion and her jaw twitched again, twice, before she spoke: "What if we don't take that as a basis of discussion? What you said. What happens then?"

"Then I deliver the gloves to Sherwood, with the proof that you hid them, and you can deal with him."

"And if we do take it as a basis, then what?"

"Then, first, I want to ask you some questions."

"Did you take the gloves? Have you got them?"

"I took them."

"Have you got them here? Show them to me."

Dol, without taking her eyes from Janet's face, sat and considered warily. She saw, from the swifter rise and fall of Janet's breast, that there had been an internal demand for more oxygen, and that looked suspicious. There was no telling what that girl could be capable of; she might, if she saw the gloves or knew they were within reach, actually try to start a roughhouse. Dol, having seen her smash a tennis ball and vault into a saddle, knew that she was far from puny.

Dol said, "Don't get any silly ideas. If the gloves were here before you, in my hand, and you tried to grab them, one yell out of me would bring an army, and then where would you be? I'm even keeping my voice low, not for my sake, but yours. The gloves are in a safe place. When I get through talking with you I'm going to turn them over to Sherwood. What I tell him, or don't tell him, depends on what you tell me."

The heave of Janet's breast was subsiding. She sat with no change of expression, and no movement save a slow gradual slumping of her shoulders; then suddenly she jerked herself back to straightness, so abruptly that Dol felt her own muscles tighten involuntarily all over her body in a reflex readiness for combat.

Janet said, "I hid them in the watermelon. What do you want to know?"

"I want to know . . . " Dol hesitated. "Look here, Janet Storrs. I'm not as tough as I thought I was. I know that people can do unspeakable things. I know that daughters have killed their fathers. I thought I was as hard as my knowledge should have made me, but I'm not. If what you tell me . . . if it appears from what you say . . . that this is as ugly as that, I don't know what I'll do. I'll probably leave the gloves on the card tray in the reception hall and let them find them there, and keep my mouth shut. I don't owe it to anybody, not even myself, to mix in anything as horrible as that."

Janet spoke into Dol's eyes. "I didn't kill my father."

"I hope to God you didn't. Who did kill him?"

"I don't know."

"Where did you get the gloves? Who gave them to you to hide?"

"Nobody."

"Where did you get them?"

"I found them."

"Where?"

"In the rose garden."

"Where in the rose garden?"

"Under a bush. Under the mulch. Peat moss. I saw the mulch had been recently disturbed, and wondered if it was a mole, and poked at it to see. The gloves were under it."

"When was that?"

"Yesterday afternoon, late. I think about half-past five. I had been reading there in the pergola, and I left because a bird was singing in the filbert thicket, and I went to try to see what it was. Then I went back to the rose garden to get my book, and that was when I found the gloves."

Dol was frowning. "What time did you first go there to read?"

"About four o'clock, a little after."

Janet cleared her throat, but it didn't seem to help her voice any. "I thought I would just keep them . . ."

"As a souvenir. Then, when you learned what had happened, and later last night when they examined everybody's hands and mentioned gloves, you came upstairs and examined the pair you had found to see if they had been used to pull a wire, and you decided that you would defend the man who owned them against the consequences of his crime, though the crime was the murder of your father. Like that?"

"No," Janet muttered. "Not like that. It was not his crime. He didn't do it."

"How do you know he didn't?"

"Because he didn't. You know he didn't. You know . . . it was Martin. . . ."

"You mean you recognized them as Martin's gloves."

"Yes."

"Obviously. I've read your poems, and I have eyes, especially for what you have made no great effort to conceal. I know that Martin is the only man whose gloves you would want to put in a drawer in your room, and certainly the only man you would want to protect from injury—at any cost. Since they were his gloves, what made you so sure that Martin hadn't done it?"

"Because he wouldn't." Janet's fingers twisted. "Would he? Why would he? You know he wouldn't. Someone else got his gloves . . . someone else wanted him to be accused. . . ."

"That could be a theory." Dol was frowning. "It certainly could have been your theory, no doubt of that.

At least, someone could have used them. It seems less clear that Martin was supposed to be accused, since it was quite possible that they might never have been found, under the peat moss." Her eyes, on Janet, narrowed speculatively. "I know you're a strange girl. A strange woman. After you learned what the gloves had been used for, why didn't you give them to Martin and tell him where you had found them, and leave it to him?".

"I couldn't. I . . . I couldn't do that. I couldn't shock him like that."

"My lord. You didn't want to shock him. You have got it bad, and him pledged to another and a richer girl. So you haven't told him about it? You just went and hid them in the watermelon?"

"Yes."

"Didn't you realize that by doing that you might be making it impossible to discover and punish the murderer of your father?—No, I take that back—what you realized or didn't is none of my business. You did it, and that's that. I think you were a Grade A ninny, but I doubt if that interests you any."

Dol arose and got the pigskin case, put it on the chair, and opened it. Then she lifted her skirt, pulled out the gloves, and arranged the tops of her stockings. She stood with the gloves in her hand: "Here they are. You see how much good it did you." She tucked the gloves in the case and shut the lid. "I'm going down now and turn them over to Sherwood. I'll keep you out of it. It would look nice in the papers, that story, wouldn't it? And that bully Brissenden would enjoy the details of your passion for another girl's swain. Wouldn't he? I say you're a ninny."

She picked up the bag and turned to go. Janet's soprano came faltering, "But they'll find out . . . you said my fingerprints . . ."

"Leave that to me. I'll keep you out if I can. If they do get onto you, you'll just have to tighten up your belt and take it. Holy matrimony, the things a woman will do!" She opened the door, passed through, and closed it behind her.

Downstairs, in the reception hall, she was very nearly tripped up by an unlucky coincidence, but she jumped it neatly without a stumble. The coincidence was the fact of Sergeant Quill's presence there, talking to a colleague, at the moment that she entered; and the additional fact that, seeing the pigskin case in her hand, he decided that he had time to spare for a little entertainment.

"Oh, Miss Bonner!" The sergeant was in her path. "I see you took my advice, only I didn't mean the whole works, I just meant the gun. I been telling Miller here about that outfit, it sure is a pippin. I'd like to show it to him." He extended a hand for it. "You don't mind, do you?"

For an instant Dol's heart stopped, as her quick imagination showed her the calamitous outcome if she refused, and the trooper insisted and got stubborn and took it—and opened it to show his brother. So she smiled at him charmingly:

"Not at all, sergeant. In just a few minutes, when I come out—Mr. Sherwood sent for me—"

She brushed past him briskly, crossed to the door to

the card room, opened it and entered; as she went to close it behind her, it was obstructed by the sergeant following her, and she abandoned it to him. Another trooper, in there, was moving to intercept her; she circled, ignoring him, and went to the table. Brissenden, who had been standing looking out of a window, turned at the intrusion; Sherwood and his spectacled assistant were at the table as before; a big man with a Morgan nose, in his shirt sleeves, was at the farther end; in the chair at this end where Dol had sat in the morning, was Sylvia Raffray.

Dol deigned no reply to Sherwood's indignant protest at her unceremonious interruption. She lifted the case to the table, opened it, took out the gloves and tossed them down.

"There they are. I found them."

"The—well, by God."

Brissenden nearly knocked over a chair getting there. The man in his shirt sleeves stood up and leaned to see. But their concentration on the find was arrested by Sylvia. She too, staring at the gloves, had stood up, and they all heard her involuntary gasp; and, looking at her, saw her eyes fixed in amazement. Sherwood's hand, reaching for the gloves, stopped in the air.

He snapped, "What is it, Miss Raffray? You recognize them?"

Sylvia drew back, and looked, horrified, at Dol. Dol was at her side, a hand on her shoulder: "Now, Sylvia. Sylvia dear! Everything—"

"Step back, Miss Bonner." Sherwood was curt. "If Miss Raffray recognizes—"

Dol wheeled on him. "What if she does? You're not afraid you're not going to find out who they belong to, are you? With all the help you've got? If she got a jolt, give her a chance. If she knows whose they are, she'll tell you."

"Do you know?"

"No." Dol was patting Sylvia's shoulder, softly. "I never saw them before. You might see what you think of the marks on them."

Sherwood had the gloves in his hand, and the others were crowded around him. Sergeant Quill was peering over the attorney's shoulder with compressed lips, slowly nodding his head. Brissenden wore a ferocious scowl. The spectacled assistant looked interested but skeptical. The man in shirt sleeves grabbed one of the gloves and went with it to the window.

The sergeant muttered, "That's it. Exactly the same as the ones we tested with, them marks."

Brissenden growled, "Where did you get them?"

"Just a minute, colonel." Sherwood reached across to lay the glove on the table in front of Sylvia. "Please look it over, Miss Raffray? Miss Bonner says she never saw them before. Have you?"

Sylvia didn't take it. Dol picked it up. "Here, Sylvia. Buck up. Don't be deducing things. All this is, it's a fact, and you don't know what other facts it leads to and neither do I. That glove *was* used to murder Storrs with."

Sylvia had it in her hand looking at it, but as Dol said that she dropped it and it fell to the floor. Quill moved to get it. Sylvia looked up at Dol: "I know it's only a fact. But Dol . . . that's a pair of gloves I bought yesterday in New York. I bought them myself."

"Good lord! No wonder it was a jolt. What did you do with them?"

"I gave them to Martin." Sylvia swallowed. "I had made a bet with him and lost. You remember I left the office yesterday with Martin and Len? On our way to lunch we stopped in at Gordon's and I bought them to pay the bet." Sylvia's chin began to tremble and her fingers clutched Dol's skirt. "Where . . . where did you find . . ."

"Sylvia!" Dol's low cry was a call to courage, a bugle to summon grit. Having herself once, just once, wept in the presence of a man, it was not to be borne that any woman in the world should ever do so again. Above all, not Sylvia. She turned to the beasts: "Miss Raffray bought the gloves yesterday afternoon in New York, between twelve and one o'clock, at Gordon's on 48th Street, and gave them to Martin Foltz to pay a bet. That should do for her. Let her alone. As for me—"

Brissenden blew: "We'll let her alone when we're through with her. You seem to think—"

"Then I'm unique around here. If I think." Dol was withering. "I know you can't investigate a murder without hurting somebody's feelings, but there's no sense in your tormenting this girl, and under the circumstances it would be a good idea for you to consider *my* feelings. I did some darned good detective work finding those gloves, and would you like to hear about it now, or would you rather read it in the paper tomorrow morning?"

The man in shirt sleeves cackled loudly and said, "Your name's Bonner? Mine's Maguire. Pleased to meetcha. I'm Chief of Police at Bridgeport. Some of my boys have been working here, and I know damn well they didn't find the gloves." He cackled again.

Sherwood was looking at him without pleasure. He turned to the sergeant: "Bring Foltz.—No, wait a minute." He switched to Dol: "Tell us about your detective work. Where did you find them?"

Dol pulled a chair close to Sylvia and sat down. She picked Sherwood to look at: "There wasn't much to it. I wasn't really looking for the gloves, but of course they were in my mind. I happened to be out in the vegetable garden, and looking at the compost heap I saw a little pile of the insides of a watermelon. It wasn't ripe, and there was no rind. It occurred to me that someone might cut out a piece of rind, remove some of the inside, stick the gloves in, and replace the rind. Of course it was one chance in a million, but anyway I went to the watermelon patch and looked. I found one that had been cut. I removed the piece of rind, and the gloves were inside. There they are."

Maguire of Bridgeport leaned to Sherwood: "Get that melon. Fingerprints.—You left the melon there, Miss Bonner?"

Dol shook her head. As she had been speaking she had changed her mind about this. "I thought of fingerprints too. I got specimens from everybody here, and then I took the melon to the compost heap and powdered it. There were none, except my own. So I wiped it off and took it back to the patch—"

Brissenden barked, "Destroying evidence!"

"Please, colonel." Sherwood raised a hand at him. He looked at Dol: "You understand, Miss Bonner, we appreciate your finding the gloves. It was a remarkable piece of work, and you deserve great praise. But searching for fingerprints is a job for experts. It was most audacious of you to tamper with the melon. Tampering with evidence. That sometimes leads to serious trouble, if it gets before a court——"

"I found the gloves."

"I know you did. But you say you took specimens from everybody? That takes time. You must have found the gloves an hour ago or more. Precious time wasted——"

"I found the gloves."

"I know. The implication doesn't escape me, that we should be thankful for what we have got, since you brought it to us. Well, we are. But . . . you say you wiped the melon off? Why?"

"Oh, it was all covered with powder. I found the gloves."

Maguire cackled. Sherwood observed drily, "So I understand. Anyway, the melon's no good now. We can get it later.—Quill, bring Mr. Foltz. Tell Grimes to make sure he knows where everyone is." The sergeant went. "You ladies will go, please? I may need you later, Miss Raffray. I don't want to torment you, as Miss Bonner puts it, but I may have to ask you some more questions about your conversation with Mr. Storrs yesterday morning."

Dol said, "You go, Sylvia. I'm going to stay here, if Mr. Sherwood will let me."

"I'll stay too." Sylvia had her chin firm again.

But Sherwood said positively, "No, Miss Raffray. I'm sorry, I can't permit it. Don't make it unpleasant, please."

Sylvia tried to insist, but had no help from Dol, and the attorney was firm. She must go. She surrendered. Dol went to the door with her, saw her out with a squeeze on her arm, and then came back to the table and looked Sherwood in the eye and told him:

"I found the gloves. What more do I have to do—"

"All right, all right." He pushed air down with both hands. "Sit over there, please. And no interruptions, you understand that."

The chief of police cackled.

CHAPTER

TWELVE

*I*T APPEARED to Dol Bonner's eye, as Martin Foltz entered the room and was conducted across to the table by Sergeant Quill, that he looked like a man who had recently been drinking too much, but she was sure it was only an appearance. With all the animadversions she might have made regarding Martin—the chief of which would have been that he was a male biped—the likelihood that he would get soused when subjected to a strain was not one of them. She thought him tender-skinned, too ostentatiously a social epicure, and intellectually and esthetically dandified, and she was convinced that he was miles short of deserving Sylvia—but no man alive could have passed that test.

As he took the chair Sylvia had just vacated, after a glance of mild indifferent surprise at Dol Bonner, he looked as if he were controlling an inward irritation only for the sake of avoiding an unpleasant scene. He raised his brows at Sherwood.

The attorney was leaning back with his arms folded; the gloves were not in view because they were in his right hand, concealed by his left arm. He cleared his throat. "I sent for you, Mr. Foltz, because there has been a development. We've found the gloves that were worn by the murderer."

Martin's forehead wrinkled. "Then—" He stopped.

He went on, "Then you know who did it." His frown deepened. "I suppose you sent for me . . . but you ought to see that I'm in an anomalous position, and it isn't pleasant. I have no standing or responsibility in this house, I am merely the fiancé of Miss Raffray. She wished me to be present at a family conference when Mr. Cabot, the lawyer, came. Now you call me in . . ."

"You misunderstand." Sherwood's eyes were glued to him. "I didn't send for you as a representative of the family. I wanted to ask you about the gloves." Abruptly he leaned forward and extended his arm, holding the gloves within twelve inches of the other's face. "Did you ever see them before?"

Martin shrank back, in reflex, from the gesture. He demanded angrily, "What is this?"

"Take them, please. Look at them. Did you ever see them before?"

He took them. Six pairs of eyes were on him. He looked at the gloves, at the leather, the fingers, the cuffs, and when he looked at Sherwood again there was perceptible apprehension in his gray eyes and pallor under his tan. Dol thought uncomfortably and scornfully, "I hope the poor lummox doesn't faint."

Martin said in a strained tone, "These are my gloves. They look like mine. Where did you get them?"

"Look at the palms. No, I said the palms. See those marks running across there? The wire made that. The wire Storrs was strangled with. Pulling on it."

Martin demanded harshly, "Where did you get them?"

"They . . . were . . . found." Sherwood leaned

back. "You understand now, Mr. Foltz, why I sent for you. Don't you?"

"No. I don't. I don't know how you knew they were mine."

"Miss Raffray told us."

"Sylvia told—" Martin stared. "She told—then did she bring—" He sprang to his feet. "I want to see her! I demand to see Miss Raffray!"

Quill moved a couple of paces. Dol thought, "There you are, a spoiled brat yelling for mama. Sylvia would do better to adopt an orphan." Sherwood said, "Sit down. Miss Raffray was here and we showed her the gloves, and she said she bought them yesterday to pay a bet she owed you. They belong to you and they were used by the murderer. Did you kill Storrs?"

Martin met his eye. "No. I want to see Miss Raffray."

"You can see her when we're through here. Sit down. Did you put that wire around Storrs' neck and use these gloves to pull him up and strangle him?"

"No."

"Okay. You didn't. Then will you please sit down?"

Sherwood waited. Martin looked at Dol, but not with appeal; scarcely, it seemed, with recognition. She thought, "The man really is hypersensitized. And intelligent too, I wonder why he's not a genius." Meanwhile Martin was sitting down, but he sat as if he might any instant be impelled upwards again.

The attorney asked conversationally, "These *are* your gloves, Mr. Foltz?"

"I think they are. They look like it."

"Miss Raffray gave them to you yesterday?"

"Yes."

"Did you have them with you when you drove out to your place from New York yesterday afternoon?"

"Yes."

"Where were they between 4:40 and 6:15 yesterday afternoon?"

"I don't know."

"Oh. You don't. Where were they at four o'clock?"

"I don't know."

The attorney's next question was forestalled by a grunt from Maguire of Bridgeport. Maguire moved, beckoning with his head, and Sherwood got up to follow him across the room. Brissenden also arose and joined them, in the far corner. Mutterings came from the consultation of the high command. Martin looked at Dol: "Something like this would happen to me. Can't you bring Sylvia here?"

Dol couldn't help feeling sorry for him. She shook her head. "Hold the fort, Martin. Mud like this splatters on everybody."

The trio came back and resumed their chairs. Sherwood looked among the papers on the table before him, found one, and slid it across to Brissenden and Maguire. Then he spoke to Martin: "Suppose you tell us the history of the gloves. From the time you got home with them yesterday."

Martin said, "This is taking it for granted that it's the same gloves."

"Of course. That can be established."

"I've already told you what I did yesterday . . . the hours as close as I could remember them. When we arrived at my place around three o'clock I carried the gloves into the house with me. I am positive of that, because when I was in my room changing my clothes——"

"Zimmerman was in there with you."

"Yes. He was talking with me while I changed. I put the gloves in the pocket of my woolen jacket. I always have a jacket along when I play tennis."

"But gloves? It was warm yesterday."

Martin frowned. "One thing should be understood. I am not justifying anything or defending myself, I am just telling you what happened. I wear that jacket riding sometimes, and I wear gloves. I do other things around the place. Anyway, I put the gloves in the jacket."

"Okay. Then?"

"As I've told you, I talked some with Zimmerman. Then I went outdoors and joined Miss Raffray and Chisholm. I put the jacket down——I suppose on the back of a chair, I usually do. Some time later Chisholm left to come over here, and shortly afterwards Miss Raffray also left. I sat there, as I've told you, and my man de Roode came to ask me some things——"

"Was the jacket still there?"

"Yes. It must have been, because when I finally decided to come to Birchhaven I put it over my arm and brought it along."

Sherwood nodded. "That's the jacket you left on a chair in the reception hall."

"Yes. I've explained about that. I entered by the sun room, but after going around by the side hall to the east terrace, I went back in that way, and in the reception hall I decided to go to the dining-room and get a drink,

"Of course not. She had enough on her mind."

Sherwood glanced aside at a noise; it was Brissenden getting up and pushing his chair back. The colonel strode around back of Dol, around the end of the table, planted himself in front of Martin, and glared down at him.

His voice rasped: "Look here, Foltz. I think you're lying. I don't know what the truth is, but you're not telling it."

Martin blurted, "Do I have to tolerate—"

"Shut up! I've been tolerating all day. I've never heard worse poppycock than your saying you put those gloves in that jacket and then didn't notice whether they were there or not all afternoon. You're a damn liar! You can't get away with it." He pivoted, in perfect military form, to Sherwood. "You're in charge here. Are we nothing but a bunch of suckers? If you'll send this woman out of here, I'll get another tune out of him and it won't take me long. Or let me give him a ride down to Station H. What the hell do I care whether he pays an income tax?" He wheeled back to Martin. "I've put out worse fires than any you can start! Don't think I can't open you up!"

"I think . . . you could." Martin was pale and his voice had tin in it. "If I understand you."

"I guess you understand me! I'll give you something you can feel! You need your memory tickled!"

Dol muttered to herself, "The darned infantile sadist. I'd like to stick a pin clear through him." She knew that Martin had an acute dread of physical pain; it was a major threat to offer to pinch him. But surely, even with the flatulent colonel, it was only a bluff; they wouldn't dare. . . .

Martin was saying, his voice still tinny, "I am not lying. And I'm not a coward, but I'm morbidly sensitive to pain. If you presumed to . . . to touch me, I would say anything you wanted to hear. What good would that do you?" A perceptible shiver ran over him. "I don't imagine you'll try it. I have told you all I know about those gloves."

The colonel was silent, gazing down at the confessed softy in manly repugnance. At length he sighed. "For the love of Mike." He threw up his hands, shook his head, and went back to his chair.

Martin spoke to Sherwood. "I would like to call your attention to something. You don't want to believe me when I say that I don't know when the gloves were taken from the jacket. But that is exactly the reason why I didn't tell you when I found that the gloves were gone. I didn't see that it could help you any." His voice was better now. "The truth is, I was tempted. I could have told you that I saw the gloves still in the pocket when I put the jacket on the chair in the reception hall, and that would have eliminated everybody but Ranth. I don't like Ranth. It would have eliminated my friend Zimmerman and . . . and Len Chisholm. But it was too serious a matter for that sort of temptation. I preferred to tell you the truth."

"Then you might have tried it," the attorney observed drily. "You didn't tell us anything until we found the gloves and you had to."

"I'm sorry if it hampered you." Martin stirred impatiently. "I can't see that it did. By the way—if I am to know—where were they found? In the house?"

"No. Miss Bonner found them. Of course it's her story, but I would prefer that she keep it to herself for the present—"

"The devil she did." Martin raised his brows at Dol. "So *that* was what you wanted the fingerprints for."

Dol nodded and grunted a yes. She told the attorney, "I can keep it all right, but Miss Raffray heard it and you said nothing to her about keeping it."

"All right. It isn't important." Sherwood leaned back with his arms folded, pursed his lips, and surveyed Martin gloomily. "You realize, Mr. Foltz, that what you tell us is completely unsatisfactory. If it's the truth, you can't help it, but that doesn't make us any better satisfied. The gloves that the murderer used have been found, and we know who they belong to, and we are left precisely where we were before. That doesn't sound possible, does it? It's a fact. We have advanced one little step, it is now certain that it must have been someone who had access to those gloves in your jacket yesterday afternoon, it was no outsider; but we were already pretty well convinced of that on other grounds."

He pulled at the lobe of his ear, which was his favorite courtroom gesture for a pause when his tone was down. "Do you know what an investigation like this means? When a prominent man like Storrs is murdered? This is Sunday afternoon. A captain of detectives is in Storrs' office in New York, with the vice-president of the firm, examining everything. We went through

everything here in Storrs' study last night. His asso-
ciates in New York, business and social, are being questioned; likewise here in the country. And so on. The
records of all of you here are being traced as minutely
as possible, particularly, of course, with regard to your
relations with Storrs. That includes you. I tell you
frankly, we have so far found not the slightest contradiction of what you told us last night, that you and
Storrs were the best of friends, that you never had a
quarrel or cause for one, that since you first met him
when you bought your place over the hill four years
ago you have been good neighbors, and that he accepted
you enthusiastically as the fiancé of his ward, Miss Raffray."

Martin murmured, "That is all true."

Sherwood nodded. "I don't doubt it. It has been confirmed. But I want to say three things. First, we've
found the gloves that the murderer wore, and they are
your gloves. I know what you say about it, but it's a
fact and there it is. Second, the attorney-general of this
state will be here tomorrow morning, and he's a much
more impatient man than I am. You'll have him to deal
with. Third, it would be a good plan for you to tell me
right now what the trouble was between Storrs and your
friend Zimmerman."

Martin, obviously taken unaware, jerked up straight
and said nothing. Sherwood snapped, "Well?"

Martin said resentfully, "Damn it, I've got nerves. I
don't know what trouble you mean. I know nothing
about it."

Sherwood was leaning at him. "You don't? Do you

know that Zimmerman called on Storrs yesterday morning?"

"Yes."

"And that when Miss Raffray met him in the hall he was very agitated and spoke to her about a mortal injury?"

"Yes. He gets agitated."

"And that a few minutes later Storrs told Miss Raffray that he would like to kill somebody?"

"Not Zimmerman."

"Who else do you suppose? You or me or the mailman? It must have been Zimmerman, he had just that moment left. Zimmerman refuses to tell us what the talk was about. All right. Zimmerman is an old and close friend of yours, you have known him for years. Storrs was also your good friend. Is it likely that there could have been hostility between them and you wouldn't know about it? Certainly you know! Are you going to tell me that that was something else you didn't notice, like the gloves being gone?"

Martin turned up his palms. "I simply don't know."

"You don't? You stick to that?"

"I have to, or make something up. Storrs and Zimmerman never liked each other. It was too bad, but they didn't. Storrs was a puritan and thought modern psychology was not clean, and Zimmerman was contrary and enjoyed baiting him."

"You stick to it that you don't know why Zimmerman went to see Storrs yesterday morning?"

"I do. I am compelled to."

"By God," Brissenden growled, to no one but Mars.

He repeated it, "By God. I'd like to compel him a while."

Sherwood got up. He walked to a window and glanced out as if in forlorn expectation of spying a fact perched on a branch of a horse chestnut tree. He walked back to the table and stood gazing murkily down at the top of Martin's head, then lifted his shoulders high, held them there three seconds, and let them drop. He kicked at the leg of his chair, and sat down.

"I'd like to try something, Dan." It was Maguire of Bridgeport, up and beside him. "Let me have the gloves."

Sherwood handed them to him, and he approached Martin. "You say these was bought yesterday, Mr. Foltz?"

"Yes."

"You ever had 'em on?"

"No. Oh . . . yes, in the shop."

"Mind putting 'em on now?"

"I . . . don't like to."

"Just do me a favor. Help out the cause.—That's right." He winked and grimaced at Dol. "Miss Bonner and I like to use our heads." He grasped Martin's right wrist and held it so that the hand, with the glove on it, was before his eyes. "Bend your fingers shut. Tight. Now open 'em. Do it again. Do it a few more times." Martin obliged.

"Thanks." Maguire drew the glove off himself, carefully, took it to the window, and peered at it in the strong light. After a couple of minutes of that, he shook his head in defeat, returned to the table, tossed the glove over to Sherwood, and sat down. He explained, "Thought I might compare the creases with the ones our friend made yesterday gripping that wire, since the gloves are new. None of these new-fangled ideas is worth a damn."

Brissenden said grimly, "It depends on who has them."

Sherwood was sitting with bent head and closed eyes, rubbing his brow, back and forth. At length he sighed, deeply, and looked up.

"All right, Foltz. That's all for the present. You're on thin ice, I can tell you that. Please don't leave these grounds—that's not a request, it's an order.—Weil, get Governor Chandler on the phone—he'll be at his residence.—Quill, tell Hurley to pass the word that everybody on any other line than this Birchhaven bunch is to call it off and report to Station H and wait for orders. Then go with Miss Bonner and have her show you that watermelon and bring it in here. You might see if there's any chance of footprints. On your way, send that butler in. And send someone to Foltz's place to bring that fellow de Roode over; I'll see him when I'm through with the butler. . . ."

Dol, some minutes later, walking up the path toward the vegetable garden with Sergeant Quill, was not very good company. Nor was it concern or conjecture which chiefly possessed her; it was angry dissatisfaction with herself, and wrath at another woman. She was thinking, "So Janet lied. She lied and I swallowed it! Darn her ornery hide, she looked me in the eye and lied to me, and it looks very much as if I'm out on a limb. . . ."

CHAPTER

THIRTEEN

SYLVIA RAFFRAY sat on a large gray stone at the edge of the rock garden, frowning at a brown caterpillar, born belated, which was mounting a twig of sea lavender in decrepit desperation. She herself, not quite desperate and certainly not decrepit, was nevertheless in an unprecedented state of mind, requiring—to prevent collapse into mournful inertia or tearful hysterics, which her healthy youth despised as the easiest and weakest of feminine retorts to catastrophe—an amount of discipline and control which she had never before been called upon to furnish. Grief gnawed at her and could not be cast out; she had had deep and genuine affection for P.L.; she understood why, in a less restrained civilization, women had torn their hair and beat their breasts when their dear ones had died. And as if grief were not enough . . .

Now Martin was in it. He was in there now with those men, shrinking from their noise and their questions—she could see him—explaining about his gloves. The gloves she had bought for him. Sylvia shivered with repugnance, and with terror at the ugliness of it. No faint doubt of Martin's blamelessness was in her unsuspicious mind; but characteristically—for she was indubitably fortune's spoiled darling—she was irritated with him because of those gloves. The gloves she had bought herself . . . and those horrible marks across the

198

palms . . . what were they saying to him now . . . and what was he saying. . . .

"Sylvia. Er—Miss Raffray."

She looked up. She had not heard him approach; apparently he had walked on the grass. She said listlessly, "Make it Sylvia." She made an effort to flop her mind over to this intruding object; it might help. She observed, "You certainly look sick."

Steve Zimmerman nodded. "That's nothing to worry about." He looked down at her, his pale eyes intent and his nostrils twitching, then sat cross-legged on the grass, facing her, six feet away. "I mean for me to worry about. I was never calculated to get very far on my looks. It is popularly supposed that a man devoid of physical grace and attractiveness feels inferior about it. I never have. Of course, I'm not normal."

"Oh," Sylvia said. "You're not?"

"Certainly not. Normal? My God. I am hypercerebral."

"I see. 'Hyper' means too much, doesn't it?"

"No. It means above measure. It can mean excessive." His nostril twitched, and he rubbed it with the back of his finger. "Ever since lunch I have been deciding to have a talk with you. I saw you come out here a little while ago."

"Well?"

Her face was a foot higher than his; he looked up at her. "It's easy enough for you to say 'Well.' Your brain is accustomed to react almost exclusively to the simpler sensory impulses. That's a loose way of putting it, but you wouldn't understand a correct technical statement.

I have been led to this decision by the most tortuous and difficult path I have ever followed. I have a proposal to make to you. To clear the way, and anticipate a question you will want to ask, I should tell you that I wanted first to inform Martin about it, but I have had no opportunity since I decided. He was in the study with the rest of you, and from there he was taken to the card room. So I've had no chance—"

Sylvia put in, "You don't know what they sent for him for. Do you?"

"I suppose some more of the same questions that they've asked a dozen times—"

"No." Sylvia shifted on the stone. "They've found the gloves they were looking for. Dol found them. They are marked the way they said they would be. It's a pair I bought yesterday and gave to Martin, to pay a bet. They belong to him. That's what they're asking him about."

Zimmerman, his pale eyes fastened on her, said nothing. All at once, apparently, he was not even breathing; he might have been offering a display of suspended animation.

Sylvia demanded sharply, "Well? Why are you staring at me?"

"I beg your pardon." But his eyes didn't move. "You say Dol found the gloves? Where?"

"In the garden. Hid in a watermelon."

"You mean the vegetable garden?"

"Yes."

"But—" Zimmerman stopped. At length he sighed, as if he had been needing air for minutes. "Then they found them. And they belong to Martin. What good does that do them?"

"I don't know. It certainly doesn't do Martin any good, or me, or anyone else."

"What does Martin say?"

"I don't know. What can he say? That he doesn't know how they got there. What else could he say?"

"Nothing." Zimmerman slowly nodded his head. "I see. That was the bomb they had to explode for him— a watermelon with his gloves in it. He should not have had gloves. But he had." He frowned and shut his eyes as if the light hurt them, then after a moment opened them again to look at her. He said abruptly, "Anyway, that has no bearing on the proposal I want to make. Certainly I am not making it in the orthodox manner, and I suppose I strike you as pretty clumsy, but you must consider the circumstances. I want to ask you to marry me."

He sat with his pale eyes on her. Sylvia was simultaneously convinced of three things: that her ears had gone back on her, that the man's brain had cracked clear through at last, and that everything stored up for her, tragic and grotesque and merely comical, had decided to happen all at once. All she did was to ask weakly, "What?"

"Naturally," Zimmerman said, "you're astonished. I don't flatter myself that the idea has ever occurred to you. Why should it? But I have some considerations to advance that probably haven't occurred to you either. I know that young as you are, your mind is not entirely frivolous. Our marriage would promise advantages, not only to us but also to society, which could not be expected from any other probable choice you would make. I want to tell you about them, but before I do that I must clear your mind to make room for them. Otherwise you won't even hear them. The obstacles must be removed first."

He sounded, incredibly, completely serious, earnest, and sane. Sylvia, stupefied, could only gape. He went on:

"The most obvious obstacle is your engagement with Martin. I cannot remove that; I can only tell you that I disregard it and I think you should. He is my closest friend, but there are three considerations which with me rise superior to friendship. First, you—I'll explain that later. Second, the egoistic satisfaction I get from my work. Third, the object of my work, to lift our race from the animal mire it is sunk in. So I ask you to disregard Martin. I offer a comment to help you: the phenomenon called, much too vaguely, love, has many different factors and manifestations. The sexual factor is easily transferable, as has been proven millions of times, unless it has become romantically or neurotically fixed. With you it has not. Aside from that, your attachment to Martin is predominantly the functioning of your maternal instinct—I dislike these silly romantic terms, but I don't want to be technical—and that can be just as well satisfied with a lapdog, and much better satisfied with a child of your own, or even an adopted one. It is bad for Martin too; a grown man shouldn't be mothered, it keeps him flabby. Your maternal instinct is obviously strong; that's why you picked a man like

Martin, a ready object for it with his faulty adjustment to an adult world, which you intuitively and unconsciously felt."

Sylvia was enough recovered from her stupefaction to have found words, but she did not interrupt. She stirred on the rock, and listened; surely not because there was a drop of sense in what she heard. . . .

"So we'll disregard Martin. There are many minor obstacles, as of course there are to any human proposal, but I think only one other major one, namely, that I am utterly unqualified as an object of romantic devotion. Look at me. My nostrils are equine, my physique is totally undistinguished, my eyes were faded at birth. I don't know what the devil is wrong with my hair; possibly something could be done with it; I've never had time to try. But I am not asking for romantic devotion. If you decide to accept my proposal, and it develops later that you have a capacity for romantic devotion which requires exercise, and you find an object for it, we can work that out when the time comes. It is just possible that by that time I can fill the bill. Of course, looking at me now, that strikes you as preposterous, but the chronicle of romantic attachments through the centuries, judging from portraits and photographs and other evidence, is an almost continuous series of miracles.

"For the advantages, take the personal ones first, and we can confine ourselves to yours, because mine are obvious and you're not interested in them anyway. You would acquire all of the social conveniences of marriage and would assume an irreducible minimum of obligation, except financially, and you can well afford that.

You would be free to give or to withhold. You could satisfy your maternal instinct under your own roof, with objects as temporary or as permanent as you cared to make them. You would have my intellect at your service when you wanted it, with the assurance that it would not be thrust upon you when you didn't. You would have constantly within reach a man who adores you more humbly, and at the same time with more true pride and intelligence, than any other man you have known or are likely to know. I met you only a year ago, when I left my job in a western college to accept the offer from Columbia. I adored you, utterly and passionately, the first day I saw you. I worship you as I worship my work —as the justification of life and the only acceptable evidence of pure truth and beauty in the human world. And you have enriched me; esthetically, I was born the day I saw you. . . ."

Sylvia could not remove her gaze from his pale intent eyes; the rest of his face she did not see. She made herself speak: "Don't go on . . . please. Please don't."

Zimmerman's hand fluttered and dropped to the grass again. "All right. I don't want to make you uncomfortable. I mention my personal feeling for you only that you may know, first, that it exists, and second, that it can be articulate if ever it should have the good fortune to be welcome. Otherwise I promise positively that you shall never be annoyed with it—as you have not during the past year. Only, as I said, it may amuse you—it might even some day be of service to you—to know that it is constantly within reach.—Another personal advantage to you—I hope you would consider it so—would be your assurance that some day your husband will be a famous and respected man. I am destined to dominance in my field. I am sorry I can't prove that; I can only assert it. I have precisely those qualities—temperamental, intuitive, and analytical—which are needed to grasp the probe that psychology is sinking, like a dagger of knowledge, into the human brain, and to sink it to new depths. I also have a rigorous and passionate determination to perform that job. It was my only passion, before I saw you. But don't be apprehensive about that —my passion for you can be controlled. I can control anything that is sensible to the operations of my brain."

He disregarded a bee which lit momentarily on a strand of his stringy hair limp on his forehead. "So much for the main obstacles and the personal advantages. I want you to consider now the biggest advantage of all, to society, to science, to all men and women alive and yet to be born. Martin professes not to know the amount of your fortune, but I understand it is between three and five million dollars. You could keep a third of it for your personal needs—mine are negligible—and with the remainder we can establish a psychological research laboratory with me in charge. On account of your total ignorance of the matter, it is difficult for me to give you an idea of what that would mean. Locating it here in New York, in roomy but inexpensive quarters, we would have an inexhaustible supply of material for experiment —men and women, children, babies—to be hired cheaply and discarded at will. We would not need to spend more than 5% of our capital for original equipment, which would leave us an ample income for development and current expenses. I have already prepared in detail a proposed program for three years' independent research and experiment, with an estimate of the cost, and the probable results, under my direction, are absolutely staggering. Within ten years, at the most, our laboratory would be recognized as the center of authority, and of hope, by psychologists throughout the world. The ultimate effect on human society, on the daily lives of men and women, would be incalculable. It would increase their knowledge, their happiness, and their effective functioning as the most highly developed of organisms. And you would have made it possible. You would have furnished the fuel that kept the fire going. Not only that, you may, if you want, take part in it. I have completed an outline for a series of experiments with babies —based on an entirely new concept of the relation of heredity to environment—which you could manage perfectly under my general supervision. I would like to go over it with you, it is fascinating. You could handle the babies perfectly, after you had acquired a sense of the strictness of scientific discipline. That one outline would take you about two years, at ten hours a day. You would have not only constant association with twenty or thirty babies—I believe I settled on twenty-five—but also the deeply satisfying knowledge of the importance, the vital significance to all mankind, of your work."

Sylvia had been, for minutes, weakly shaking her head. She had, in spite of everything, a point of conviction within her, well buried, that some day she would laugh at this scene—but that would be after she had pretty well forgotten the piercing intentness of those water-pale eyes. She stammered at them, "But I . . . I mustn't let you go on this way. Really. I'm not at all that kind of girl—the serious worth-while kind. I'm as selfish as the dickens. Oh, maybe I could give you some money to start a laboratory . . . six months from now, when I get it. . . ."

Zimmerman shook his head. "That wouldn't do. You would give only a comparatively small amount; you wouldn't turn loose anything like two-thirds of your fortune when it came down to it; and I would have no assurance that future needs would be taken care of. But the main objection . . . apparently I haven't made myself clear. The laboratory would be merely one of the advantages of our marriage. I am young, and in any event I shall have a career. But it will be only half a career unless you share it. It will be a monster with brains and nerves and bones, but no heart. That is poetry. A year ago I couldn't have said anything as unscientific as that, but when I met you I learned that there is not one truth, but two: a truth that lights the way, and a truth that warms us. I never felt the need for warmth before, just as a man born deaf doesn't feel the need for music. I mean now, specifically, merely the warmth of your presence near me. I can be frugal—though God knows your presence would not be frugality."

He paused. He sighed, and muttered at her, "That's my proposal. I want to talk you into it, not out of it."

Sylvia thought, the poor guy. The poor, poor guy.

He said, "I did poor work last spring. All summer I

have been no good." He sounded all at once, startlingly, ferocious. A ferocity pale like his eyes. "I must clear my mind at any cost. I have work to do."

Sylvia looked at him, and her eyes widened, because she had never had to bother about concealing her feelings in obedience to any necessity other than that imposed by good manners. So, when the thought came to her and she accepted its plausibility, she blurted it at him: "Steve Zimmerman! Is this what you went to see P.L. about yesterday morning? Is this what you talked to him about?"

He looked at her in surprise, but after only an instant's hesitation he shook his head. "No. I didn't mention it. I wasn't fool enough to mention it to him."

"Then what did you go there for? You won't tell those men. You won't talk about it. What did you mention?"

Zimmerman shook his head again. "I can't tell you." He frowned. "You're changing the subject. I know I'm making my proposal to you when you're under the first real stress you've ever had to bear. I can't help it; it's my opportunity, and I must seize it."

"But I want to know. Won't you tell me?"

"No." He was emphatic. "Some day, perhaps, if you still want to hear it, if we are married . . ."

Sylvia shivered involuntarily. Not at, directly and specifically, the idea of Steve Zimmerman for a husband; it was merely the state of her nerves. She said, "I couldn't ever marry you. I told you, I'm selfish."

"That's all right. So am I. Even from the selfish standpoint, I've shown you the advantages—"

"No. Please." Sylvia got up from the stone. "I don't like—there's no use." She moved a step.

"Wait a minute." Zimmerman, still cross-legged on the grass, did not tilt his head to look up as she stood. "I have put all this . . . with restraint. But I can plead with you—I can display the most acute suffering for your compassion—I can show you the most vital necessity—"

"Don't! Please don't." She moved again.

"Wait," Zimmerman demanded. "Are you refusing me on account of Martin?"

"I am engaged to Martin."

"But is it on account of him—"

The sentence hung in the air, unfinished. Sylvia was gone. With no concession at all to good manners, and no compassion for the torment of unrequited love, she simply went.

Zimmerman's back was toward the direction she took, and he didn't turn to watch her go. His head bent forward, his chin on his chest, his lids dropped to give the pale eyes a rest, and the only visible movement was his right index finger slowly poking in and out of a beetle hole as his hand, propping him, nestled in the grass.

Sylvia, reaching the top end of the flagstone steps— for the rock garden was at the foot of a declivity— looked from right to left indecisively. Would Martin be out of the card room? Would he be out of the house? She must know what had happened. Would she tell him of Steve's incredible proposal? No, it would only upset him and exasperate him . . . but she knew she would tell him. Anyway, for months now she had thought that it didn't do Martin any good, his close association with that mental morbid freak, just because they had been friends before Steve had gone out to his job in the western college. . . .

She went past the filbert thicket, around by the rose garden, but it was empty. On all the spreading slope there was no one in sight except a trooper in uniform on the east terrace. To avoid the necessity of ignoring him in passing, she struck off to the right, and at the top of the slope circled the rear of the house. The kitchen girl Ellen, the cook's helper, was there struggling with a bag of something, and Sylvia saw that her eyes were red from weeping and thought, "She can cry and work at the same time and I can't do either one." Then, crossing the drive to the garage, to the west lawn, she saw that two chairs near the tennis court were occupied, and headed for them.

It was not Martin; it was Dol Bonner and Len Chisholm. Sylvia hesitated, then went on to them. Len, who had a drink in his hand and provisions for more in a bottle and pitcher on the table, got up and pulled a chair around. Sylvia shook her head and demanded:

"Where's Martin?"

Dol told her, "I guess in the house. I didn't see him come out after we left the card room."

"What happened?"

"Nothing. They showed him the gloves and Martin said they were his. He put them in the pocket of his jacket when he changed yesterday, and took the jacket to the tennis court, and later brought it over here. The last he remembers seeing the gloves was in his room when he put them in the jacket. So anyone might have got them. Martin did very well, especially with that blooded colonel. I think Martin went back to the study. I'd leave him alone a while if I were you, unless you feel you should go and smooth his brow. I went to the vegetable garden with the sergeant, and then I saw Len was down here drinking again, so I came down to tell him to stop. He responded magnificently by thickening his drink."

Sylvia felt her heart a little less heavy. She sat down on the edge of the chair which Len had pulled around. "What did you want the fingerprints for?"

"You heard me tell them. The watermelon."

"What did you want with Janet?"

"You're too inquisitive. Face powder. I was out. She uses Valery's Trente-trois."

"Liar. It wasn't like that. Tell me."

Dol put her finger to her lips. "Not with Len here. He's in no condition to keep a secret. I'll tell you some day."

Len growled, "No matter what condition I was in, I wouldn't be able to remember what anybody wanted with Janet. Unless for a meat grinder. She might make good sausage."

Sylvia said, "All right, if you won't tell me, I'll tell you something. I suppose I shouldn't, but I tell you everything. I have just had a proposal of marriage."

Len growled again, "I know, that trooper that chews gum."

"Shut up, Len." Dol knew Sylvia's face. She asked it, "Who?"

"Steve Zimmerman."

Len spilled some of his drink. Dol gasped.

"What! He . . . seriously?"

"Yes. Very. The idea was for him and me to get married and take a couple of million dollars and start a psychological laboratory. He says he is passionate about his work and his career, and I . . . I am esthetically all right. I am to help out by experimenting with babies. You can't laugh at it either. Even—even if we felt like laughing."

Dol's eyes were narrowed. She muttered, "Pathological. He's unbalanced."

Sylvia shook her head. "You wouldn't think so if you heard him. He covered everything: his friendship with Martin—he disposed of that—his physical shortcomings, the certainty that he will be a famous man, my maternal instinct—the devil. Here comes one of those confounded cops. Now what do they want? My God, Dol, won't this ever end?"

"It will, Sylvia dear. What you can't jump you have to straddle. Quit biting your lip in two."

The trooper approached. "Mr. Chisholm? They want you in there."

"Me?"

"Yes, sir."

"Tell 'em to write me a letter." Len reached for the bottle, poured another inch in his glass, and added a dash of water from the pitcher. "Tell 'em returned undelivered, party has moved." He arose with the glass in his hand and backed off. "Excuse me, ladies, I don't want to miss the next act, they say it's the best." He followed the trooper, in long strides.

Dol looked after him, and shrugged. She turned and demanded, not at all as a young lady ready for gossip, "Tell me about it, Sylvia. What did he say?"

CHAPTER

FOURTEEN

*A*T TEN o'clock that Sunday night the small room
which served as an inside office at the Station H
barracks of the state police, three miles from
Birchhaven on Route 19, was filled with tobacco smoke,
tension, conflicting theories, and half a dozen men. The
bulky one on the wooden bench, chewing at a cigar in
the side of his mouth, was Inspector Cramer of the New
York Homicide Bureau; beside him was Maguire of
Bridgeport, looking sleepy but indomitable. A nondescript trooper leaned against the door jamb. Colonel
Brissenden, still miraculously elegant as to uniform and
intransigent as to demeanor, sat erect at one side of a
small table, and across from him was Sherwood, looking
harried and weary but obstinate. The middle-aged man
threatening to go bald, slim and saturnine with slanting
eyes, was the attorney-general of the state, E. B. Linnekin, who had just driven from a Vermont week-
at sixty miles an hour to fend disaster, share kudos, ̣ ̣d
retrieve justice.

Sherwood was saying, "That's the picture the way it
stands now. The only two for whom we can demonstrate
any motive at all are Chisholm and Ranth. Chisholm
certainly had opportunity, by his own admission—he
went there and saw Storrs asleep on the bench, and he
could have got the gloves before he left Foltz's place.
But that's not enough even for a coroner's charge, let

alone a jury. And his motive—just because he got kicked out of a job? And he was sore? Whoever went to the garden house and got that wire and went there and rigged it up and poked it under Storrs' neck was as cool as a cucumber and as malignant as a snake. And he had an awful good reason for it, of some kind or other."

Linnekin declared, "I say there's a woman in it."

"Hell, there's four women in it. One of them is batty, one thinks she's too hot to handle, one's rich and sweet and innocent, and one pretends she's floating around somewhere over your head when you ask her anything. I've told you. You try it in the morning."

"I shall."

"That suits me, with no reservations. As to motive, the only thing we've got that's satisfactory is Ranth. It looks like he did it. But even if we are all convinced he did it, we're in a hole. With the evidence that we have from three people, Mrs. Storrs and the daughter and the butler, that after seeing Storrs Ranth returned to the house before 4:30, and Chisholm's testimony that Storrs was alive at 4:40, we've got to show that Ranth went there again *after* 4:40, or at least make it extremely plausible. In fact, we have to show that he went there after 5:20 or 5:25, because that was when Foltz put his jacket on the chair in the reception hall, and Ranth couldn't have got hold of the gloves before that. The butler says that at five o'clock Ranth was in the card room writing letters. He could have left the house by the sun room, after getting the gloves from the hall, and returned the same way, but no one saw him go or come. Another difficulty is that note on the grass. Is

it likely he would have left it there after he strung
Storrs up? He might, if something put him in a panic,
but he doesn't look addicted to panics. Understand, I'm
not trying to read Ranth out of it, I'm just showing
what we're up against. It looks to me very probable
that Ranth did it. What does it look like to you, Inspector?"

Cramer grunted, without removing his cigar. "Nothing looks like anything. Whoever did it certainly got
all the breaks. It's a bad one. You've either got to put it
on Ranth or uncover some motives somewhere. If it was
him, and you try it on a jury with no more than you've
got now, they won't bother to leave the courtroom.
Did I tell you? One of my men found Storrs' secretary
down at Long Beach, and she says she didn't hear any
of the talk with Zimmerman yesterday morning, and
no one else could have."

Sherwood nodded. "I got it on the phone from your
office." He shot a sidewise glance at Brissenden. "The
colonel brought Zimmerman to the barracks late this
afternoon and tried to pry him open. Nothing rough,
just tactics. It only closed him up tighter. He's an educated mule, the worst kind."

Brissenden growled, "We should have locked him
up, the damn insolent little squirt."

"I disagree. Tomorrow will do for that. If he won't
talk at the inquest, we'll throw him in. That right, Ed?"

"Certainly, we'll have to." The attorney-general
looked somberly judicious. "I think you've acted with
proper discretion, Dan. These people, except possibly

Ranth, aren't the kind you can put the screws on. But it's murder, and they'll have to talk. I say there's a woman in it." He licked his lips.

Cramer nodded at the table. "Those gloves." They were lying there. "You say you tried them on everybody?"

"Yes. They were loose on Zimmerman, and pretty tight on Chisholm, but they went on all right." Sherwood sighed. "I tell you, Inspector, as you say, it's a bad one. I would appreciate it if you would go over the ground thoroughly in the morning. Now here, once more, look at this diagram. . . ."

Maguire of Bridgeport closed his eyes.

On the grounds of Birchhaven were the peace and stillness of night, but it was a peace under surveillance. At the entrance to the estate a motor cycle leaned against one of the enormous granite pillars, and a trooper stood at the edge of the driveway, moving now and then to keep himself awake. Down by the fish pool, thirty paces from the entrance to the nook under the dogwoods, stood another trooper. He was not stationed there; he, and a colleague who was at that moment seated on a chair by the tennis court, removing a piece of gravel from his shoe, were on patrol. At the house, Belden had locked the outside doors at ten o'clock as usual, but had left the door to the main terrace on the latch because there was a trooper there also, now tussling with boredom on a straight-backed chair in the reception hall, then going to the terrace for a cigarette, an easement of his muscles, and a look at the night. When in the reception hall he could hear, very faintly if he strained his ear, a murmur of voices from the study.

Or more properly, a voice, for chiefly it was George Leo Ranth speaking. After dinner, which had been socially a replica of lunch, he had, with most admirable and exquisite finesse, maneuvered Mrs. Storrs from the room, around to the side hall where she had had no intention of going, and into the study. It was a stroke both bold and adroit for him to pick the study as the field of the skirmish; it was the room most privately and exclusively her husband's of all in the house, where his spirit might be expected to linger if it tarried there at all; it was as if Ranth told her, "Let us be where your husband can challenge me; I surmounted him in life; I shall not evade him in death."

Now, at ten o'clock, he had won the first trench; she was listening to him without either acquiescence or response, but without protest. The light was dim, from the reading lamp in the corner. Mrs. Storrs was seated on the divan by the radio, her hands clasped in her lap, her shoulders sagging, her eyes veiled by drooping lids. Ranth was ten feet away, easily and gracefully erect on a Turidan rug which P. L. Storrs had once brought back from Persia with his personal luggage; he talked better standing.

". . . but that is beyond the interest of all who fail in comprehension, and to fail in comprehension is the most trivial failure of all. There is no demand from Siva that he be understood; no rite in ancient or modern Sakti that can be explained grossly to intelligence alone. Three steps: contemplation, acceptance, introgression. We cannot understand what we adore. Three fulfillments: dispersion, infiltration, homoousia. The second can be reached only through the first; the third is inaccessible until the first and second have been perfected. Three sacrifices: I, self, I myself. Shreds of identity are the tatters of incompletion. To be whole presupposes and requires infinity. There is no other way to glory. There is no method by which the eternal cycle may be entered save by dissemination of the personality into an infinitude of *disjecta membra,* to follow the unnumbered radii from the quivering center of all flesh . . ."

The apostate stirred on the divan, unclasped her hands and clasped them again, and became again immobile.

". . . into the movement that can never cease. The rites of Occidental Sakti command spiritual destruction only as the prelude to humility and the sublime restoration; they are superior to the grossness of physical destruction and no longer demand the sacrifices of the ancient temples. I, George Leo Ranth, am the priest, the hierophant, and the talapoin, and it is I who beckon from the eternal cycle which I have entered. . . ."

The trooper in the reception hall could hear the murmur only if he stood perfectly still and held his breath.

Upstairs, in her room at the end of the hall, Janet Storrs sat at her flat-topped desk of Brazilian cedar, with a pad of paper before her and a fountain pen in her hand.

She had formerly used a lead pencil when composing, on account of the convenience of erasing, but two years ago had changed to a pen, because in the event that the manuscripts ever became valuable, it would be much better to have them in ink. She had not yet dressed for bed, but had kicked off her shoes and got into mules. She sat with her eyes focused on the swaying window curtain, but seeing nothing; her vision was inward. At length she sighed deeply and looked at the pad of paper:

> *If I should say to you, "My heart is dead,*
> *My blood is still, and even pain is gone;*
> *I stand here lifeless in the night; and dawn*
> *Will find me here; and day will come; and red*
> *Will set the sun again;*

A shiver of despair ran over her. She thought, "It's no use; I can't finish it. It was said that poetry is an emotion remembered in tranquillity . . . but God help me, I am not tranquil . . . no . . . no, I am not tranquil. . . ."

She buried her head on her arms, on the desk, and her shoulders shook violently, though there was no sound.

Three doors down the hall from Janet's apartment, on the opposite side, was the room assigned to Steve Zimmerman. It was not the finest that Birchhaven had to offer guests; it had only a lavatory in a niche instead of a bathroom; still, it was far more luxurious than the accommodations Steve permitted himself to pay for on 122nd Street in New York. Belden, or the maid, or both, had apparently been demoralized by the event of Saturday afternoon, since there were no towels on the rack, the ashtray on the bedstand still held cigarette butts and match ends from the night before, and when Steve went to the closet for a coat hanger he found that the door would not open and had to drape his coat on a chair.

These annoyances manifestly glanced off of the shell of Zimmerman's consciousness; he was obviously pre-occupied. Having found the closet door locked or stuck, and hung his coat on the back of a chair, he crossed to a window and opened it wider and poked his head out into the night; from below and to the left he heard the scrape of a footstep and saw that it was a trooper on the terrace. He pulled himself in, went and sat on the edge of the bed and scratched his elbow, and stared at a row of books, between bookends, back of the light on the bed table.

Ten minutes later, still sitting there, the edge of his consciousness noted the sound of voices entering at the open window, apparently from the terrace; he distinguished no words. Finally he muttered half aloud, "I'll go on with it. I have to. I've started it and I'll see it through. It is not credible that I can be shattered by events. Irony does not go that far. It would be like Einstein getting run over by a truck."

Arising to go on with his undressing, he heard foot-steps muffled on the carpet of the hall passing his door. He got stripped, put on the pajamas which had been brought over from his bag at Foltz's the evening before, sat on the edge of the bed and scratched his elbow again, and finally twisted around and stuck his legs between the sheets—at least the maid had not neglected to turn the bed down. There was one blessing he could count on, no matter how events exploded around him: he could sleep. He always did. He had, even that night in June when he had first admitted romantic terms into the austerity of his personal vocabulary, with regard to Sylvia Raffray. But first, before he put out the light, he would lie there and tidy up a little more in his mind. He lay on his back, his eyes closed, his lips compressed, his wide nostrils expanded. . . .

There was a knock at the door, a low discreet trio of taps. Steve opened his eyes, twisted and raised on his elbow, and muttered to himself, "Damn it, not tonight. It must be him." The taps sounded again, and Steve sat up and said, "Come in."

The knob turned, the door silently swung open and, after the intruder was in, as silently closed again.

Steve's pale eyes betrayed surprise and his voice irritation. "What the devil do you want?"

The impression Wolfram de Roode produced, more by structure than by size, of brute physical power, was even more striking in this bedroom than it was out of doors. And his intelligent face, as he stepped smoothly and quietly across to the bedside, showed the strain of some emotion which he was obviously controlling with difficulty. He spoke low, in a tone of husky menace:

"Where is he? What have you done with him?"

Steve was sitting, his knees drawn up, looking up at

the face above him. "What do you mean, done with him? I suppose he's in bed."

"He is not. I've looked in his room. Where is he?"

"I don't know. Maybe downstairs. How do I know?"

"He is not." De Roode's hands, at his sides, clenched into fists. "Damn you. You murderer! Where is he?"

Steve said, with a good imitation of composure, "You're a fool, de Roode. Say it louder, why don't you? Someone else might like to hear it. You call *me* a murderer? I tell you, I don't know where he is. And for God's sake, do you think I'm afraid of you? We're not in a jungle.—Well, maybe we are. Anyway, he's around somewhere. Possibly under his bed. I haven't seen him since dinner. Don't stand there looking as if you ought to have snakes in your hair . . . you look silly. . . ."

He would have to talk this neurotic ape out of the room. . . . He went on talking to that end. . . .

Thirty yards away, in a room in the other wing, Len Chisholm sat in a chintz-covered chair in the cushion of which a cinder from one of his cigarettes had burned a hole as big as a dime without his taking any interest in the phenomenon. He had not undressed for bed, and betrayed no inclination for that enterprise. Sections of the Sunday Gazette were scattered around the floor; also on the floor was a tray with a bottle, pitcher and glass. It had originally been deposited on the bureau by Belden, but Len had changed it to its present location to save mileage.

He kicked feebly at a newspaper section which appeared to be in the way, though he had no present intention of moving, picked up the glass and swallowed a couple of gulps, grimaced indignantly at the tastelessness of it, and muttered hoarsely because his windpipe was constricted by his posture: "I'm nuts. Nuts very nuts. That sounds like Gertrude Stein. You can't fight it, you can't give in to it, you can't strangle it, you can't even get drunk. I'm only a pathetic imitation of a drunk. I'm no more drunk than you are. Drown it in liquor. You can't drown anything that won't sink. I don't mean that. I mean I'm already sunk. I'm already drowned. So any liquor I swallow is merely tautology. . . ."

It was midnight when the trooper went upstairs to knock at the door of Martin Foltz's room to see if he was there. It might have been much earlier than that but for the erratic behavior of Wolfram de Roode; if he had, for instance, on leaving the Birchhaven house at 10:40, seen fit to communicate his anxiety to the trooper. But it appeared from his actions that he was already convinced that the trooper was not in a position to be of any help to him; at any rate, he said nothing whatever when he came downstairs, made a detour to the study to speak to Mrs. Storrs, passed through the reception hall, and went out by the main door. The trooper was momentarily minded to halt him, but, knowing the circumstances, saw no point in it, and let him go. The time consumed by de Roode in trotting back to Foltz's place by the path through the woods was of course a necessary delay, since he had to get his car.

The first that the men at Station H heard of him was at 11:20, when there was a call for Maguire of Bridgeport on the telephone. The conference was still in progress, and Maguire went to the front office to take the call. It was the deputy warden on the night shift at the county jail.

"Chief? This is Cummings. There's a gorilla turned up here that wants to see a guy named Martin Foltz, and by God I'll say he wants to see him. He says Foltz is here in my hotel, and I say he ain't. I was getting ready to throw him out on his ear, when it occurred to me that that's one of the names I saw in the paper about that Birchhaven murder, so I thought I'd better call you. This bird just stands here and says he knows Foltz is here and he wants to see him. That's all he says."

"What's his name?"

"Deerudy or something like that."

"Hold the wire."

Maguire left the receiver dangling and went to the inner room. In a few minutes he came back to the telephone.

"Cummings? Listen. We want that man here at Station H. Right away. Can you send him?"

"He's got his own car. He wants to know if you've got Foltz there."

"To hell with what he wants. His own car is all right, but you'd better send a man with him to make sure that he gets here."

At 11:50 they arrived. The inside office was much denser with smoke than it had been before, and everyone looked weary and irritated and their eyes were bloodshot. They had been about ready to call it off for the night when the call had come from the deputy warden. De Roode walked in with the jail keeper trailing him, swept the room with a swift glance, and stopped at the table.

Sherwood demanded, "Well? What did you go to the jail and ask for Foltz for?"

De Roode's mouth worked. He controlled it.

Brissenden barked, "You got a tongue?"

De Roode said, "I want to see him. Where is he?"

"In bed asleep. I suppose he is. Where did you get the notion he was in jail? What's the idea?"

De Roode said, "You have him here. I want to see him."

Brissenden stood up. "Damn you, will you answer a question?"

Apparently he wouldn't. Not, at least, until his own had been answered to his satisfaction. He wanted to know where Foltz was, and Brissenden's snarls seemed to have no effect on his desire. Finally Sherwood told him in dreary exasperation: "Look here. If you can understand plain English, Foltz is in bed at Birchhaven, as far as we know. We left him there. Maybe we should have locked him up, but we didn't. Where did you get the idea we did? Who told you?"

"No one told me." De Roode's massive chest expanded like a heavyweight prizefighter's as he took a deep breath. "I went to Birchhaven at six o'clock to take him some things, and he told me about the gloves. I understood then why you had asked me what you did this afternoon, about his jacket and gloves in it.

But you are wrong." He looked around slowly at the faces. "I say you are all wrong! Mr. Martin didn't do it!"

"Didn't do what?"

"He didn't kill Mr. Storrs."

"Who the hell said he did? What did he tell you about the gloves?"

"He said you had found them, and they were his gloves, and they had been used to kill Mr. Storrs."

"Right. What about it?"

"That was all. But I could see that he was worried, I could see that he expected something. I went home. But at ten o'clock I couldn't go to bed without seeing him again. You understand, I have cared for him for many years. I went back to Birchhaven. The trooper in the hall told me that everyone had gone up, except Mrs. Storrs and Mr. Ranth in the study. I went up to his room and knocked, and there was no answer. I went in, and he was not there. I went to Mr. Zimmerman's room, and he was not there. I went down to the study and asked Mrs. Storrs, and she did not know. So I knew you must have taken him, on account of the gloves. I thought you would take him to the jail, and I went there."

De Roode straightened his slumping shoulders. "Where is he?"

"For the love of Mike." Sherwood was disgusted. "He's human, he was probably in the bathroom."

"No. I looked."

"Well, he was somewhere. You're a fathead. I thought maybe . . . what does it matter what I thought?" Sherwood turned to the trooper on a chair by the door. "You might as well call Birchhaven and tell the man there to see about Foltz. See if he's in his room. Tell him to call back right away."

The trooper went. Sherwood got up and stretched thoroughly, with a cavernous yawn. "You're coming with me, Inspector? That's better than going back to New York; you wouldn't get more than three hours' sleep if you're going to be out here at eight o'clock." The others moved and looked for hats. Maguire was muttering to the man from the jail. The attorney-general spoke darkly to Brissenden, who nodded a scowling agreement. Inspector Cramer crossed to the table and helped Sherwood get his papers gathered up and deposited in his brief case. No one paid any attention to de Roode. They talked desultorily, then straggled towards the outer room.

The phone rang, and the trooper answered it. He talked a brief minute, then hung up and turned to his superiors.

"Hurley says Foltz is in his room, in bed."

"Did he go in? Did he see him?"

"Yes, sir. He went in, and Foltz was sore because he had waked him up."

"Hunh. Where is that damn fool?" Sherwood turned and saw de Roode. "Did you hear that? He's in bed asleep, where we all ought to be. Except you, you ought to be in jail yourself, anyone as bright as you are. Come on, Inspector."

Sylvia slept. She had not expected to; she had not slept Saturday night. And now, at ten o'clock Sunday

evening, the turmoil in her head and breast was surely
in worse confusion than it had been twenty-four hours
before; there had been the discovery of the gloves,
which she had herself bought; the grotesque proposal
of Steve Zimmerman—she could not forget his eyes;
the detached imperturbability of Martin when she told
him about Steve, not like Martin at all; and Dol's antics
which she would not explain. So, though Sylvia went
upstairs early because the others did, she dreaded the
long dark hours of futile resentment at the net of grief
and apprehension and suspense that she was tangled in.
In fact, it scarcely amounted to long dark minutes after
she had changed to pajamas, performed a minimum of
toilet ceremonies, got into bed, and turned out the light.
Tired young nerves, which in twenty years had had little occasion for the development of detours and block-
ades in their canals, demanded respite and got it. By
10:30 she was sound asleep.

The trooper named Hurley, in the reception hall, did
not have as tiresome a night of it as might have been
expected by a man who had been assigned to watch over
a sleeping household. There was the interruption by de
Roode, coming and going, by Mrs. Storrs and Ranth
leaving the study and going upstairs some time after
eleven, and, at midnight, the phone call from Station
H and his resulting expedition to Foltz's room. It was
half an hour after that that another little diversion offered itself. He had just returned to the hall after a
trip to the terrace for a cigarette, when there came
faintly from the floor above the sound of knocking. He

listened, and after a moment the sound came again. He debated with himself a little whether it was any of his business, finally decided that it might be, since Sergeant Quill had given him a pencil diagram showing which rooms the various guests were occupying, and mounted the stairs.

He had turned off the hall light after his visit to Foltz's room, and now switched it on again. No one was visible in the corridor to the right, and he turned the corner to the other hall. Halfway down its length a man stood, and Hurley saw it was the big guy who the sergeant had told him had been drinking all afternoon, by name Chisholm. Hurley walked down the hall to him, quiet on tiptoe but assured. He had been feeling a little out of his element on night post in a house like this, but a drunk was a drunk anywhere.

He spoke in a rough undertone. "Who you looking for?"

Len Chisholm leaned against the jamb of the door he had presumably been knocking on, raised his brows superciliously and kept them there. He disdained to reply.

"Come on, what do you want?"

Len left the jamb in order to get his lips within ten inches of the trooper's ear, and whispered as one conspirator to another, "Sit down and I'll tell you. Let's both sit down."

Hurley grunted, "You're pie-eyed. What do you want with Zimmerman at this time of night?"

Len attempted a frown, but it wouldn't stay in place. He leaned to the jamb again and abandoned the whisper for a rumble. "Zimmerman?" He was scornful. "I wouldn't speak to that runt if you offered it to me on a silver platter."

"What are you knocking on his door for?"

"I'm not knocking on his door. I intend to visit Miss Bonner. The only job I have ever cared for."

"This is Zimmerman's room."

"What!" Len turned and peered intently at the door's upper left panel, his nose almost against it. He touched it with his finger. "By God, it is." He wheeled unsteadily. "I am not in the habit of going into rooms occupied by men in the dead of night. You can take my word for *that*. My mistake." He propelled himself forward by placing his back against the door jamb and using it for purchase, abruptly brushed past the trooper, and was off down the hall, tacking some but by no means staggering.

Hurley followed him, muttering, "Thank God he can navigate. I'd hate to lug that lump of meat." There proved to be no occasion even for steering it. Len turned the corner into the main corridor without mishap, proceeded to the door of his own room, opened it, passed through, and shut it with a bang.

The trooper grimaced as the door banged, gazed at it a second, and then turned and went back downstairs.

The banging of Len's door a little after 12:30 may or may not have been heard by various others—except Sylvia, who was sleeping too soundly,—but it was heard quite distinctly by Dol Bonner, because her room was not far away from Len's, across the main corridor, and she was not asleep at all. She had not even undressed. She sat at the little table between two windows and put things down on paper, or on the window-seat with her knees up and her chin resting on them, or paced the floor in her stocking feet, frowning at a chaos which she could not shape. She did harder thinking between ten and two o'clock that night than she had ever done in her life—most of it abortive, some of it painful, and none of it conclusive.

Most of the first hour was spent at the table with pencil and paper, setting down individual schedules for Saturday afternoon, theories with pros and cons, probabilities balanced against implausibles. At length she saw that she would never get anywhere that way; there were too many hypotheses and permutations. She went and sat on the window-seat and considered Janet and the lie she had told. Should she go now to Janet's room and have it out with her?

She had been tempted, as soon as she learned that Janet had lied, to confront her with it and demand the truth. She still was. But still she held back. She wanted first to have the possibilities well enough arranged in her head so that, if Janet sought refuge in another lie, it would not be gulped down so easily as the first one had been. Also there was the likelihood that Janet would simply stand pat and refuse to elucidate at all, in which case it was better that she should not know that her lie had been detected. And in addition, the Janet business was extremely ticklish anyway and already perhaps bungled beyond repair. The only pressure that could have been applied to her no longer existed, and Dol could have kicked herself for her quixotic impulsiveness in wiping the fingerprints from the watermelon. Granted the humanity of her desire to keep Janet out of it, surely a little reflection and ingenuity could have provided a better method; for instance, she could have hid that melon somewhere, and cut a hole in another one and substituted it. Sherwood and Brissenden had been indignant that she had wiped off the melon because it contained no fingerprints; if they knew that what she had done was to remove the prints of the person who had actually cached the gloves . . .

All of which was particularly pertinent and vital because the certainty that Janet had lied, and the most obvious inference to be drawn from it, put a new face on the whole matter and made it seem extremely likely that the destruction of those fingerprints might prove to have been a major mistake. And even if that inference was wrong, any other possible inference from Janet's lie was equally pregnant with perplexity.

Dol felt incompetent, bewildered, exasperated, and determined. She could not go to bed and go to sleep. In the morning those men would be back here. They didn't even know about Janet and her lie, nor about Zimmerman's strange and curiously timed betrayal of friendship—nor even Len Chisholm's camouflaged infatuation. But they would be here; and, for one thing, they might lose patience with Zimmerman's obduracy and take him away and lock him up. They might do anything. . . .

During those four hours from ten till two, sitting at the table, or on the window-seat, or pacing back and forth in her stockings, various noises came to Dol in the night-still house. Steps in the upstairs hall, the voice of Ranth saying goodnight, presumably to Mrs. Storrs, faintly the ring of the telephone bell in the card room which was beneath her; then, later, more footsteps, and after an interval again more, and the loud banging of Len's door. It was still later by an hour, around 1:30, that she again heard footsteps, this time on the gravel outdoors, and she went to the open window and leaned out. After a moment she made out a form below on the path, then a round blotch that could only have been a face upturned to her lighted window.

A voice came up, "All right, ma'am, patrol."

Her nerves were ragged. She blurted, "Well, patrol on the grass," and withdrew herself from the night.

She went to the bathroom, having her own, got a drink of water, and came back and sat on the edge of the bed. They would almost certainly take Zimmerman. They might take more than him. She sat with her shoulders drooping, her eyes half closed with weariness, her brow wrinkled in miserable uncertainty. She had tried to pull the thing together in her mind, and it was no good; or if in fact it was, what in the name of heaven was she to do next? Should she drop the whole darned thing, empty it out of her mind, confess herself licked?

No. She sat for a while merely hanging on to that no.

Her teeth came together and she stood up. This was no earthly use; her mind was played out. And if she was on the right track, and if they did take Zimmerman away in the morning, she would be blocked, and all she could do then would be to go to Sherwood and spill the whole thing to him, including Janet's story and the lie in it, and the truth about the prints on the melon. In that case, she must do something now. She looked at her wrist; it was two o'clock; they would be here in six hours. It still might be best to have a try at Janet—but she tossed her head impatiently, surely she had considered that enough—if she knew Janet half as well as she thought she did, that would be a mistake. All right, then the only thing left was Zimmerman. She had two levers to use on him, if her main supposition was correct, and time itself, and suspense, must have worn him down a little, not to mention the fermentation made manifest by his proposal to Sylvia.

Good. Zimmerman. She felt relieved and instantaneously purposeful. She went to the mirror and saw that she couldn't possibly look worse, and that therefore dabs at betterment wouldn't repay the trouble. At the door she turned the knob quietly but firmly, pulled on it, and was in the hall.

She left her door standing open to have the light, and went to the widening of the corridor at the head of the stairs, and turned the corner. Here it was much darker, quite dark, and she stood a moment for the adjustment of her eyes. She moved when she could see well enough to distinguish a break in the wall for a door-frame, and at the first one on the left she paused; that was an empty room behind a locked door, left vacant by the departure of P. L. Storrs; the next would be Zimmerman's; she followed the wall to it, located the door-panel with her fingertips, and with her knuckles tapped on it gently, and waited. No sound came. She tapped again, and still there was no response. She had no desire to rouse anyone else, particularly the trooper in the downstairs hall, so she quietly turned the knob, learned that the door was not locked by its give to her tentative pressure, and pushed it open and entered. Her low-voiced "Steve. Steve!" got no more response than had the tapping. Thinking, "He certainly can sleep," she softly shut the door and heard it click, then turned to address the darkness in a louder tone, "Steve! It's Dol Bonner." No reply; and all at once she knew that the room was much too still, too still even for the peace of sleep; it was as still as death. The room was empty. Her heart thumped and she turned and groped with her fingers on the wall beside the door, found the switch, and flipped it on. Then she turned to look, and stood transfixed, with no blink in her stare for the sudden flood of light.

For seconds she didn't move, and when she did it was to put her hand out behind her to feel for the door knob, but she couldn't find it that way. She turned and grasped it, and the hold on it steadied her. She opened the door gently, and from the hall closed it gently behind her. She stood and caught a tremulous breath that was almost a sob, and that too seemed to help; then she glided back to the main corridor, passed through the door she had left open into her own room, found her oxfords on the floor by the window-seat, and sat there and put them on with trembling hands impossible to control. She went to the corridor again and descended the stairs to the reception hall. The trooper, there on a chair, arose in surprise at the appearance of this fully dressed young woman at something after two in the morning.

Dol said in a shaky voice, "Come upstairs. There's a man dead up there."

CHAPTER

FIFTEEN

*T*HUS it happened that the high command resumed operations on the Birchhaven affair five hours before the time they had appointed.

Inspector Cramer said, "That don't mean anything. There's three ways to account for the cord being tied in a double knot like that around his throat. One would be if he did it himself. He might. Another would be if the guy that did it was so powerful that he could pin him down on the bed and hold him down with his knees and do as he damn pleased, only in that case he'd have to choke him with one hand to keep him from yelling while he tied the knot with the other. The third would be if you got the cord tight around his throat and kept it there until he was unconscious, and then tied the knot to make it good. Offhand, I like that way best. Almost anyone could do that if he wanted to bad enough."

"I don't know. I don't see how." Sherwood, unkempt and bleary-eyed, was glowering down at the body of Steve Zimmerman which, since it would not be moved until Doc Flanner arrived, still lay, twisted and contorted diagonally across the bed with its head dangling over the edge, and the electric cord from the night lamp taut with a double knot around its throat. "Say he's lying there asleep, how are you going to get the cord around him, and pulled tight, before he has a chance to let out a yell? You're not going to poke it under his neck like you might a wire. Do you think he wouldn't yell?"

"Maybe he wouldn't have time to. Look." The inspector pointed at the wall near the floor, to the right of the head of the bed. "That's the outlet that cord was plugged into, it's the only one close enough. Ordinarily, of course, the cord passes from the lamp along the wall behind the bed to reach the outlet. But let's say you were thoughtful enough to make preparations. You could come in here ahead of time, detach the cord from the outlet, go to the lamp and pull the cord to you, and then pass it across on top of the bed and plug it in again. Then where the cord crosses the bed you tuck it under the edge of the pillows, and if the bed is turned down and ready to get into, who's going to see it? Nobody, unless he happens to move the pillows, which is a chance you take. Later, when he's asleep and you come back, you don't have to poke it under his neck, it's already under. All you have to do is quietly remove the cord from the outlet, and you've got him."

"You have if you're quick enough and strong enough."

Cramer shook his head. "You don't have to be a giant. If you once get that cord crossed on his throat, and a good hold on it, and enough grit to hang on for about a minute in spite of hell, he couldn't do a damn thing but bounce around on the bed and claw at you, and he would be much more apt to claw at the cord, it's an instinct when something's tight around your throat. Then when he quiets down on account of lack of air, you can tie all the knots you want to."

Brissenden, standing at the foot of the bed, growled, "Fingerprints on the plug and the outlet."

"Sure, try for 'em. I doubt it. Everybody is finger-print-conscious nowadays. You notice that melon didn't have any—at least, let's hope it didn't. There's one thing I observed that seems to support my guess as to how it was done." The inspector stepped closer to the dangling head with the purple face and the protruding tongue, and bent over it. "Look here, Sherwood. See that mark across the side of his neck, half an inch from where the cord is now? Two things about that. First, it's another indication against suicide, the others being that it would be a world's record for a guy to tie a knot as tight as that around his own neck, and he wouldn't be likely to throw that pillow on the floor and muss up the bed like that. If he did tie his own knot, there would be no reason for another mark like that alongside it. Whereas, if it happened like my guess, the preliminary strangling would make a mark, and then the cord might get shifted when he pulled it tight again with the knot. Of course, that doesn't settle it. He may have had a crack on the head first to knock him out. How soon is your doctor coming?"

"Let's get out of here." Sherwood, stooping to look at the mark obedient to Cramer's suggestion, had straightened up with a shudder. "Flanner should be here any minute. There's nothing more here you want, is there?" He held his hand to his mouth, swallowed twice, mastered the crisis, and turned. "Quill, you tend to Doc and the men doing the pictures and fingerprints when they come. Keep a man outside in the hall. We'll be downstairs. All right, Colonel?"

Brissenden grunted assent. "Tell 'em about that plug and outlet. Cover the whole room." He strode behind Sherwood and Cramer to the door, and out.

In the main corridor a trooper who was standing there stopped them. He spoke to Brissenden: "Mrs. Storrs has gone downstairs, sir. What about the rest of them?"

"Everyone is to get dressed. No one is to leave the house."

"Yes, sir."

Below, in the reception hall, was a group, all in uniform with holsters and cartridge belts. Brissenden sent two of them up to join Quill, and another pair to find the men outdoors on patrol, relieve them and send them in. Sergeant Talbot was dispatched to the card room with telephone calls to make. It was learned that Mrs. Storrs was not awaiting them there, but had gone with Belden, who had dressed himself to perfection in four minutes, in the direction of the kitchen. The high command proceeded to the card room. It was lit; Talbot was on the stool at the telephone stand; and one of the chairs at the table was occupied. Brissenden, seeing that, scowled. Sherwood motioned Cramer to a chair, sat down himself, and took out a handkerchief and thoroughly wiped his face; he had been too infuriated to stop to wash when the phone call had got him out of bed.

He said, "This is Inspector Cramer of New York. Miss Bonner."

Dol nodded.

"Oh, you're the one that found the gloves in the watermelon." Cramer got out a cigar. "Don't be alarmed, I'm not going to light it. Neat piece of work. I understand you're a detective."

"Thank you. I run a licensed agency." Dol shifted her eyes to Sherwood. "I'm here because I found Zimmerman when I went in his room and I thought you'd like to ask me about it."

"Naturally." Sherwood sat for a minute's silence, gazing at her. Finally he asked, "What did you go to his room for?"

"To ask him something." Dol touched the black spot on her cheek with the tip of her finger. "Maybe I can save you time and a lot of questions. I was in my room from ten o'clock until two o'clock, without leaving it, and no one else entered it. I didn't undress because I was thinking about this case, and I had an idea I might solve it before you did. I didn't know what you might do in the morning, you might even make an arrest, and I knew if I was going to get anywhere I had better not lose any time. I decided that my best bet was to see Zimmerman and try to get out of him what he went to Storrs' office for Saturday morning, and what happened there. If I waited until morning I might not get a chance at him. I went to his room and knocked on the door. I opened the door, and when I called his name and there was no answer, I turned on the light and saw him on the bed. Then I went downstairs and told the trooper."

"Why did you think we were going to arrest Zimmerman?"

"Because he wouldn't talk."

"Where did you get the idea you might solve this case before we did?"

"I just got it. I guess finding the gloves had puffed me up."

A windy snort came from Brissenden. Sherwood observed drily, "You seem to have a knack for finding corpses. When you found Storrs Saturday you kept it to yourself while you went to the tennis court to study human nature. Did you try that tonight? After you found Zimmerman did you go to your room to get it solved before you let us in on it? Or somebody else's room?"

"No." Dol touched the black spot again. "I don't see why you bother with sarcasm. I told the trooper within two minutes after I found him. I went to my room first to put on my shoes, because I was in my stocking feet and I didn't want to go downstairs that way."

There was an ejaculation from Inspector Cramer. Sherwood glanced at him inquiringly, but he shook his head. "Nothing. It just occurred to me what she must save on smelling-salts."

An interruption came from the door; it opened and Mrs. Storrs entered. In a pink negligee and slippers, with her hair gathered under a contraption at the back of her head and the night grease imperfectly removed from her colorless skin, she was not a joyous sight. She approached the table and told Sherwood:

"So you're back here. You needed more facts, and one has been furnished you. All this in my house." There was a faint hissing as she breathed in. "I came to tell you that I misled you yesterday. I was lost in darkness. And to tell you that Belden will shortly have coffee for your men, and for you if you want it."

"Thank you, Mrs. Storrs. You mean that you no longer believe that Ranth killed your husband?"

"I mean what I say. I misled you. I think you should know that I am no longer in the sphere that holds you. I have nothing to tell you. All . . . all this in my house." She turned to go.

Sherwood stopped her, but got nothing for it. He did manage to elicit a statement that she had left the study with Ranth and gone up to her room a little after eleven o'clock, but he had already learned that from his brief questioning of Hurley upon arrival. As regarded this second item in the cycle of destruction, Mrs. Storrs had heard nothing and seen nothing, and knew nothing.

As the door closed behind her departure, Cramer bit deeper in his cigar and muttered to Brissenden, "There seems to be an unusual assortment of women here." The colonel grunted hearty agreement. Sergeant Talbot, having finished with his telephoning, was sent to bring Len Chisholm. A trooper entered and reported that Doc Flanner and the photographer had both arrived and were upstairs, and that the man was back from Foltz's place with de Roode. Sherwood instructed him to tell Talbot that he would take de Roode first, before Chisholm. Then he informed Dol that he would send for her when he needed her again.

Dol said without moving, "Look, Mr. Sherwood. One of three things about me. Either I'm engaged on the other side and not to be trusted, or I'm a feeble-minded female freak and just a nuisance, or I really do want this case solved and might possibly have another piece of luck like finding the gloves. Which do you think?"

Sherwood frowned at her. "Which do you?"

"I want the case solved. I have no other interest that might interfere with it. Once yesterday I thought I might have, but now I know I haven't. I have . . . some ideas. They may be no good, but on the other hand they may, under certain circumstances, prevent a mistake."

"What ideas? Do you think you know who killed Zimmerman?"

"No, not so I can say it. Not so it's any good. I have to find out, for instance, why you sent for de Roode—oh, here he is. I'll know now."

Sherwood, still frowning at her, finally shrugged and turned to the newcomer, but before he got further than a survey of him there was another interruption—Belden arriving with the coffee. The butler filled steaming cups, passed a tray heaped with sandwiches, distributed plates and napkins, and bowed himself out as from a social table of bridge.

Sherwood said: "Well, de Roode, we've got you."

The man stood with his head bent as though in weariness, but Dol could see the cord of muscle at the side of his neck and the gleam of his hostile and careful eyes as they focused on the attorney.

"I don't know what you mean, you've got me. You sent for me."

"And you know why. Don't you?"

"No."

"You don't. Down at the barracks you said that you came to Birchhaven around ten o'clock to see Foltz, and you left a little after ten-thirty. Is that right?"

"Yes."

"And when you didn't find Foltz in his room you went to Zimmerman's room?"

"Yes."

"What did you do in there?"

"I asked Mr. Zimmerman if he knew where Mr. Martin was, and he said he didn't. Then we talked a little, and I came out."

"You must have talked quite a while, and you thinking Foltz was in jail and wanting to see him so badly. The trooper says you were upstairs between twenty and thirty minutes. What was Zimmerman doing when you left?"

"He was in bed."

"What was he doing? What did he look like?"

"He wasn't doing anything. He was sitting up in bed talking. But . . ."

"But what?"

"Nothing. I was only going to say, he got out of bed. Because when I left his room I stood in the hall a minute, deciding what to do, and I heard him locking the door on the inside."

There were grunts from Brissenden and Cramer. Sherwood demanded, "You what?" He scowled. "You don't mean that."

"I do mean it." De Roode remained imperturbable. "I heard him turning the key."

Sherwood sighed. "In that case, it looks like the next thing is to arrest you for Zimmerman's murder."

De Roode's chin went up. "He—" He stopped, his eyes boring into the attorney's gaze. He said gruffly from his throat, "He hasn't been murdered."

"Yes, he has. He's up there now the way you left him."

"Not the way I left him. If I had left him murdered, he couldn't have got up and locked the door after I was out of the room."

"Certainly he couldn't. And no one else could have got in afterwards to kill him. And the door was unlocked when Miss Bonner went to his room at two o'clock. So you didn't hear him lock it. So you're lying. Got that straight in your mind? You might as well come clean with it, de Roode. What did you do it for?"

The man made no reply. Dol could see the swelling of the cord of muscle on his neck, and the slow lift of his powerful shoulders as he took in air long and deep. It seemed minutes before the shoulders began to sink again. When they had reached bottom he said, not as a challenge nor yet as a surrender:

"If you think I murdered him, arrest me."

"What did you do it for? Because he knew you had killed Storrs? Was that it?"

"Arrest me."

"Why did you say you heard him lock the door?"

"Arrest me."

Sherwood leaned back. Cramer muttered, "Uh-huh, you've gagged him. That's the way it goes sometimes."

But to an explosive suggestion from Brissenden the inspector objected, "Not a chance. Look at his mouth, he'd wear out a squad."

He did wear out Sherwood. He did no more talking. The attorney fired questions at him, tried to browbeat him, reasoned with him, but Cramer was right, de Roode had been gagged. He said "Arrest me," or said nothing, not even bothering to shake his head. Finally the attorney told the trooper:

"Take him out and have one of the men keep him. De Roode, you're being held as a material witness. Don't let anybody talk to him. Send Chisholm in."

Brissenden watched them go and then growled, "If you had let me keep Zimmerman he would be alive now and we would have got it out of him today. I say that Talbot ought to take that bird down to the barracks and work on him. I want it on record that I say that."

"Okay." Sherwood gulped his cup of coffee, now lukewarm. "I'm not trying to make a record, I'm trying to stop this damn massacre." He poured hot coffee and sipped at that. "He can take him later if it looks that way. First let's see what we've got. What we haven't got is motive, and we can't get a line on any. Why in the name of God would de Roode want to murder P. L. Storrs? Or Foltz? Or even Chisholm? We have a motive for Ranth, but where would Zimmerman fit into that? And if de Roode did hear Zimmerman lock the door, how did Ranth get in the room? If de Roode did it himself, why did he tell such a silly lie about hearing the door locked, and why did he kill Zimmerman, and why the devil did he kill Storrs? And if the two jobs were done by different people, who were they and why did they do it?" Sherwood glared at Dol. "What about it, Miss Bonner? How are the ideas coming? You wanted to know why I sent for de Roode. Because he heard Zimmerman lock his door. How do you like that?"

But Dol had no opportunity to tell how she liked it. Len Chisholm came in.

From the standpoint of elegance, he was a wreck. Dol, looking at him, thought, "They might at least have brushed some of the cigarette ashes off of him." His tie was on one side, his shirt needed tucking in, and his face was either comic or heroic, as it might move you, with a desperate dignity.

He ignored the men and squinted at Dol. "Oh. So there . . . there you are. Investigating a murder?" It was obvious that he meant it for a friendly question.

Dol said nothing. He frowned at her, gave her up, and turned to the men. "My God. Are you fellows still here?" He pointed an accusing finger, not too steady, at Cramer, who was in the chair Maguire of Bridgeport had occupied twelve hours before. "You've been monkeying with your nose. It's not the same nose at all. Do you know Cyrano de Bergerac? Let's hear *you* say it, Cyrano de Bergerac." He abruptly shifted to Sherwood. "Mind if I sit down?"

Cramer grunted in disgust. "You might as well ask questions of a weegie board. Is this the one your man found knocking on Zimmerman's door?"

"Yeah. And the one who saw Storrs asleep on the bench Saturday afternoon."

"Huh. He gets around." Cramer chewed on his cigar,

and watched Len's elaborate performance of lowering himself into a chair. "If he's putting on an act, he's good. If you let him sleep it off he'll claim he can't remember anything. If you duck him he'll have a fit."

Sherwood stared at Len. "Look here, Chisholm. Do you know what your name is?"

"Certainly." Len smiled at him indulgently. "Do you?"

"How drunk are you?"

"Well . . ." Len's brow wrinkled. "I'll tell you. I'm too drunk to drive a car. I've got too much sense. But I'm not too drunk to know where I am. I know exactly where I am."

"That's fine." Sherwood sounded encouraging. "Then you probably know where you've been, too. For instance, when you went to Zimmerman's room. What did you do in there?"

Len shook his head emphatically. "You must mean my room. You're mixed up. You must mean what did I do in my room."

"No. I mean Zimmerman's room. The one around the corner from yours, in the other hall. More than two hours ago you went there in the dark and knocked on the door. Remember? And the trooper came up and spoke to you, and you told him you thought it was Miss Bonner's room? And before the trooper came, you turned the knob of that door to open it? That's why you ought to be able to remember whether the door was locked. Just concentrate on that: was the door locked?"

Len looked cunning and superior. He waved a hand. "I see what you're doing. You're trying to get me to compromise Miss Bonner. It's a fallacy. If Miss Bonner's door was locked, how would Zimmerman get in?" He frowned. "That's not what I mean. I mean how would I get in. And I didn't get in. That's why I say you must mean my room. I got into my room whenever I felt like it."

"Sure you did. But that door you were knocking on— when you tried to open it was it locked?"

Len shook his head. "You don't understand anything. There wouldn't be any *use* trying to open a door if it was locked. It wouldn't do you any *good*."

"Okay." Sherwood sighed. He leaned forward and demanded abruptly, "What did you have against Zimmerman? Why did you hate him?"

"Hate who?"

"Steve Zimmerman."

"Oh. Him." Len nodded. "That runt."

"Why did you hate him?"

"I don't know. I never stop to think why when I hate anybody. Hell, I don't like you either."

"Did you kill Zimmerman? Did you strangle him with that cord?"

Len squinted at him. "You don't mean Zimmerman. It wasn't him that was strangled, it was Storrs."

"I'm asking you, did you kill Zimmerman?"

"No." Len looked disgusted. "Did you?"

Sherwood sighed. He turned: "Do you want to try this a while, Inspector?"

Cramer grunted. "I'd hate to offend him. I might try." He came around and stood in front of Len's chair.

He had about the same amount of success as the attorney. Whether Len's elusiveness was the sharp cunning of a man defending himself against peril, or merely what it seemed to be, an excess of alcohol causing a cerebral traffic jam, the effect was the same. He slid down the question marks like an ant down a corkscrew. Cramer, after ten minutes of it, was ready to call it off when a trooper entered with the information that the doctor was ready to report.

Sherwood nodded at Chisholm. "Take this man and put him in his room and keep him there, and see that there aren't any bottles around. Don't let him out until I ask for him. Maybe you'd better feed him, if he'll eat. Tell Talbot to send another man down to the entrance, it'll soon be daylight. As soon as I get through with Flanner I want to see Foltz."

Len said, "There's a butler in this house that tends to the bottles." But he got up and went, without protest and without ceremony, more unsteadily than he had entered, not permitting the trooper's hand on his arm.

"That's the last you'll get out of him," Cramer declared. "When he comes to again he'll be a blank."

Sherwood said in a voice too weary to be savage, "I know I'd like to roll him on a barrel. Damn it, I've got to get some sleep. Only four hours last night, and now tonight—hello, Doc. What about it?"

Doctor Flanner's report was brief. To all appearances, death by strangulation, with a remote chance of any different conclusion from the autopsy. All symptoms typical. Two areas of pressure, one where the cord was fastened by the knot and the other evidenced by a mark below that, apparently caused by a previous pressure from the same or a similar cord. Both areas well beneath the hyoid bone. No contusions or other external evidence of violence except the strangulation. Been dead from three to five hours.

The attorney nodded. "Much obliged. I'll phone you some time before noon, we may have to postpone the Storrs inquest." The doctor gone, he turned to Dol Bonner. "I'd like to ask you something. After you took the trooper upstairs and showed him what you had found, in between that and the time we got here, which was about half an hour later, did you happen to see Chisholm and tell him what had happened? Was he in his room?"

"I don't know. I didn't see him. I went to Miss Raffray's room to wake her and tell her about it, and stayed there with her a while. I didn't see Chisholm at all."

"You didn't." Sherwood put up his brows at her. Then, at an intrusion, he turned. It was Martin Foltz. The attorney put sharp eyes on him. "Sit down, please, Mr. Foltz."

Martin was visibly agitated—chiefly, it appeared, with anger. His voice trembling, he burst out at Sherwood, "My man de Roode is out there and they won't let me speak with him! They say by your orders! Outrageous insolence!"

"Calm down a little." Sherwood patted the air. "Your man de Roode is under arrest."

"Under arrest for what?"

"We call it, detained as a material witness. Sit down, Foltz. You ought to know better than to start shooting off about insolence. If you insist on it nobody can stop you, but it won't get you anywhere. Sit down."

Martin stood. His mouth twitched. Finally he said, "I have a right to talk to de Roode. I have a right to know what's going on. Steve Zimmerman was my oldest friend. They wouldn't let me in to see him."

"Do you know what happened to him?"

"Yes." Martin's mouth twitched again. He controlled it. "Miss Raffray told me. I . . . they wouldn't let me in the room. I have a right to know . . ."

"Sure you have," Sherwood agreed. "I know, you've had a shock. So have I. If you can pull yourself together enough to be seated in that chair . . . thanks. Probably you already know as much as we do, if Miss Raffray told you what Miss Bonner told her. Zimmerman was strangled with an electric light cord some time between ten and two o'clock. Murdered. Miss Raffray told you that?"

"Yes."

"Okay. So I'm trying to find out what different people were doing around here, and I'm not having much luck. Miss Bonner was lucid and succinct, but no one else. Mrs. Storrs is congenitally obscure. Your man de Roode is either a liar or a murderer or both. Chisholm is either drunk or foxy. I am hoping you'll take after Miss Bonner. The man that was here tells me that you went upstairs with Miss Raffray around nine-thirty and didn't come down again. Is that right?"

"No." Martin clipped the word. "I went up with Miss Raffray, but I came down again."

"The devil you did. When?"

"It must have been around ten o'clock, or a little later. I talked with Miss Raffray a few moments at the door of her room, and then went to my room. I walked up and down and smoked a couple of cigarettes, trying to quiet my nerves. I haven't got the kind of nerves a man ought to have. I never have had. It affects my stomach too, when I'm upset, and I didn't have any of my tablets with me. I thought of going down to phone de Roode to bring some over, but if I did that I would have to pass that trooper in the hall again, and I didn't want to. I hated his being there and what it meant, and anything I hate has a bad effect on me." Martin fluttered a hand. "You wouldn't understand that, you haven't got my nerves. I hadn't slept Saturday night, and I knew I wouldn't sleep with my stomach like that, and I might not anyway. I went down the back stairs to the kitchen, and got some baking soda and a spoon and a glass. I opened the door and went out to smoke a cigarette, because it calms me down to smoke outdoors more than it does with walls around me. I returned to my room and took the soda and went to bed, and I had just managed to get to sleep—at least that was how it seemed—when that damned trooper knocked on my door and insisted on coming in. He said you had phoned to ask if I was in my room. I took some more soda, but I couldn't go to sleep again, and I was awake when Miss Raffray came to tell me what Miss Bonner had told her." Martin stopped, took out a handkerchief and wiped his forehead, and crumpled the handkerchief tight in his hand. He said, "I . . . I hope I made it lucid and succinct."

Sherwood nodded. "Thanks. When you went down to the kitchen did you see anyone?"

"There was no one there."

"On the stairs or in the hall?"

"No."

"Did you leave your room except for that trip downstairs?"

"No."

"Did you hear any noises before the trooper knocked on your door?"

"I heard footsteps. It sounded like Mrs. Storrs, she walks on her heels. I heard a door close, I think two doors. That was before I went to sleep. After the trooper woke me up, a long time after, I heard knocking, very low, and low voices, and then I heard a door bang."

"Any other noises? Anything at all?"

"No. Nothing. Until later I heard footsteps and voices again. That must have been Miss Bonner and the trooper, because it was soon afterwards that Miss Raffray came to tell me."

"You heard no sounds from Ranth's room? It's next to yours, between yours and Zimmerman's."

Martin shook his head. "The closets are arranged here to separate the rooms, and Ranth isn't noisy."

Sherwood regarded him in silence. Then abruptly he demanded, "What was de Roode's grudge against Zimmerman?"

Martin stared. The attorney waited. Martin said, "I don't pretend to know what it's about, this business about de Roode. You say you're detaining him as a material witness and that he's either a liar or a murderer. Now you ask me . . . why the devil would he have a grudge against Steve Zimmerman?"

"I don't know. I'm asking you."

"All right, I'm answering. He didn't. I have a right to know why you're holding him!"

"Maybe," Sherwood conceded sourly. "I'm not particularly excited about your rights just at present. There's been two men killed here. Did you know that de Roode came here last night a little after ten o'clock and went to Zimmerman's room and stayed in there fifteen or twenty minutes?"

"No. Who told you that?"

"He did. Anyway, the man we had there in the hall wasn't blind. De Roode says he came to see you and couldn't find you, and went to Zimmerman's room to see if you were there. Zimmerman was there and spoke to him, so de Roode was the last one to see him alive. He says he left him alive."

"What reason have you to assume he didn't?"

"None at all. But it's a cinch that someone didn't leave him alive, and besides, there's another item in de Roode's statement that doesn't fit at all. I'm saving that item, for the present. And I'm holding de Roode. If you want his rights attended to, get a lawyer. Just now I'm more interested in other rights that have been violated—the rights of Storrs and Zimmerman to go on breathing. And the right of the people of the State of Connecticut to know who did the violating. There are a couple more questions I'd like to ask, Mr. Foltz, and I put them to you as the closest and oldest friend of Steve Zimmerman. Do you know of any grievance that de Roode had against Storrs, or reason to fear him?"

"No."

"Do you know of any motive that anyone here might have had for killing Zimmerman?"

"No."

"You haven't the faintest idea of why Zimmerman was killed, or who did it?"

"No."

Sherwood leaned back. He pulled at the lobe of his ear, sighed, and finally turned an inquiring glance on the colonel and the inspector. Brissenden shrugged, and Cramer shook his head. Sherwood returned to Martin:

"I guess that's all for now, Mr. Foltz. Your man de Roode is under arrest and I don't want him talking with anyone for the present. You of course are not, but I ask you to keep yourself within these grounds. If you wish to get a lawyer for de Roode, which doesn't seem to me an urgent necessity, you may use the telephone or send a message by one of the men." He shifted to the trooper: "Send Miss Storrs in."

Martin stood up. He looked at Dol as if he would say something, but ended by turning away wordless. He had Sylvia to go to, and Dol watched him go. Then, with a wrinkle in her brow that threatened to become permanent if this kept up much longer, she leaned back and closed her eyes. She was wishing that she dared confront Janet with her lie here in front of these men and let them worry the truth out of her, but she knew she could not. It was too great a chance to take. That truth could not be worried out of Janet, it would have to be forced out. Somehow . . .

If the illumination got from the others had been

scanty, that received from Janet Storrs and Sylvia Raffray was considerably less than scanty. Ten minutes for each of them was enough. Janet, self-possessed, fully clothed and toileted, and inscrutable, said she had not left her room after entering it at something before ten o'clock, had gone to bed about midnight and lain awake, and had heard nothing of any significance. Sylvia, not toileted at all but with a steady chin, which Dol saw with relief and inward gratitude to heaven, had heard nothing, had slept almost from contact with the pillow, and had awakened only for Dol's knock on her door. To questions regarding the possibility of a motive for de Roode to kill either Storrs or Zimmerman, or both, she offered ignorance, reinforced by an obvious disbelief.

Awaiting Ranth, Sherwood went to the window and stretched himself comprehensively; outside was no longer a black opacity but a gray and dingy blur. Brissenden shifted in his chair and sent Dol a brief scowl, the thirtieth, perhaps, of a series. Cramer deposited a horribly mangled cigar in an ashtray and got out another one.

George Leo Ranth entered and walked to the table, sat down and crossed his legs and looked patiently and politely receptive. Sherwood crossed from the window and stood frowning down at him with his hands thrust into his trouser pockets and his shoulders hunched up.

"Well, Mr. Ranth. I suppose you know what we're here for now."

Ranth nodded. "Mrs. Storrs told me. I am sorry. Violence is inherent in all natural processes, but the kind of violence displayed in murder is proof of the lack of spiritual development in man. I deplore this second manifestation of it, though it is an advantage to me as an individual. You had some reason to suppose me involved in the death of Mr. Storrs, but certainly not in that of Mr. Zimmerman, since I scarcely knew him."

"Yeah. Thank you for calling my attention to that. Of course out of all the possibilities we have to consider —if you killed Storrs and Zimmerman knew it, you might have had to remove him to protect yourself. That has been known to happen."

Ranth faintly smiled. "Nevertheless, it does complicate things for you. It probably does in any event, even with all suspicion of me removed; but on the other hand, it might simplify it for you by presenting fresh considerations. I should think it might."

Brissenden barked, "What does that mean? What do you know about it?"

"Nothing. I know nothing. But pardon me, I believe there is one thing I do know. If you would tell me this: is it true that Zimmerman was found on his bed, strangled by an electric light cord around his throat?"

Sherwood grunted a yes.

"Was that cord tied there against his struggles, or held against his struggles while he died? Or was he first rendered unconscious by a blow or a narcotic?"

"I don't know. I think he struggled. The bed looks like it."

"If he did—if he struggled—I do know one thing that may help, in case time is significant. I know that he was killed before 11:25. At that time I went to my room, which is next to his. There are closets between the rooms, but my hearing is acute, and I did not go to sleep. I went to bed and lay relaxed. The sound of two men struggling on that bed would surely have reached me. I heard other sounds plainly—for instance, quite late, a knocking that seemed to be on a door not far from mine, followed by two men talking in low voices, and that followed by footsteps and the banging of a door. I also, as you probably know, heard the trooper and Miss Bonner; at the agitation of their voices and movements I went to the hall to investigate. The trooper would not let me enter Zimmerman's room. Miss Bonner had gone downstairs to get the men from outdoors. My assistance was not required—it appeared, not wanted. I re-entered my room and dressed."

Sherwood sat down. He eyed Ranth with no visible satisfaction or gratitude. Finally he grunted, "So that's your story. I'll be damned if you mightn't think this is a deaf and dumb asylum. A man gets strangled in bed with the house full of people, and nobody saw anything or heard anything or even dreamed of anything. You put it that the fact that you heard nothing after 11:25 proves that Zimmerman was killed earlier than that. It doesn't at all; it only proves that if he was killed after 11:25 you did it yourself. I'm not accusing you; I tell you frankly that I have nothing whatever on which to base such an accusation. I'd like to ask you this: have you anything to add to what you've said that might help us? Anything at all regarding events here, or anything you knew or suspected or that you now suspect?"

Ranth slowly shook his head. "Nothing whatever."

"Okay. That's all. Please stay on the premises."

When Ranth had gone there was silence. Dol closed her eyes again, Sherwood sat with his chin on his chest,

Cramer chewed his cigar and stared at the opposite wall.

Brissenden stood up. "I'm going to tell Talbot to take de Roode down to the barracks." He licked his lips.

The attorney nodded wearily. "Go ahead. I'm not sanctioning anything but questioning of a suspect. Tell your men that."

"You wouldn't," the colonel snorted contemptuously, and stalked out.

The inspector arose, poured himself half a cup of cold coffee and gulped it down, coughed a couple of times, and replaced his cigar. He moved around and stood in front of Sherwood. Dol let her black lashes lift a little to see what he was doing, then dropped them again.

"Well," Cramer said, "you're up against the same thing as you are with Storrs. Motive. That's the place to dig, and I don't see how I can help you any. I doubt if they'll get anything out of that de Roode, granting that there's anything to get. I suppose it has occurred to you that he may not be a liar or a murderer either one; it could have happened, his visit to Zimmerman's room, just the way he said it did. He might have heard Zimmerman locking the door, provided that there was someone hid in Zimmerman's room while de Roode was in there. Then after Zimmerman went to sleep the guy unhid himself, did the job, unlocked the door and went to his room to take a rest, of course expecting to have until morning for that. He must have been exasperated when he was got out of bed again so soon afterwards. If it happened that way, it must have been Foltz or Chisholm, it couldn't have been Ranth. If it was Ranth, either de Roode is lying or cuckoo about hearing the door locked, or Zimmerman himself unlocked it later; maybe he went to the bathroom and neglected to lock it again when he went back. If de Roode did it, you'll certainly have to find out why."

"Yeah." Sherwood was forlornly sarcastic. "Much obliged."

"Don't mention it. But there's one little experiment we might try. We might satisfy our curiosity about that, if we don't do anything else. Ranth said if there was any struggling on that bed after 11:25 he would have heard it. I wonder if he would. I also wonder if it might not have been heard from Miss Bonner's room, or even Foltz's. What do you say we shoo everybody downstairs and make a few tests?"

Sherwood dragged himself to his feet. Dol opened her eyes.

Thus it was that the lovely and happy flush of dawn, as its rays reached the second story windows of Birchhaven that September Monday morning, would surely have danced gaily with laughter if it had been blessed with a sense of humor and ignorant of the significance of the ludicrous antics to be observed there. First in Ranth's room, then in Foltz's, then in Dol Bonner's, a woman and three grown men stood motionless and silent, in attitudes of strained attention, while, in the room from which Zimmerman's body had been removed on its journey to the dissecting table, a 190-pound trooper rolled on the bed and bounced up and down, rolled and bounced some more like a boy in exuberant play, while three of his comrades stood there and scowled at him.

CHAPTER

SIXTEEN

Six hours later, at eleven o'clock, Dol Bonner sat on the window seat in her room, sipping a cup of hot tea and staring out at the sunny lawn.

She had reached the conclusion that there was no safe detour for her, no trail that might be found or blazed to avoid the risk she must take; she must either leap the crevasse or give it up. There had been a chance; but when, around ten o'clock, de Roode had been brought back to Birchhaven by a couple of troopers and released from custody, that chance had disappeared. She had seen de Roode clamber out of the car and heard him demand to see Martin; he had not, apparently, suffered mayhem, and he certainly did not look crushed.

Sherwood, having departed at dawn, was now back again, as was Brissenden; they were in the card room with Len Chisholm, who had informed the trooper stationed outside his door that he had awakened, by a series of deep and lugubrious groans. Inspector Cramer was gone.

Dol had not slept. She knew her head was not clear; the sunny lawn outside was like a landscape in a dream, in appearance fair and cheerful, but with a sinister and threatening quality that could not be defined. And her brain was muddled. She knew it but couldn't help it. She could not lie down and sleep. She must first leap that crevasse; she knew that she must, all the hours that she had been shrinking from it. Those hours had begun when she had heard de Roode's story in the card room; she had been convinced then of what had before been only incredulous conjecture. With that conviction in her head it was not strange that she could not sleep. For one thing among others, she was tormented by the practical certainty that if she had gone to Zimmerman at ten o'clock, with what she had known then, instead of waiting until two, he would be alive now and it would all be over.

Now there was no Zimmerman to go to, and that made the situation desperate.

She had considered presenting Sherwood with her facts and surmises and leaving it to him, but from what she had seen of his methods she doubted if he would be equal to the job—and now the job *must* be done. The murderer of Storrs and Zimmerman *must* be unmasked. She had considered a direct attack on de Roode with whatever weapons she might command, but dismissed that as hopeless. She had considered, again, the possibility of coercing Janet into disclosure, and had dismissed that too. One false step might be ruin, for when she once betrayed her knowledge all the defenses of cunning and despair would be erected against her, unless she demolished them in advance.

So, finally, she was led to her decision. Her head still was not clear, but her determination was. She would take the jump. There was nothing else for it.

She swallowed the last of her cup of tea, got up and went to the mirror and peered at her reflection and muttered at it, "You look like something left on the bank when a river goes down. Also you feel like it." She brushed at her hair a little, patted with a powder puff, scraped her lips with her teeth and renounced lipstick; and went to the pigskin case where it rested on the table, opened it and unstrapped the Holcomb pistol from the lid, looked to make sure the pistol was loaded, and put it in her handbag. With the handbag under her arm, she left the room, descended the stairs, and told the trooper in the hall that she wished to speak with Sherwood. The trooper went to the card room and in a moment returned and told her to go in.

She ignored Len Chisholm, who sat with his elbow on the arm of his chair and his head supported by his hand; likewise Brissenden, who stood, by now permanently truculent. She spoke to the attorney:

"I want to go for a little walk with Martin Foltz. I'm telling you in case your men have been instructed not to let any of us out of their sight; I don't want that; I need a tête-à-tête with him. I'll tell you about it after I see how it comes out."

"What's the idea?" Sherwood regarded her without enthusiasm. "You'd better tell me about it now."

"No, I can't do that. Maybe there's nothing to tell. I'm not going to elope with him; we won't leave Birchhaven. You can trust me. I'm not going to strangle him, either."

Sherwood appraised her. Finally he shrugged. "Go ahead, if you don't leave these grounds."

"Tell your men, please."

Sherwood turned. "You hear, Quill? Tell the men Foltz and Miss Bonner are going for a walk and don't want to be disturbed."

The sergeant went, and Dol followed him.

Another inquiry of the trooper in the hall got her a direction to the sun room. There she found Martin and Sylvia. Martin was stretched out on the couch in the recess, with his eyes closed, and Sylvia sat on the edge, leaning over his head, smoothing his brow with the tips of her fingers, passing them back and forth gently, soothingly. The motion was suspended as she looked up at Dol with tired and cheerless eyes; and Martin stirred and sat up.

"Anything . . . anything new?"

"No, Raffray." Dol was crisp. "What would a man be without a ministering angel? But I'm going to supplant you. Something has occurred to me that I want to discuss with Martin."

"I'm not discussing with him. He won't discuss."

"He will with me. Won't you, Martin?"

"Sure." He wasn't eager. "Shoot."

Dol shook her head. "Not here. I'm going to cart you off. I'm proposing a tête-à-tête. Come along."

Sylvia, her lips compressed, stood up. "I knew . . . it was something. It always is when you walk like that. Dol . . . I can't stand any more of this! I don't see how anybody can! And you . . . you're so damned mysterious. . . ."

"I'm not mysterious. I just want Martin to come with me somewhere outdoors. I want to consult him about something. That will do his nerves more good than having you baby him. You ought to do something too, anything, it would do you good. Go to the kitchen and bake a pie. Come along, Martin."

She finally got away with him, leaving Sylvia stand-

ing there gazing after them. Instead of leaving the house
directly from the sun room, she led the way the length
of the side hall, emerging onto the east terrace—flooded
with sunshine, as was the whole expansive slope, stretch-
ing away from their feet. Dol said, "Let's go this way,"
and started on a bee-line across the grass, ignoring the
path. Martin, beside her, observed querulously, "I don't
like to go more than twenty yards from the house, because one of those damned cops comes snooping around."

Dol grunted something. But in another fifty paces
Martin suddenly stopped short and demanded, "Where
are you headed for? I don't want to go down there."

Dol faced him. "It's the best place. The nook. The
cops won't follow us—you know I am supposed to be
helping them—and I don't want to be overheard."

Martin shook his head stubbornly. "Nobody can hear
you right here. What do you want to discuss?"

"Now, Martin," Dol chided him. "And you usually
so gallant? I want to talk with you in that nook. I'm
not capricious, am I? Lord, if I wanted to I could have
a squad of troopers conduct you there—I stand high with
them since I found the gloves. I'd much rather it was
just you and me."

She thought she was smiling at him, she wasn't sure,
but she was sure that her heart was thumping. She must
not give herself away ahead of time, she must do it
right or it wouldn't work; and she knew that he was
perfectly capable of turning on his heel and returning to
the house. If her smile looked the way she hoped it did,
he probably wouldn't. . . . She turned, with assurance,
and started down the slope again.

He was with her. She wished now her heart would stop thumping; cool composure would be better. They passed the fish pool, circled the end of it . . . and were at the dogwoods. They stooped under the low branches . . . and were in the nook.

Dol said, "You haven't been here since it happened, have you?" She pointed. "That's the tree the wire was fastened to—that's the limb. That's the bench that was overturned; they've set it up again. What's that? Oh, I guess they drove those pegs there to show the position the bench was in." She sat down on the bench, and a shiver ran over her. "I suppose it isn't really cool in here, but it seems so coming out of the warm sun, and as dark as the devil. Sit down, Martin. Don't stand there as if you were ready to run, I really do have something to say to you."

He lowered himself to the bench, towards the other end, four feet from her. He told her petulantly, in what Sylvia called his off-key tone, "All right, say it."

Dol did not look at him. She had a feeling that it would be better, at that point, not to. She looked at the grass at his feet, and made her voice as casual as she could: "What I want to talk to you about is confession. The different ways people have of confessing things. All sorts of things. They confess sins to priests, and injuries, big ones and little ones, to their wives and husbands and mothers and friends, and of course they confess mistakes all the time, either because they have to or because they want to. It seems to be an instinct, and often it gets so powerful that it's irresistible. Don't you think so?"

She looked at him; but she saw that he wasn't going to answer, because he wasn't breathing; he was rigid, with his eyes fixed on her. She went on: "Of course, whether it's an instinct or not, I don't suppose anyone ever confesses to anything serious unless there's some good reason for it. You confess to a priest because you want absolution. Sometimes a man confesses to the police to make them stop hurting him. And so on. But I suppose the commonest reason for confession is to distribute the burden of guilt. It becomes intolerable, and you have to share it. This may all sound elementary to you, I don't know; if Steve Zimmerman were here he could phrase it in technical psychological terms, but I can't do that; anyway, that's what I want to talk to you about, the different reasons for confession. Of course, I'm not silly enough to think that you're going to break down and confess just because I talk about it, and that's why I'm saying there must be a reason for it."

She heard him breathe, and looked at him, and saw that he was trying to smile. He said, "I'd just as soon confess to you as not. You confess to me and I'll confess to you. I'll bet it will take you longer than it will me." Suddenly he was petulant again. "Why the devil did you bring me down here to talk about confession? I'm no priest."

"I brought you here to tell you the reasons why you must confess." Dol got his eye and held it, and her fingers tightened on the leather of the handbag under her arm. "There's nothing else for you to do. There are various reasons, but the main one is the one piece of bad luck you had. That was what gave you away. I mean, of course, that it was Janet who found the gloves."

"What the hell are you talking about?" Martin's voice was doubtless meant to be harsh with resentful bewilderment, but it was not a proper harshness; the tin was in it. His expression was better than his voice. "Is this supposed to be funny? Janet didn't find the gloves; you found them yourself."

Dol shook her head. "Janet found them. Haven't you been wondering who the dickens put them in that watermelon? Of course you have; but you might have known it was Janet, because no one else would have done it." The handbag slid to her lap; she opened it and put her hand in as if to take out something, but instead let the hand stay there. She did that without taking her eyes from Martin's face. "But I must explain why that gave you away. After I found the gloves I tested the melon for fingerprints, and it was covered with Janet's. She had hid the gloves. I went to her, and she said that she had found them under the peat moss in the rose garden, and recognized them as your and took them to her room. Then, when her father was found murdered, and hands were examined and gloves were discussed, she looked at the pair she had found and saw that they were marked with the wire. She didn't think you had killed her father, but she didn't want you dragged into it by having them recognized as your gloves—so she told me—and besides, it would have been embarrassing for her to explain why she had concealed them in her room." Inside the bag, the pistol grip was now snug in her hand. "But yesterday afternoon it came out that the gloves had been bought on Saturday. The only time that Janet could possibly have seen them was in the pocket of your jacket in the reception hall Saturday afternoon, and even that was not possible, because she had not been there. She had been in the rose garden, and she had not seen you or anyone else. Her statement that she had recognized them as your gloves was a lie. But her action in taking them to her room and later hiding them in the watermelon could only be explained on the theory that she *did* know they were yours. She could not very well have recognized them as belonging to anyone else, and even if she had, who besides you would she seek to protect? So she must have known they were yours, and there was only one way she could have known it: she must have seen you hide them in the rose garden. While you were doing that, you didn't know that Janet was in the filbert thicket looking for a bird, did you? She was. And she saw you stooping over, doing something in the peat moss under a rose bush, and after you had left she went to take a look, and she found the gloves."

Dol suddenly withdrew her hand from the bag, with the pistol in it. She spoke to his face: "Look here, Martin. I can shoot this thing, I've practised with it. Don't think I won't. I show it to you so you won't get any notion about treating me the way you did Storrs and Zimmerman. I wouldn't kill you if I could help it, but I would hurt you, and I know you can't stand the idea of being hurt. So don't make any sudden movements."

Martin's eyes lifted from the pistol to her face. She had, on various occasions, seen his eyes petulant, or plaintive, or contumelious, but she had never seen them ugly before—little round hard pebbles of fear and hate, so painful to see, so odious as human eyes which she thought she knew, that an uncontrollable shudder ran over her. He said, in a voice that was also new to her, "Put that . . . thing away. Put it away, I tell you!"

"Don't you move." Dol's hand with the pistol rested on the bench. "You look as if you might jump and run. Don't try that either, or I'll shoot." She forced herself to keep her gaze at his intolerable eyes. "I'll finish about Janet and the gloves. I don't know whether you knew they had been taken from the rose garden or not; maybe you didn't go near there, thinking that if they were found you could explain that they had disappeared from your jacket, and that that was safer than getting them and trying to dispose of them. You must have been astounded and pretty flustered when you learned that they had been found in a watermelon. I was sitting looking at you when you learned that, and I'm remembering how you handled yourself; that's why I'm taking no chances now, I'll pull this trigger if you make a move. As for Janet, of course she knew Saturday night that you had killed her father, since she actually saw you hide the gloves. I don't pretend to understand her; of course I'm aware that she's infatuated with you, God knows why. Maybe she doesn't believe in vengeance, or maybe she offered her filial love as a sacrifice to another kind of love, or she may even have counted on impressing you some time with the tale of what she had done to protect you. It doesn't matter.

"So I knew yesterday afternoon that you had killed Storrs. At first I knew it but I didn't believe it, because I couldn't conceive of any motive you could have had.

I knew it must be so, but it wasn't credible. Everything else about it was all right: you had the gloves, and you had the opportunity because no one really knows what time you left your place Saturday afternoon to come over here, except possibly de Roode, and he is yours body and soul. But there was no motive and no hint of one. I got my first hint yesterday afternoon, when Sylvia told me that Steve Zimmerman had asked her to marry him. Steve was your closest and dearest friend, and he knew that you worshiped Sylvia. But now all of a sudden two things: first, he wanted to marry Sylvia, and second, he didn't want you to. But why? Granted that he had been wanting Sylvia for some time, and had concealed it because of his friendship for you, why was he suddenly not only willing, but desperately anxious, that you should be deprived of her? Because, possibly, he knew you had killed Storrs? That could be. But how did he know that, and besides, why had you done it? Then I thought, the fact that Steve had proposed to Sylvia yesterday afternoon was no proof that he had that moment decided that you should not have her. He might have decided that a month or a week or a day ago and merely have awaited an opportunity. Or he might have decided it and taken some other step—for instance, he might have gone to Sylvia's guardian about it. And he had in fact gone to see Storrs Saturday morning, about something which apparently wasn't trivial, judging from what he said to Sylvia when he met her in the hall, and from the fact that he refused to tell what his errand there had been. You see how I arrived at that? You see how it was Steve's proposal to Sylvia that gave that away?"

There was no answer. Dol no longer had to endure Foltz's eyes, for she couldn't see them. His head was bent, his hands were gripping the edge of the bench, and his body was moving slowly to and fro, slightly forward and back again, forward and back, as rhythmic and as ceaseless as a metronome. But she kept her eyes steadily on him:

"Last night I was fitting pieces of things together, and I tried that. It fitted, all of it. Zimmerman decided you should not have Sylvia, and went to Storrs and told him so, and told him why. Storrs was well enough convinced so that he told Sylvia he could kill you with his hands, though he didn't say it was you, leaving that task, probably, for the evening at Birchhaven. At my office you learned from Sylvia that she had met Zimmerman coming out of Storrs' office very agitated, and you knew then that he had told Storrs—whatever it was. When you and Len and Sylvia got to your place Saturday at three o'clock Zimmerman was there, and you and he went to your room, and he confirmed your fears: he had told Storrs. You knew you had lost Sylvia—both her person and her fortune—I have sometimes wondered which you worship more—I suppose you don't know yourself. So you had to kill Storrs, and you did so. You must have been aware that Zimmerman would be morally certain of your guilt as soon as he learned of it, but I presume that you figured that your lifelong friend could not bring himself to denounce you and have you executed for murder. I wouldn't be surprised if Zimmerman offered that night not to expose you to that fate if you would give up Sylvia. That would be logical. Did you agree? Did you refuse? I don't know. Anyway, yesterday afternoon Zimmerman asked Sylvia to marry him, and last night you killed him.

"I fitted those pieces together, and finally, at two o'clock last night, I determined to go to Zimmerman and confront him with them and insist that he tell the truth. I thought I could crowd him into it. When I got to his room he was dead. Of course that settled it; I was right; but my resolution to act had come too late to save Zimmerman. And there was still one other remote possibility: that it was de Roode, passionately devoted to you, who had actually done the killing; but I abandoned that when I heard his story to Sherwood this morning. It was obvious that he hadn't known that Zimmerman had been killed, not because he said that, but because he said that after he left Zimmerman's room he heard the door being locked from the inside. If he had killed Zimmerman he would have known that we had found the door unlocked, and there would have been no earthly reason for him to invent such a tale. So it must have been true; he really had heard the door locked. In that case, you must have been concealed in the room at the time that de Roode was in there; you heard his talk with Zimmerman and knew that he had been to your room and found you gone; and to account for your absence you concocted the story about going to the kitchen for soda. Possibly you had actually gone to the kitchen, but not at the time you said you had. You couldn't have, because at that time you were hid in Zimmerman's room, waiting for him to go to sleep so you could sneak to the bed and get that cord around his throat. I suppose with Zimmerman dead you thought you were safe. Didn't you? You thought that with him silenced no one would ever discover your motive for killing either of them, and without motive there can be no real suspicion, let alone proof. Didn't you? Wasn't that what you thought?"

Foltz's body no longer moved, to beat its rhythm, but his head was bent and he did not look at her. He was not inert with despair; she could see the rapid rise and fall of his shoulders betraying an inward activity which was demanding air, and more air—oxygen for the swiftly racing blood. He was far from inert, but he made no movement and said nothing.

Dol stirred, shifted on the bench a little. Her left hand gripped the bench's edge, out of his sight should he turn, against her hip under a fold of her skirt. She gripped so tight that her nails dug through the paint. She said, as curt and incisive as she could make it:

"Don't think you're not going to talk, Martin. There's something you're going to tell me before we leave here. I want to know what it was that Zimmerman told Storrs about you Saturday morning. I need to know that. That's what I meant when I spoke about confession; you don't have to confess anything else, I already know it. What was it?"

No movement and no reply.

"Come on, I intend to know it."

Nothing.

"Look here." Dol's voice cut. "Then don't look. I've got this gun, and there are six shots in it. I haven't the faintest shred of compassion for you, not because you're a murderer, but on account of Sylvia. I don't need to explain that, you know how I feel about Sylvia. That's why I have no pity for you. I knew when I brought you here what I would have to do, and I resolved to do it. You're going to tell me what Zimmerman told Storrs. If you don't, I'm going to shoot you. I'm a pretty fair shot. I won't kill you. I'll hit you in the legs and the feet, right from here where I'm sitting. Of course, people will come. I'll tell Sherwood everything I have just told you, and I'll say that you attacked me and I had to shoot in self-defense. Then he'll start on you, he and Brissenden and the others. They'll get it out of you. . . ."

He had moved at last, away from her with a convulsive movement, and he was staring not at her but the pistol. Then his eyes raised to her face: "Goddam you!" It was the rage of imminent fear, superimposed on the helpless despair that had been penetrating his flesh and bones. "You wouldn't!"

"Yes, I will. You sit still." Dol knew now—she had been afraid till this moment—she knew now that she would do it. She was cold and certain. "I know you don't like to be hurt. I'm going to hurt you. A bullet hurts more, much more, if it hits a bone. I'm only six feet away from you. I shall count twenty. I warn you not to move—if you do I won't wait. At twenty I'll shoot." She raised the pistol. "One . . . two . . . three . . . four . . ."

At twelve he cried, almost a scream of terror: "Stop! Don't!"

"Then talk. Quick."

"But let me . . . good God, let me—"

"Talk!"

"I . . . I . . . put that down!"

She let her hand go to the bench. "Talk."

"I . . ." He was staring at her, and it was harder to meet his eyes than it would have been to pull the trigger, but she did it. "There was a girl killed . . . many years ago. Nothing was done to her . . . only . . . she was killed." He gasped for a breath. "Steve knew about it. I was not suspected—there was no reason why I should be! I was a small boy. She was strangled with a wire. Steve knew I killed little animals—I couldn't help it, I tell you! I had to see them . . ." He shuddered, and stopped.

Dol, without mercy, demanded, "Go on. Not with that. With this. Here."

"But there's nothing . . . only Steve. When the pheasants were strangled he knew I had done it. He discussed it with me. We discussed it many times . . . the psychology. Then he met Sylvia, but I didn't know —at first—then about a month ago he told me I must give her up. I must go away. I refused. Good God, Dol, could I give up Sylvia? Could I give up . . ."

"I don't know. Cut that. Go on."

"That's all. I refused. I continued to refuse. Then he said he would tell Storrs. I didn't think he would do that. I didn't know he wanted Sylvia himself—him! Steve! The dearest and closest friend I ever had—the only one who knew—except de Roode—but I—I—you see—"

It was his stammering that warned Dol—that, and seeing his eyes leave her for an instant, to something behind her, and then dart back to her—but they were different eyes. To her everlasting credit, she did not turn her head. She sprang from the bench and forward, leaped toward the tree, wheeling as she leaped, and from there, with her back to the tree, she could see them both: Martin, quivering from head to foot, on the bench, and de Roode standing ten feet from it, where he had emerged from the thicket with her back to him.

Martin was pleading hysterically, "Get her, de Roode! She won't shoot! Get her!"

Dol had the pistol up. "Don't come any closer!"

The man with the ape body and the intelligent face ignored that. He was moving, slowly and deliberately, towards her, with his eyes straight at hers, and as he came was speaking, not to her, soothingly and reassuringly: "All right, boy, don't you move. All right, boy, don't you worry, she won't hurt me . . . boy . . ."

"Stop! I say stop!"

"All right, don't move, boy—"

She pulled the trigger, twice. De Roode went down. She saw that, definitely, saw him floundering on the grass, saw him pull himself to his knees and start crawling towards her. . . .

"You! Halt!"

That was not her voice . . . was it? No, it was quite different, it was a manly military voice, and he came crashing through the dogwood branches. . . .

Dol went down too.

CHAPTER

SEVENTEEN

O N Thursday, at something after twelve o'clock, in
the office of Bonner & Raffray, Len Chisholm said:
"I don't believe a doggoned word of it. You just
wanted to steal the show. Foltz wouldn't have stood a
chance."

"Don't you fool yourself." Dol, seated at her desk,
brushed back her hair. "The chances would have been
ten to one in his favor. If I had turned it over to Sherwood, he wouldn't have got anywhere with Janet or
Martin either one—even granting that he would have
accepted my interpretation. Janet's fingerprints were
gone. He had nothing on her; she could have denied
what she had said to me. And without that he had absolutely nothing on Martin either, and, knowing that
he hadn't, he would have been cautious, and it was no
time for caution. Not to mention the fact that I would
have had to admit to Sherwood that I had deliberately
erased those fingerprints."

"You had to admit it anyhow."

"Yes, but it was all over then. He had what he
wanted . . . and I had given it to him. . . ."

"So you had indeed." Len leaned back comfortably
and sighed. "I was up at Sherwood's office yesterday
afternoon. I suppose you've seen today's paper. Martin
has made a signed confession, and Sherwood has got
a statement from Janet, and de Roode is in the hospi-

tal with a shattered ankle bone. You must be a pretty good marksman; I suppose your second shot went right through the hole the first bullet had made."

"It went in the ground. I was only trying to stop him. What did you go to Sherwood's office for? What did they want?"

"I was there on business." Len was supercilious. "Don't you think us newspaper men ever work? How do you suppose the Gazette gets the coverage it does on all the big news?" He tapped his chest with his finger. "Me."

"Oh. You got your job back."

"I consented to go back, yes. Which reminds me of what I really came here for. You realize, Miss Bonner, that our readers like the human interest touch. Unquestionably, the item that appeals to them most about the Birchhaven affair, the thing that twangs their heartstrings, is the fact that when Dol Bonner, the delicate and dainty detective demon, fainted, she was caught in the arms of who or whom? Some nondescript pedestrian or passing motorist? No, sir; by the brave and puissant colonel himself, North Wind Brissenden! Now if you would let me have an exclusive interview, describing your delicious sensation as you felt his powerful protecting arms enfolding you—"

"I will. On the telephone. Go somewhere and call me up."

"I'll write it with a good approach, working up suspense. I'll describe how de Roode saw you going off with Martin and got suspicious, and finally succeeded in sneaking off to follow you without a trooper seeing him, and how Brissenden, looking from the window of the card room, happened to see de Roode going in the same direction you and Martin had gone and that made *him* suspicious, and how I saw Brissenden suddenly beat it from the card room and that made *me* suspicious—"

"Shut up. If you really have got your job back, don't you think you'd better—well! Hello there!"

Len stood up. "Hello, Sylvia."

Sylvia greeted them. The gray woolen Beauchamp suit and the dark gray toque would have been more becoming to her if her cheeks had been flaunting their accustomed happy coloring, but even so she could not have been called a frump. She sat down on one of the chromium and yellow chairs, sighed, and used her gloved hand for a fan.

"It's hot as the dickens for September. I've just spent two hours in that lawyer Cabot's office, and he's a pain in the neck, but I guess he's honest." A little spasm went over her face, like a shadow, and disappeared. "I ought to hate you, Len, because you're a newspaper man— good lord, they're awful. You're looking very trim— isn't that a new shirt? A new tie too, quite handsome. Aren't you proud of him, Dol? Should I call you Bonner instead of Dol, since you're famous now? By the way . . ." She stopped, flushing a little, showing what she could look like in gray, with her own pigment. "I . . . I want to say . . . I'm proud of you, and I'm grateful to you, and I want to go on being your partner if that's agreeable. . . ."

"Forget it." Dol brusquely cleared her throat. "I mean the pride and gratitude. The partner part is okay."

"Good." Sylvia went to the desk and put out her hand. "Shake. Till death do us . . . oh. I didn't mean . . ." She shivered a little, bit at her lip, and then went on, "What about some lunch? I'm hungry. The three of us, on the firm."

Dol shook her head. "Can't. I'm leaving on a one o'clock train for Gresham. On account of—I didn't get to see Dick off Sunday and I must run up to see him and take him some things. You and Len run along."

Len muttered something. Sylvia demanded, "What? *Your* Len? He wouldn't go."

"He will if the firm pays for it." Dol's caramel-colored eyes flashed a glance at him under long black lashes. "Huh, Len? Equerry of the Steering Wheel?"

Len made her a low bow from the hips. He straightened up. "Did you ever try taking a dive into a vat of boiling tar? I know where I can find one for you." He turned. "My credit's good at George and Harry's. Come on, Sylvia."